CAUGHT

A River Bend Chronicles Book

Renee Kumor

Habent Sua Fata Libelli

Manhanset House
Shelter Island Hts., New York 11965-0342

bricktower@aol.com
absolutelyamazingebooks.com

All rights reserved under the International and Pan-American Copyright Conventions. No part of this publication may be reproduced, stored in a retrieval system, or transmitted in any form or by any means, electronic, or otherwise, without the prior written permission of the copyright holder.
The Absolutey Amazing eBooks colophon is a trademark of
J. T. Colby & Company, Inc.

Library of Congress Cataloging-in-Publication Data
Kumor, Renee
Caught, a river bend chronicles book
p. cm.

1. FICTION / Romance / Suspense. 2. FICTION / Thrillers / Crime. 3. FICTION / Mystery & Detective / Private Investigators.
Fiction, I. Title.
ISBN: 978-1-955036-52-8 Trade Paper

Copyright © 2024 by Renee Kumor
Electronic compilation/ paperback edition
copyright © 2024 by Absolutely Amazing eBooks

February 2024

CAUGHT

Number 21 in the

River Bend Chronicles Series

Renee Kumor

To healthcare providers
who deliver care to
the underserved in every community,
whether quiet sparsely populated coves
or forgotten neighborhoods.

Books in the *River Bend Chronicles* Series

Small Town Secrets

Taking A Chance

'tis The Season

An Act Of Charity

Someone Cares

Forever, Sonny

Season Of Revenge

Who Am I?

Old Debts

Deadly Politics

500 Kisses

There's No Explaining Love

Brewing Terror

Girlfight

Decorating For Death

Where Is She Now?

Brooken Hearts, Broken Promises

Too Fat To Fly

Masking Murder

Kudzu Summer

Caught

CHAPTER ONE

The kitchen door rattled, getting her attention. Lynn Powers, executive director of the River Bend Philanthropies, had stopped home to grab lunch and find a more comfortable pair of shoes. She heard the door fly back and the knob hit the wall. Who could that be? Someone breaking in? At lunch time? She heard the dog come racing from his favorite morning spot on the sofa and run into the kitchen acting delighted. She was right behind. "Dad!"

Jim Hoefler held out his arms. "I came for hugs. I've been storing them up since lockdown." Everyone in River Bend seemed to be coming out of pandemic miasma since the vaccines had become available. She ran into her father's arms. "Marianna and I got our shots. We're open for business." Vaccination sites were active in River Bend and folks were eager to make the covid virus a thing of the past, or as the CDC projected - develop herd immunity.

She hung on to him and laughed. "You know I haven't had any shots. And it might still be possible to get the virus." Age and occupation regulated shot access. Lynn's first opportunity for immunization was still a few weeks away.

He kissed her cheek and kept one arm around her shoulders. "I know. But I've quarantined long enough. Marianna and I agreed that we'll come out, but with caution."

"I just came home for some lunch," she said, "can I get you something?" They stood with arms still clinging to one another.

He patted his stomach. "I think I spent the lockdown eating. We're dieting now." He looked around the kitchen. "What you got?"

She laughed and released him. It was so good to have him back in her kitchen. She poured him a glass of iced tea, no sugar, and pulled out a chair at the table. "Sit. I'll find something low-cal for you." Before she started food prep, she had one question. "What do you mean back with caution?"

"We won't take trips. If we dine out, it will be outdoors. No theater, yet. And no big indoor gatherings." She placed a sandwich in front of him. "But several of our friends have gotten their vaccines so we're back to playing bridge and other small gatherings." He winked at her. "Like lunch in your mask-free zone. And maybe breakfast after some big crime wrap-up."

"Happy to say crime seems to be in lockdown, too." Lynn's husband, Dusty Reid, was chief detective with the James County/River Bend Joint Investigation Unit. The family liked to gather in Lynn's kitchen for breakfast after a dramatic close to one of Dusty's investigations. He was not happy about the family tradition, but everyone else liked being in the know on crime.

Early in the pandemic Lynn had declared her backyard picnic area a mask-free zone. It had become a popular gathering spot for many of her friends and relatives. She gave her father another hug and decided it was time to celebrate. "I think we'll do a cookout this weekend to welcome you back."

Lynn refilled Jim's glass of iced tea and tempted him with a bag of chips. "This is all I can offer now. I have to get back to my office. We're almost up to operating on a face-to-face basis. We just limit meetings to small committees."

Jim settled the bag of chips alongside his sandwich. "Any cookies?"

"Really, Dad, I have to go." She threw out her hand toward the pantry. "Help yourself. Save some snacks for Dusty. Let the dog out when you leave." She kissed him on the cheek.

He waved with one hand while the other rummaged through the chip bag. He and the dog would share the sandwich. He reminded himself to check for chip crumbs on his clothing before he went home. Or Marianna would know he had fallen off the diet wagon.

* * *

Lynn got back to her office in a great mood. The country was coming out of this weird time. She looked around her office. She and the staff still worked both from home and onsite. Staff, she loved the term. During the last months she had hired her old friend Rory Prentiss to become grant manager. He joined Nelda, the best assistant in the world.

Caught

Things were great at the Philanthropies. Local nonprofits were coming to terms with the fallout of the past months. Some, like Rory's old employer, the Arts Council, had closed their doors. Others had decided to merge, and a few had become very sophisticated in providing services as well as become expert in virtual fundraising. Everyone was getting an understanding of the support available through federal grants and loans for both businesses and nonprofits.

Even though the world had been locked down, life had gone on. Thanksgiving and Christmas had happened, but on a much smaller scale. Schools were operating, masked in place or from home. Parents had made choices. The school board had made choices and because everyone was human, not everyone was pleased.

Life had gone on for Dusty's unit. Mars and his wife Trina had a baby boy. Mars' mother had been trapped in London but had taken advantage of the vaccine availability and would soon be quarantined in some U.S. entry port for a few weeks. Lynn had to laugh. Mars had entertained everyone with his birth angst. Trina had threatened to have him quarantined far away until the baby arrived. After the birth he had taken Trina and the baby to Hank Seymour's hunting cabin on the fringes of the national forest. The three of them had spent two days resting before returning to life with their two other small children.

Thinking of this mythical hunting cabin made Lynn smile. She had never been to the cabin. Her friends Sean and Lee Hennessey had used it as a getaway for their honeymoon. Last summer theirs had been the first Zoom wedding Lynn had ever attended. She smiled to herself as she remembered Lee and Sean's marriage taking place in a field on Lee's brother's farm, family and friends zooming in virtual celebration. Some pandemic memories were delightful.

* * *

Kip Mahaffey was one of the golden boys of River Bend. He wasn't a boy anymore, but he was still golden. He was even aging golden. His hair was showing attractive glitters of gray within the blonde and his physique was almost as trim as in his younger days. After twenty plus years as a practicing attorney and all-round community leader, he had finally decided with much encouragement from others, to run for mayor of River Bend. It was time. This pandemic had everyone disenchanted with the old local leadership. Of course, everyone knew those in office hadn't caused the pandemic, but voters were tired of the current state of affairs and were ready for a change, hoping change meant a journey back to normal. Kip was ready, too. He was always ready when opportunity knocked. That's how he had always operated. Sometimes opportunity was a little shady, and sometimes opportunity didn't knock so a fellow had to just push himself through the door. But life was good for Kip. And as long as his public life never caught up with his underworld life, and the false impressions he wove about his character held, he was, as always, golden.

Rachel Teague, a beautiful, blonde woman with a solid reputation as a hard-working community leader, parked her car in the river park lot. She was, as always, dressed to perfection. Style was her trademark. She liked dressing and grooming with flair. She also liked community volunteer work, and everyone seemed to like her and appreciate her talents. Except maybe her husband, but that was another story, another part of her life, the dull, quiet part. The pandemic had made her life too quiet. All community work had almost stopped. She had had nowhere to volunteer her time and energy. Finally, the blanket was lifting. She was ready for some new adventure and community challenge. Anything was better than a quarantine life with her husband, especially now that the children were all out of the house and leading their own lives. These last months had been lonely, quiet, and sad. Rachel was ready to be busy again.

Today she was meeting Kip Mahaffey, one of the players in her exciting community life. Together they had helped lead, organize, or direct several community successes. They had done committee work for the Hunger Alliance, the Philanthropies, and, most recently, worked with a team on organizing centers to deliver vaccines.

It was getting harder and harder for Rachel to work with this man. Kip was everything charming and respectful. Yet, she had recently begun to want more from their relationship than a similar work ethic. She wanted love, affection, and yes, she wanted sex. Her marriage was a stifling, sad union. Her husband had been withdrawing for the last few years. She had no idea why. Owen Teague continued to provide for her and was always ready to join her in social events with their friends and family. But when home alone together, he was not the man she married over twenty years ago. She snorted at the term, alone together, an oxymoron and maybe the description of more marriages than hers. She took a deep breath. Owen's appeal did not compare to Kip's. That's why she couldn't be with Kip more than necessary.

Today Kip had called and asked for a private meeting. He said he wanted to talk about something away from prying eyes. They were never alone in their community work. That's how thoughtful Kip was. They met with others or in public places to accomplish all the good they did for River Bend. So, the caution of 'prying eyes' and her own emotional yearnings had her very anxious.

Kip waved as she drove into the park, indicating that he had staked out a park bench at the edge of the playground. Surveying the site, she realized that he had still kept their meeting in plain sight. Nothing secret or sly about this charming man. Rachel pulled her mind back from the sexual fantasies that had plagued her recently and returned his wave as she left her car.

He pecked her cheek per his usual pre-pandemic greeting, and Rachel's ingrained poise served her well. Over the years she had held steady under some comical and dreadful situations. Today that poise, that personal reserve, kept her from throwing herself at Kip and demanding a sexual release away from her dry life of marriage to Owen. She took a deep breath, seated herself on the bench and arranged her skirt across her knees. "What are we keeping from prying eyes?"

He laughed and seated himself beside her. "You don't know?" He threw his arm across the back of the bench. "I want to run for mayor, and I need a campaign manager." She looked at him. He dropped his hand to her shoulder and sort of caressed her neck. "This is a municipal election. Short and sweet. Don't say 'no' before you give it some thought."

She enjoyed his touch but held herself steady. These touches were so Kip. Did he do this to everyone? Or was she the only one? And was he sending her some sort of sign? Was he asking to move their relationship forward? Was she ready? And what about Owen and what about Kip's wife? And why was all this going through her mind now? "I don't know what campaign managing would involve," she finally replied, "I've never done anything political."

"But you know all the politicians. You've lobbied them for various causes." He was correct. She had gone to Raleigh to speak to the legislature on issues pertaining to childcare and education over the years. He continued, "I can give you some names to ask for guidance. The election is in November, and we'll need time to raise some cash, announce my intention and run a small campaign, probably not do much actual campaigning until September." He shrugged at the simple organization he suggested. "And this would be the beginning." He waited for her to understand.

"The beginning of what?" Obviously, she didn't understand.

"My political career." He almost said 'ta-da' before he continued. "Next the state legislature and maybe even Congress to follow. Folks tell me I have the chops to meet the challenge." He turned a pleading, charming eye on her. "I just need the right team. With you I know I can win this election and any others I try." He stood looking as though he were ready to deliver an acceptance speech. "We're a team. Work with me and you can go as far as I do."

Rachel immediately sensed that a political campaign would place her and Kip hip-to-hip for several months. She also understood that her current state of confusion, frustration and sexual tension would make this impossible. "Let me think about it for a few days. And let me talk with Owen."

"Owen?"

"My husband."

"Don't worry about our spouses," he said. "Anita will go along. She really has no choice. I provide her some sort of standing in the community. Besides why would Owen object? He never seems concerned about your community work."

She had no response to that because Owen never seemed interested in anything she did. He worked, came home, ate dinner, and never seemed to hear what she reported about her day. She had quit asking about his day and telling him about hers years ago. And she was certain that working at this intensity, a political campaign, would make the chasm wider in her marriage. Rachel was also caught off guard by the rest of his comment. Kip never spoke of his wife. In fact, Rachel had never really met her. She and Owen socialized with a different crowd.

She offered him a weak reply. "I have to see if this would fit with my other obligations."

"We always fit," he said as he reached down to take her hand and help her to her feet. "I'll wait to hear from you." Releasing her hand, he walked out of the park along the greenway and back toward his office in town.

She watched him go and thought over his last comment. Did he always speak with double meaning phrases? Had she never noticed before this? What was happening to her? She knew one thing. She had to stay away from Kip Mahaffey. She was reading too much into their association. Or was she?

* * *

The priest walked into the church body from the sacristy. He had refilled and put away some of his oils. Visiting the sick and burying the dead seemed to be what he did these virus days. He looked out from the altar into the empty pews. Would they ever come back? This virus was celebrating its first year. He had his shots and had committed to visit as many of his elderly parishioners as possible.

This had been a year like no other for the entire world. No one knew what normal was any more. He knelt at the front of the altar and prayed for all those in the community who had been lost. Percentage wise River Bend was like every other place but still many of those who had died had been friends, not just parishioners but friends in his life here. His poker group of bachelors was a great support group. They snuck into the rectory a few times a month to vent and pray and smoke cigars. He chuckled to himself; old Doc Noah left the group. He found himself a lady friend. Nick was happy for the man. And Sean Hennessey had only joined them for a few months when he found his lady. Two happy men. But Tilly, the Lutheran minister, and Reverend Mike from the Church in the Pines still came to play. Three single preachers, three single men.

Father Nick stood, interrupting his short prayer, because he heard a sniffle. It echoed through the old church. He turned and squinted behind him. The sound seemed to come from the side aisle. He started toward the noise. A shuffling sound, a rattling breath. In the dark near the old confessional booth, a place where the lighting fixture seemed to be surrendering, he thought he saw a shadow. A homeless person? The priest moved slowly forward, clearing his throat, "Can I help you?"

Someone seemed to gasp for breath. Father Nick found a bulky figure slumped in a pew. "Sir? Do you need help?"

"Ah, Nicky?" sighed the stranger, "I was hoping to find you before I check out."

Nick knelt beside the man. "Do I know you?" He studied the figure in the weak glow of the tired fixture assisted by the late afternoon light pushing through the stained glass. "Father Gillespie?"

"Ah, you do remember." Cough. A struggle for breath.

Nick reached for the man. "Let me help you. We have a fine hospital here."

The old priest moved his hands in a weak motion that suggested he wanted to stay in place. "I'm fine. I had to see you." Gasping for air. "I'm ready. I just had to explain."

"I thought you were dead." Nick wrestled with his memories. "One day you were teaching seminary classes and the next day you were gone. I never heard an explanation. I was ordained and at my parish by then. I guess I lost track of you."

The man chuckled, a very weak but joyous sound. "I left. I found love." Shocked, Nick tried to speak. But the man continued. "Just listen. I want to tie up," a gasp for breath, "loose ends." He struggled to sit up straight. "I met a woman. And it was love, not sex, not lust, love." Phlegm. Cough. "I followed her up to her mountainside, moved in with her. God knows," weak chuckle, "He really knows how much I loved her." His hand touched Nick's arm. "She was beautiful. This virus got her a few months ago. I learned love, Nicky. We teach about the God of Love, Jesus the Son of God loves us. I learned that He loves us in many ways. Sometimes He loves us through another person."

"It's been what, fifteen years?" Nick struggled to hold the man upright.

"About. We survived. She had a family. They don't know who I am. They just accepted me." The man was fighting congestion, trying to find a breath. "I worked nights at an all-night gas mart." He patted Nick's arm again. "A lot of folks need a priest in the middle of the night." He looked up at the younger priest. Found his eyes in the dusk of the church. "I never stopped being a priest. Heh, heh. Sometimes I thought this was what life was like for the missionaries in Africa or some place. I never talked religion. It would have been like talking to some African tribesman. Can you imagine discussing the Trinity or Papal infallibility or St. Augustine? Heh, heh." He tried to take a deep breath. "They aren't dumb. But religion to many is in the heart, not in the mind."

"But Father."

"It's John, Nick."

"John, let me find some assistance for you."

"No. I'm ready to be with God. I do need you to help me, though."

"Anything."

John started to slip from Nick's grasp. The priest helped the old man to lay down. "Papers in my pocket." The sick man clutched at his jacket. "Address for our house. Key in the envelope." Speaking was getting harder. "Go to house. Get my gear. They won't understand it if they find it. Closet. The other key."

Nick pulled the papers and envelope out of John's pocket. The man struggled with every breath. Nick ran back to the sacristy and grabbed his oils to anoint the dying. He found a purple stole in the confession box and slipped it around his neck. He anointed John as he had been doing for all the dying through these months of the virus. He whispered the prayers and John's lips moved saying the prayers with him.

"Thank you, Nicky. Do what I ask." He struggled with his words. "I never stopped being a priest. I never stopped loving the Church."

Nick sat with his old professor in the darkened church. Night settled and John ceased to struggle for breath. Nick bowed his head and cried.

* * *

It was a quiet evening. Lynn had picked up a meal from the grocery store. Of all the positive virus-related services, the grocery stores had become the most efficient - online shopping, curbside or home delivery and an increasing number of ready to eat meals that were not fast food. Tonight, she had snagged a lemon caper salmon with couscous and asparagus. She finished cleaning the kitchen and joined Dusty in his office to watch some early evening talking heads.

The news seemed to be the same. Folks who wanted vaccines around the world and folks who disdained vaccines as a diabolical mind control plot. "Isn't there other news?"

Dusty looked at her. "We're living in vaccine politics. I hope we come out the other side soon." He watched the scroll along the bottom of the screen, saw nothing encouraging and opened his mouth to offer a critical thought when his phone rang. "Reid." He listened, nodded. "I'll be right there. . . . . Yeah, I'll bring her."

That got Lynn's attention. "What? Who?"

"Father Nick wants our assistance."

In Lynn's mind that answered no questions. How could she or Dusty assist a priest? Her mind raced through several scenarios. She was still puzzling the request as she hopped into Dusty's car, and they raced out of the neighborhood. "Do we know why?"

He glanced over at her. "He's got a dead body."

"Someone got murdered in his church?" Lynn paled.

He shrugged. "We'll find out when we get there. But he did ask that you come, too."

The church parking lot was empty, but they found Tilly, the Lutheran minister, standing at the entry to St. Bridget's waiting for them. He signaled them to follow as he disappeared behind the doors. Entering the church, they could see Father Nick standing next to a pew looking forlorn.

They stopped beside him, noticed the body on the pew, and waited for an explanation. He sighed deeply, then began his story. "My old professor, Father Gillespie, came to me this afternoon. He had left the priesthood many years ago and married a woman who lived further west near Murphy. She died of this virus, and he contracted it. He came here to give me his will and end-of-life instructions. He died about an hour ago. I called Tilly. He came and suggested we call you, something about an unattended death." Now Nick looked puzzled. "It wasn't unattended. I was with him."

Dusty followed the priest as he walked into the pew to inspect the body resting on the seat. "Why didn't you call an ambulance?"

"He didn't want one. He wanted to give me his instructions and then he wanted to be left alone. We prayed together and he died." Nick wiped his eyes.

Caught

"Does he have any ID?"

Nick shrugged.

"How did he get here?"

Nick shrugged again. "He came to give me his final instructions." Dusty raised a questioning eyebrow inviting more information. "He gave me keys to his place and asked me to claim his possessions. I called Tilly because I didn't know what to do. He said call you."

"Can I see the papers?" Nick handed Dusty the packet. After reading Dusty said, "He came to die and wanted you to take care of wrapping up his life." Nick nodded. Dusty pulled out his phone and gave some instructions. "He'll have to be transported to the hospital and death verified." There was one more question. "Why did you want Lynn here?"

Nick shrugged for the millionth time. "Tilly thought it would be a good idea. He said it would keep you from thinking I murdered him." Dusty glared at Tilly. They had a checkered past.

Tilly grinned. "I know you sometimes need a calming influence." Dusty swore.

Lynn gasped. "We're in a church."

"It was a prayer," snarled the detective.

The EMTs came racing into the church and things became very organized and professional. As the body was carried out, Dusty said, "Just come into the office tomorrow and we'll do the paperwork. Do you need anything else?"

"Thank you," said Nick. "I've got to notify the bishop and figure out what Father Gillespie wanted of me." He gripped the papers in his hand tighter.

Dusty and Lynn left the church as Nick and Tilly walked into the sacristy. "They seem to be good friends," Lynn remarked.

"The two preachers?" She nodded. "They play cards together with some other guys."

"Do you join them?"

"No, Tilly says it's just single guys. Sean and Noah used to play but," Dusty grinned, "as Tilly says, they found religion."

Lynn laughed because her two friends had found love. "Have you and Tilly buried the hatchet or something and declared peace between you?"

Dusty laughed. "We have but the good Reverend Tilly likes to rattle my chain when he can and still stay on the side of the angels."

Lynn laughed again. She always enjoyed thinking of her old school friend in his surprising career as a man of God. Who would have thought the local hellion would hear a call to serve?

CHAPTER TWO

Lynn found herself having breakfast at Piper's elementary school - again. After the last breakfast Piper had pleaded with Lynn to provide more shelter locations for homeless families with school-aged children. She wondered what the dedicated principal would ask of her this morning.

Piper Zubov was Lynn's best friend and her sister-in-law. Their friendship had started in kindergarten when Lynn, a gangly dark-hair imp, met the tiny blonde, blue-eyed fairy-like demon. Sitting in the school cafeteria, Lynn thought back to her carefree childhood days and chuckled as she recalled two sets of parents wondering what the future held for their mischievous daughters.

And here was the future - Lynn the executive director of the River Bend Philanthropies and Piper, dedicated elementary school principal in a school serving low-income families with children. Piper was delighted to have her students back in school. She had worried about their safety and living conditions during lockdown. She had convinced Dusty and his team to routinely pass through their neighborhoods to check on her students. Now they were back under her protection and influence. She could make certain they had enough to eat and were safe during the hours they spent in the classrooms.

Youngsters dropped masks and ate breakfast. Teachers kept their masks in place and worked to make certain the students didn't fall further behind with any more virus induced education delays.

"Why am I here today?" Lynn asked through her Board of Education mandatory mask.

"My staff has come up with an idea and we may need help from the Philanthropies." Piper was interrupted in her presentation as she picked up a mask from the floor and tossed it in the trash. "We want to initiate a school-based health clinic. Not just a school nurse, but all the things my students need - dental checks, eye checks, behavioral health support."

"Doesn't the school nurse provide this care?" Lynn's eyes skimmed over the busy cafeteria.

"The school nurse has to maintain immunization records, be ready to deal with the big scourges, you know, lice and flu." Piper rolled her eyes along the top of her mask. "This virus! Besides, we share her with another elementary school. And she works for Public Health, not for the schools."

"Shouldn't you be asking the Board of Education to fund this?" Lynn was morphing into a grant reviewer before Piper's eyes. "You're asking for something they could provide. Or Public Health? Isn't that their job?"

"Public Health is doing their job," said Piper, "We want more for our students and it will cost more money than either budget provides. The plan is to ask the Philanthropies for a planning grant to prepare our case, possibly work with the hospital, or South End Clinic." Piper watched as the students lined up and were led to their classrooms. "I can make a request, but the better it's put together, the better chance we have of success. There are models in Henderson and Buncombe counties. We won't be creating something out of the blue. We can show numbers and budgets and I'm certain that we can demonstrate success like we did with Sharing Shelter." Piper and her staff had been the impetus behind developing more shelters for homeless families because they had documented improved grades and behavior from students whose families had received shelter through the program.

"How much?" Lynn watched as the last students exited the cafeteria.

Piper waved a hand urging Lynn to follow after the students. "Let's go to my office."

* * *

"Wow," gasped Lynn. "That's quite a proposal." She had been sitting in Piper's office for almost two hours. "Are you going to make the request?"

"No," said Piper. "I've learned something about the nonprofit world. I've formed a board of directors, they're incorporating as a nonprofit and you'll be dealing with them." Lynn raised her eyebrow in question. "Sherri Vonder is my chair and she's convinced her old friend, Amelia Rawlings, to join us." Before Lynn's eyes Piper wrapped up the whole presentation. "And Amelia has told us that Zachary will match the Philanthropies funds." Lynn's eyes grew large. "And," continued Piper, "he'll fund half of our first year of operation as a school health clinic."

"Wow," Lynn whispered again. Amelia Rawlings was the owner of Amelia's Maids, a business that employed many clients from the domestic violence shelter or newly released prisoners looking to build a work ethic and employment history. Her husband, Zachary, was a retired international banker. They had only been married for a few years after meeting as surviving spouses of murder victims. And Sherri Vonder was a woman with children at the school who had always provided safe shelter for Amelia during her first marriage to an abusive spouse. The friendship had lasted even after the murder of the abusive spouse and Amelia's fairytale wedding to a wealthy, loving man.

Piper was triumphant. "When do we get our money?" She smiled at Lynn as she sat, hands clasped before her at her desk.

Lynn laughed. "After my grants committee accepts your proposal and decides that you should be funded." Lynn hung her head in thought. "I think you may have to resign from the Philanthropies board. This is going to be a big request and your presence on the board would raise conflict of interest issues."

"You need some new blood anyway. I've been on there long enough and we have term limits, don't we?"

"We put them in our bylaws three years ago. Don't you remember the discussion? You all decided that term limits wouldn't apply to current members so that you could all continue to serve or not. I think it was so Robert O'Hara could stay on the board, as our last founding member." Sadly, Robert O'Hara had succumbed to the virus in the early months of the pandemic.

"I think I should leave the board at the end of my term and we should recruit Zachary Rawlings." Piper tried to look innocent.

Lynn laughed. "Who taught you how to be so Machiavellian? You know Zachary's going to protect your project." Piper grinned. "But I have a better idea," offered Lynn immediately drawing Piper's interest. "You're proposing something that would benefit children in all our schools. Maybe the Philanthropies' board would like to explore this concept with your committee as an even bigger idea."

"That will delay my clinic!" argued the protective principal.

"No, think of your school as the pilot project," suggested Lynn, accepting a hug from her friend as Piper showed her support for the idea. "'I'll put it on the agenda for our meeting next week," Lynn promised.

* * *

Rachel had thought about Kip Mahaffey's request for a long time. Today she had finally told him that she would decline his request that she become his campaign manager for the mayoral election. He had not been happy. In fact, it was the first time she had ever heard the hint of a different, meaner, Kip in his voice. She had held firm and he had abruptly ended the phone call. But she knew in her heart that she couldn't take on another project that would throw her and Kip together. Especially not a political campaign. He would have to start his climb to congressional success without her.

She stared at the phone, her knees were still shaking. Two days ago, she had been ready to throw herself into his arms. Was she that desperate for affection and sex? What had her marriage come to? As she thought over the state of her marriage she moved around her kitchen like a zombie, getting another uninspired meal ready. She didn't think her husband even noticed any more. He had told her after a recent medical check-up that he didn't want spicy foods, or too much chicken and, oh, maybe he should eat more fish but not often, and how about beef, but no steaks, and pork, but only if she served it with her special orange sauce.

What was left? Not much, because he hadn't suggested that salads or any vegetables were acceptable as good foods. She sighed. Tomorrow she would stop at the fancy grocery store and pick up a ready-made dinner. Tonight, it would be whole wheat pasta with a jar of spaghetti sauce. And what did it matter? He would come to the table, eat, barely speak, and then settle in front of the TV for the rest of the evening unless he had a meeting or they had an engagement with friends like a bridge game or a dinner planned.

Caught

But his final edict, wrapping up their sterile marriage, had been his comment, "Oh and by the way, maybe we should hold off on the sex. It doesn't do much for me anymore." It was a comment to which she had been unable to reply. She had been too shocked!

It was about time she started facing the desert that was her marriage and started to think about what she would plan for the rest of her life. Maybe her husband would have some ideas. Maybe he was bored and ready to leave the desert, too. Maybe he had a girlfriend someplace. Or not, because she heard the garage door open. He was home on time. He was never unaccounted for.

Owen Teague walked into the kitchen, nodded to Rachel, glanced at the stove and sat at the kitchen table clicking the remote to turn on the small kitchen TV. Owen was still a handsome man with thinning hair and a little extra weight. He had always worked hard and provided Rachel and their children with a very comfortable life. The children were getting on with their own lives. Owen and Rachel's empty lives echoed through the empty nest.

After dinner, she cleaned the kitchen while Owen moved to the den and an evening watching TV. Rachel went into her small office beside the laundry room and wondered how to start a conversation to end her marriage.

CHAPTER THREE

Lynn and Dusty had decided to join Reverend Tilly, Sean Hennessey and Doc Noah for the quiet funeral of Father Nick's old friend and mentor, John Gillespie. For several days the mechanics of death had played out: ME report, case opened and closed by Dusty's staff, formal diocesan paperwork, and informal contact with the bishop and an assortment of clergy throughout the Charlotte diocese. Even with all the activity and all the required notifications, Lynn expected only a small gathering for the formal service. She was surprised when they arrived at St. Bridget's to find the church parking lot filled with cars.

Inside the church Nick, robed for a celebration of John Gillespie's life, pulled them aside saying, "The bishop has even sneaked into town for this service." Lynn was certain he wanted to rub a handkerchief across his brow. "I don't know how word got around."

"Social media," whispered Lynn.

Nick shook his head, perplexed. "Anyway, it seems every priest in the diocese and a few from other places have come to celebrate John's life. This is not what I expected." He looked around. "I'm going to have to feed them," he almost sobbed, "and the bishop!"

Dusty looked at Lynn and raised an eyebrow. She pulled out her phone. "I'll take care of it."

Nick looked so grateful she had to laugh. He checked his watch. "Mass begins in about five minutes." Lynn nodded and walked away texting on her phone. The priest straightened his shoulders and nodded to the organist.

The celebration of Father John Gillespie's life was uplifting for all who attended. Several priests, including the Bishop of Charlotte, spoke to John's gifts and his devotion to his church. It was revealing to learn that over the years John had offered guidance and support to several of those attending. He may have moved to the mountains of western North

Carolina, but he seemed to have stayed engaged in many lives throughout the state. His friends had stories of shared loss and shared joy. As usual, Lynn left the service regretting that she had not known the deceased. She marveled at how often she had those thoughts after a funeral. Life moved so quickly, in her opinion, that we never had time to appreciate the talents and develop meaningful relationships with enough people.

At the close of the personal statements Nick glanced to her pew, she nodded and he said, "Please come to our family center for some refreshments and time for us to visit more."

Walking into the parish center the priest gasped. Yolanda Valeri, parishioner, and Dave Wetzel, local restauranteur, welcomed guests into a room with tables set, and a buffet loaded with food. Lynn recognized several other parishioners ready to serve food and pour coffee.

"How did you get all this done?" Nick asked as he watched his guests attack the buffet.

"Social media!" Lynn held up her phone for him to read the text display. *Fr. Nick surprised by bishop visit. Food needed in one hour, parish hall. 50 mouths.* He was touched by the responses as he scanned all the replies promising help and food that scrolled across her screen.

He laughed and took her arm. "Let me introduce you to the bishop."

* * *

Lynn looked at Piper, the beta version. That's what she thought of the Piper that plopped, flopped, and moaned about life in her kitchen on a regular basis. Piper 2.0 was the topnotch, dedicated, focused teacher, principal and child advocate who got things done. Beta Piper was the faded, incomplete image, a person always looking for help with problems while always ready to bitch and moan. Who was the real Piper?

"What do *you* want?" Lynn demanded of the woman half sprawled across the kitchen table. "I'm trying to get ready for the cookout tonight." The morning funeral had taken time. She looked around for dishes, or boxes, or stuff that Piper should have carried in. "Where's . . . . everything?"

Piper raised a weak, listless arm toward her house. "It's there. Will is bringing it."

"What's wrong with you?" Lynn had no patience with Beta Piper because this was Jim's celebratory coming back from lockdown cookout and she wanted everything perfect and drama free.

"Graduation." Piper barely managed to raise her head from the table to speak. "Wedding."

Lynn marveled at the speed of time. It was only last summer that Piper's son Doyle announced his engagement to Lori Santiago, daughter of Will's best friend, Miguel. As the young couple had told the family, they wanted to be married after graduation. That meant graduation from college in May and a June wedding.

"Yes," agreed Lynn. "And we have it, or them, all under control." She sat at the table and tousled Piper's curls. "Remember, you're the mother of the groom. Justine and Lori have the wedding all planned. I think it will be beautiful at the club on the lake."

"I know. I should be doing more." Piper's voice sounded as though she were very happy to be the mother of the groom and let Justine, the mother of the bride, take the lead.

"No, you shouldn't!" Lynn knew that if Piper were more involved in the planning that meant she would be, too. And she didn't have time to organize Lori and Doyle's wedding! "Besides, you and Will have been busy getting your old house ready for them." Doyle and Lori would be living in River Bend, moving into Piper's old house, the house her parents currently lived in until their move last week to a small apartment addition in Piper's current house in The Heights. The newlyweds would be settling in River Bend. Doyle would be working for Will and Lori had accepted a job with Kevin Dowd's IT firm, the business technology consulting firm for almost everyone in town. Lynn knew the new hires would be busy. Everyone in the family looked forward to the next generation taking up life in River Bend. Lockdown, pandemic or not, life moved forward.

"Graduation," moaned Piper as a reminder that she was overwhelmed by two events.

Lynn rolled her eyes and got up to open a bottle of wine. Pouring a glass for herself and Piper she said, "Again, it's all organized. We'll have a graduation party in the yard." Because Doyle and Jason, Lynn's son, were both graduating from college, but attending different universities, the locations and times didn't coincide. Piper and Lynn had planned a combined graduation and sort of late engagement party for a few weeks before the wedding.

"Should we invite more people? Did we leave anyone out?" Piper found the strength to sit up and down her wine.

"Will's suggestion was good," Lynn said. "Keep this party to family and close friends. Then have your usual summer party welcoming the newlyweds to their new life in River Bend."

Piper moaned again. "Another party to plan!"

Lynn poured her another glass of wine. "We'll just do what we've done in the past. Rent tables and chairs and cook tons of dogs and burgers." She hoped her yard survived what would almost be a party a month!

"The virus?"

"It'll be outside as usual. No problem." Lynn poured herself more wine. "We'll let invitees self-select. If they feel nervous about a germy gathering, they can stay home." She was starting to feel really hostile toward something she couldn't see and couldn't punch.

* * *

The cookout was going as planned. The evening had a little chill, but that's why everyone had sweatshirts or sweaters handy. Lynn sat on the back porch glider with her friend, Harriette Mitchell. Since Harriette's son Ricky always appeared for cookouts in the area formerly known as the mask-free zone, Lynn had invited his mother to join the family this evening. And Harriette was expressing her delight. "Thank you for inviting me tonight. This pandemic has certainly curtailed our lives. We haven't met with our widows' group for ages." Harriette was a small woman with a charmingly round figure and a warm, welcoming personality.

Lynn was the informal head of an even more informal widows' group in town. The reference to the widows' group always made her chuckle. She continued to point out to the others that she had remarried, but several of the women involved always replied that they owed her for the support they received from her while navigating unexpected widowhood. "I haven't seen Sara since Janet returned from Japan," Lynn commented.

Sara Margolin, a widow with three children, was a partner with Janet Bergman in an IT consulting firm.

"They're so busy. We've been hired to clean Janet's house." Harriette was the office manager and scheduler for Amelia's Maids. "I think Sara is considering hiring us, too. She has those three children to raise." She looked at Lynn with a sideways glance. "You helped me get through those days with Ricky. And now he's finishing his first year of college."

"How has that worked out?" Lynn knew that Jason's senior year in college had been irregular, but he would graduate in a few weeks and had been accepted into law school.

Harriette smiled. "Ricky got good advice about enrolling in the basic college classes at the community college because they would transfer to a four-year college. He's ready to move on to college life at the end of summer. He saved a lot of money and we were able to buy him a better car."

"You'll have your empty nest." Lynn looked at her and raised an eyebrow.

"And it will stay empty. I have no man in the background ready to slip in." She looked down at her hands and sniffed.

Lynn remembered one morning over a year ago when she found Harriette sharing breakfast with her neighbor. Something had happened and the man had moved on. Harriette had never wanted to talk about him. "Now that we're unmasking more and more, we should catch a beer at Frank's. Get everyone together to catch-up." The informal widows' group usually met at Frank's Tavern, a local bar frequently offering venison stew and other game recipes depending on supplies.

Harriette nodded. "I think Frank is back to almost full operation. We love our beer in River Bend." They watched the activity in the yard for several minutes. "Your father looks happy to be here tonight."

Lynn agreed. "This is his come-out. He and Marianna stayed close to home in the early pandemic days. They feel ready to get out now that they have had their shots."

"I know what you mean. Our maids have had to be very cautious working with many of our regulars." Harriette rolled her eyes. "And you know the precautions we have taken with our commercial clients."

"We appreciate it," confirmed Lynn. "Just knowing how conscientious your maids are makes people more comfortable meeting at our office. What about your in-laws?" She was referring to the parents of Harriette's late husband.

"They've been as cautious as your father," she replied. "I check with them regularly and Ricky goes over to help when he can. They are lovely people and after all this time are still in shock after losing their only child."

Lynn wanted to point out that Harriette also seemed to be mourning and staying in her widowhood when she should be getting out in the community more often socially. Then she remembered what Dusty had told her years ago, that she could stay a widow or she could move on to the next stage of life. She suspected Harriette hadn't met a man who challenged her widowhood yet - and might never.

"Hey, you two," shouted Jim, "where's dessert? I promised Marianna our diet would be on hold tonight." Everyone joined in demanding dessert because they all knew Harriette had brought her famous chocolate ice cream extravaganza cake.

CHAPTER FOUR

Rory Prentiss was delighted with his new job. He liked working for the Philanthropies and was not sorry to leave behind his old job as director of the Arts Council with the nonprofit angst of constant fundraising. This weekend he had loaned his small house to the committee working to design a program or new agency to help clients from several agencies learn about financial planning and to ensure these clients would not be victims of schemes such as payday loans or get-rich-quick promises or credit card scams.

The committee, working through a grant from funds Yolanda Valeri monitored, had hired a consultant, James Thurman, who stayed at Rory's place when he came to town. Rory liked to slip off to visit a personal friend for an intimate weekend in another county. As he liked to think, win-win for everyone. However, his friend had to leave town first thing this morning because of a family crisis in Georgia. Returning to River Bend earlier than usual would allow Rory to get a report from James and the consultant could return home earlier. Win-win.

Audrey Decker, the respected executive director of the nonprofit Exceptional Children, was a member of the committee to help clients of her agency and others learn and manage personal finances. She had met James Thurman when he was invited by the committee to help them develop the new idea into a proper program. Two years ago a man with financial planning expertise who would have helped her clients' families with these issues was murdered. Before his death he had told Audrey about a program he had worked with in another state. Several other nonprofits in town also had need for financial planning help of various kinds for their clients. James was the final consultant to assist them after working with several others through the challenges of lockdown in a pandemic. They were close to setting up an agency to meet everyone's needs. Throughout the process, James had been a frequent visitor to

Caught

River Bend. The added attraction for him was the Exceptional Children's group home for the developmentally delayed. James had a brother who needed that service. As his brother's guardian, he determined that the group home in Hanging Oak was the perfect spot for his aging, loving brother.

"This is the best place I've found," he always told Audrey. Once his brother was settled in River Bend, or the group home in Hanging Oak to be specific, James found opportunities to visit on a regular basis. And that's how it started, quick meetings with Audrey to discuss his brother. Longer meetings to help her and the small committee organize a new nonprofit. It all led to more time with Audrey. Then last fall, with her husband and her children working and schooling from home, Audrey had been called to her office to deal with issues at the group home created by the pandemic. James helped her manage the challenges. It was not unusual for her to rely on her husband to monitor the children as she dealt with another crisis. And it was not unusual for James with his nonprofit management experience to assist her in thinking through solutions. Time together became passion together.

James was familiar with the ways other group homes were handling the pandemic. With his brother in Hanging Oak, he frequently came to town and one thing led to another. He learned about Audrey's life, her marriage to a husband who was becoming more and more distant. James found Audrey lovely, lively, and intelligent. He couldn't understand why her marriage was in terrible shape. He had looked for years for someone like her. And the night he found her passion made him devoted to her. He knew her children came first, but it was easy for the two of them to find time to be together during his frequent visits to River Bend. Using Rory's house created an opportunity for quiet times after meetings for Audrey and James to be together.

This weekend was no different. Audrey was staying with James as usual. Her husband was attending a weekend work-related conference somewhere, and her children were with her parents in the next county. But today, Rory returned home unexpectedly, surprising everyone. James had immediately apologized to Rory, kissed Audrey on the cheek and announced that he had errands to run before leaving town. "I'll be back in an hour to brief Rory." They watched him get into his car and drive away from the no longer secret trysting place.

"He's giving me some time to pull myself together," said Audrey as she gave Rory a sad smile.

* * *

Two golfers wrapped up their Sunday morning round sitting on the club patio with iced tea having enjoyed a scenic but challenging round of golf at one of the private courses in western North Carolina. "You're getting better on sixteen," chuckled Walter Varney. A seasoned, experienced golfer Varney was meeting with Ralph Ebetts. Both were businessmen with a profitable sideline in organized crime. As Varney admitted to himself, he needed to be a successful businessman so that he could launder his crime profits through his trucking company books. He didn't know what business Ebetts ran. He just knew him as another middle manager in a drug and weapons distribution organization.

Ebetts sipped his tea and attacked the Reuben in front of him. Around his sandwich he nodded and said, "Yep, getting better." Ebetts was a bit younger than Varney and higher up the food chain than Varney suspected. In essence Varney, a sixtyish man with gray hair, nondescript looks and an ingrained social country club polish, had accepted a proposal to manage certain activities in and around River Bend years ago when his company needed an influx of cash. Ebetts had been assigned to monitor Varney's work.

The younger balding man had honed his physique in hard labor working in quarries and lumber in the western part of the state before catching the eye of some state crime leadership. Ebetts' social country club polish was all fake. He had learned it over the years while he was learning to golf and to run drugs.

Varney finished his Cobb salad, always worried about extra weight and his health. "Things going okay for you?"

Ebetts nodded. "And you?"

"My dirty cop says the drug task force is still interested in that cabin."

"I don't understand that deal," admitted Ebetts. "What do you gain?"

Varney scowled. "Nothing. But Mahaffey and his girlfriend run those clinics giving two-thousand-dollar shots to guys who believe it gives them an edge." He shrugged.

"So what's the split?"

"They make about thirty - forty grand a weekend. I get a third. The girlfriend also buys some product from me and brings some stuff from her clinic. She mixes something and she has satisfied customers."

Ebetts thought for a minute as he toyed with the crust from his sandwich. "Is it worth it if the cops are interested?"

"I thought about shutting it down," admitted Varney, "but Mahaffey is talking about running for mayor and after a term he plans to run for Congress." He chortled. "It might be helpful to have a congressman in my back pocket."

"Hmmmm. You got a point. I guess you just have to wait and see."

Varney agreed. "As long as the dirty cop keeps me informed." They talked some more about business and concluded by setting a date for their next round of golf.

* * *

Two people stared at one another across the room in the quiet carriage house. "I'm so sorry." James Thurman hung his head.

"You have nothing to be sorry about, James," said Audrey. But she stayed on her side of the room resisting the urge to console him, to cling to him. "I knew what I was doing. And you gave my so much warmth and affection, something lacking in my real life." She couldn't resist. She took a step closer.

He studied the woman who had found his heart. He took a step closer. "Will you be safe?"

"Yes." Another step. They could almost touch.

"Hello?" called Rory from the back door. After his briefing from James, Rory had stepped outside allowing time for them to say good-by.

They looked at one another and knew how close they had come to falling back into each other's arms. "We're in here," called Audrey.

"I'm just leaving," said James as he picked up his bag and walked toward Rory's voice.

Audrey watched him leave the room and heard the door close as he left the house. Rory walked into the room. "Are you okay?"

She sighed deeply. "I have to pick up the kids and get home before Bart gets back." She swallowed a sob. Rory took her in his arms.

"Cry it out, sweetie. Take ten minutes to mourn." He held her while she sobbed.

Rory was a good friend to Audrey. He had listened to her for years. Why he had become her confidante all those years ago was a mystery - but who knew the trials of relationships better than a gay man? In fact, he had confided as much to her as she had to him. Life in River Bend wasn't easy for his alternate lifestyle. His friends accepted him, but there were not many dating options. Or as Rory liked to point out, "There aren't many gay farmers. And I refuse to troll along the river." Audrey had always grinned at the image of Rory in South End.

Today she said, "I want to talk."

Rory pulled her down on the sofa and sat beside her. "Unburden," he said gently. "Who am I to judge?"

She related the story of her relationship with James and concluded by asking, "Any advice?" She rested her head on his shoulder with a sigh.

"This project is almost finished." Rory was thoughtful a moment. "The temptation of his presence is almost a thing of the past."

She sniffled. "James'll always be in town. His brother is living in one of the group homes." Rory embraced her.

"Maybe you can steal time alone a few times a year." Rory was practical, not judgmental.

"We ended it today," she said in a soft sad voice. "He knows we can't start up again."

"I know, sweetie, I think he knows you'll stay in your marriage and with your kids. They come first, not him."

"He's correct, you're correct." She lifted her head and looked at him. "I would never leave my marriage, put my kids through a divorce." She placed her head on his shoulder, again. "I feel so guilty."

"Sweetie, I don't know what to tell you." He squeezed her shoulder. "We've worked a long time on this project. I'd hate to have some gossip spoil it."

Caught

"Do you think I've put our program at risk?" She sniffed and caught a tear before it landed on his shirt.

He shrugged causing her head to bobble on his shoulder. "I don't know. Small town gossip can kill a reputation and sidetrack a good idea." He thought for a moment. "Lynn's a good sounding board for this heartbreak stuff. And she has a fundraiser's sense of how to manage potential mine fields. Talk to her sometime during the week."

* * *

"How long has it been?" Harriette Mitchell asked as Frank placed a pitcher of beer and several glasses on the table. The tavern hadn't changed at all since lockdown. Same old cobwebs, same old fake planters, same old welcoming Frank.

"I've lost track of time," answered the bartender. "I'm just happy to have you ladies back."

He scanned the almost empty bar. "I was beginning to think no one wanted to drink anymore."

Sara Margolin laughed. "Frank, this is our haven. Germs be damned. We're back."

"What you ladies been up to?" he asked.

Sara smiled, "Business just got hotter. Our IT clients doubled."

Harriette nodded. "Amelia's Maids picked up several new clients. Folks want to be sanitized as well as cleaned."

"Glad to hear it. At least I know you can pay the tab." He looked around.

"Who else is coming?"

"Me," said Lynn as she slid in beside Sara. "I think Piper is coming because she says she needs a night out."

"She ain't a widow," Frank reminded them.

"We know," said Harriette, "but we can't get rid of her."

"Wel-ll-ll," mumbled Lynn and they all looked at her waiting for an explanation. "Since Piper is coming, and she's divorced, I invited Allison. She's divorced from Dusty's brother."

"I heard about that," said Sara. "He's turning into a real ass." She blushed. "Sorry, Frank."

"I understand. I heard he was moving to Asheville. He said there were more ladies to charm." Allison Reid walked in with another woman and Frank gave her a good look over. "That Kent Reid is a real ass. She's one classy lady." And all the ladies knew why they continued to be faithful to Frank's Tavern.

Piper walked in behind Allison and a guest, giving orders, "Frank, wings."

"You got it, general." He trailed off to the kitchen.

"Allison?" Lynn stood as the women approached the large corner booth. "Do you know everyone?" The younger woman scanned the booth and shook her head. "Sit and we'll get acquainted. We've already ordered." Once the six women were settled in the booth, Lynn began introductions. "This is Sara who has three kids and is an IT consultant. And next is the lovely Harriette Mitchell, mother of a college freshman and manager of Amelia's Maids. Piper, elementary school principal. Oh," she looked at Allison. "You know Piper."

"But we don't know you," Piper stared at Allison's guest.

Lynn held out her hand to the new woman. "I'm Lynn, Allison's sister-in-law. Piper who has no manners is my sister-in-law, too."

The woman reached out her hand. "I'm Tovah Fleischer."

"She's my accountant," bragged Allison. "She replaced Kent, and my books have never been so well organized!" Allison had taken over her family's nursery business when her father became ill.

"So are you divorced or widowed?" demanded Piper as she stared at Tovah.

Tovah glared back at the tiny principal. "Who are you, the relationship police?" Everyone, except Piper, laughed. Tovah looked at the others in the booth. "Allison invited me to meet folks. I'm new in town." She scowled at Piper. "And to answer your question. I'm happily divorced. I left him in New York City."

"Children?" Piper was a topnotch interrogator.

"I have custody of my niece. Her mother is dead and her father travels a lot." Tovah's look dared her to ask more questions. Piper got the hint.

"I apologize for Piper," said Lynn, "but if she wasn't this obnoxious, we wouldn't learn as much so quickly." She refreshed everyone's beer mug.

Caught

Tovah smiled. "I'm just glad you shake hands. I feel I haven't touched anyone for years." She looked at her new friends. "And that includes my ex. In lockdown, my company sent us all home to work and I found out that he liked to use our lovely apartment as his playpen. Any stray woman he could find. Mostly nurses. He's a surgeon."

"My ex was a doctor, too," gushed Piper in amazement. "I feel like we're sisters." Tovah rolled her eyes. Piper continued, "He slept with everyone within a hundred miles. I came back here to raise our sons."

"Wow," marveled Lynn. "Three widows and three divorcees. We're becoming more diverse."

"Here's the food," interrupted Frank. "Nachos for everyone and wings for the general." He placed the platter of Greek nachos and a dozen wings on the table along with another pitcher of beer and small dishes. "Enjoy!"

They all dug in until Harriette asked, "What's new with everyone? I feel like I've been under water for a year."

"I'm going to DisneyWorld in a month or so," announced Sara. "We were hired as subcontractors. They used some of the pandemic time to upgrade internal computer operations. I'm going to take the kids with me for a week. It will be our first real vacation since we moved back here." She caught Tovah's eye. "When I was widowed, I came back here. I was raised here and needed family support with three kids."

"Like me." Piper chirped around a buffalo wing.

Sara continued, "I joined my cousin Janet's consulting firm because her husband had just been sent to Japan by the Navy. I kept up the business here and she consulted from Japan. Now she's home and I can get away."

"Is she divorced or widowed?" Tovah was trying to stay abreast of these new friends and trying to get a wing, but Piper was hoarding.

"She's married to Tim and he manages our business. He said it's more interesting than the Navy." Sara lowered her voice. "He also helps us with the government contracts."

"I get to talk next," ordained Piper.

"When haven't you talked?" asked Lynn.

Piper whined and Beta Piper appeared in the booth. "Graduation, wedding." She took a drink and grabbed some nachos. Then remembered she was helpless and slumped in her seat.

Lynn looked at Tovah. "Piper has a son graduating from college and getting married a month later. She has nothing to do. The mother of the bride has the wedding all organized and she has no role in the graduation weekend except show up. Never show her sympathy. She'll take advantage." Piper moaned but grabbed the last wing.

Tovah sat back and grinned, feeling comfortable sitting with such entertaining and accepting women. This move to River Bend might just be what she needed to begin a different, slower paced life. Like Piper and Sara, she had moved here for family support.

* * *

Bart Decker walked into the house Sunday evening. "Daddy," called out one of the kids. "We bought your favorite pizza. Mommy said you would be home for dinner." He ruffled the curly head.

"I'm home and hungry, pal." The man hung up his jacket and walked into the kitchen with his young son. He nodded to his wife. "Audrey, did you have a busy weekend?"

She looked as guilty as hell, he thought. He had driven by the house this morning and the group home in Hanging Oak and hadn't seen her car. Of course, he couldn't challenge her because he wasn't supposed to be in town, he was supposed to be at some non-existent seminar in Winston-Salem. As long as she wasn't suspicious, he'd let her lies stand. They were piling up and he'd have to think about his reaction. He didn't like to think some bastard was having a sweet time with his wife. But he couldn't give up his own secret activity. He needed the drugs to stay on top of his game.

"The kids are ready to eat, Bart," said Audrey as she poured soft drinks and iced tea. "We just got back from Mother's." She looked at him out of the corner of her eye. He was suspicious, she was certain.

"Grandma played Monopoly with us," offered one of the kids. "We had a good time."

"Let's all wash up," said Audrey. "Dad and I are hungry."

Caught

There was a lot of bustle in the kitchen and soon everyone was seated around the table. "Bart, if you brought home some laundry, I have to wash the playthings the kids brought home." She smiled at him.

"I'll get my stuff out of the car after dinner." And that was how a very benign dinner progressed around secrets.

CHAPTER FIVE

When Lynn got into her office Monday morning she found Audrey Decker, the executive director of Exceptional Children, waiting for her. She was surprised to see the strain on the woman's face. "Let's go up to my office." Lynn knew that Audrey's look indicated more than some funding crisis but had no idea what it could be.

Without offering coffee she got down to business. "Is there something wrong?"

Audrey, a slender woman with dark blonde shoulder length hair, nodded. She had been the driving force in the establishment of the Exceptional Children agency offering services to developmentally delayed children and adults. It was a successful program that had garnered statewide attention and made Audrey one of the state leaders and advocates for her client population. "Rory told me I had to talk to you," she whispered.

That surprised Lynn. She knew Rory and Audrey were friends and were working on a project under a Philanthropies' grant. "About the new agency? Or finding money?"

Audrey shook her head. "This is personal." After a big sigh, she began, "As you know we have been working with the consultant for several months. Our plan is almost ready for unveiling." She hung her head, gathering her thoughts and her courage. "We've worked closely with our consultant, James. And .... maybe .... I worked a little too closely." Lynn gave her a puzzled stare. Audrey sighed again. "He brought his brother to live at the group home. He helped me with some management issues..... and we had an affair."

Lynn gasped. "Had?"

Audrey nodded. "During our last meeting, I told him we had to stop. I think my husband is getting suspicious." She looked at Lynn with tears in her eyes. "I think that's why it started. My husband, Bart, has been acting so strange. I found James a good listener. I unburdened myself. He had his own personal issues. We shared. We commiserated and then we had an affair."

"Is it over?"

"Yes." A definitive answer. She dried her eyes. "We talked it over before he left town. He agreed. We'll make certain to keep our distance during these last few meetings. This project is too good to ruin with my misbehavior."

"Why is Rory involved?" Lynn could see Audrey's pain and confusion.

"He has let James stay at his place when he's in town and that's where we got together after the committee meetings." Lynn remembered Rory telling her that he gave his place over to the project working committee and left town to stay with a friend on those days. "He caught us Sunday. James and I were taking advantage of Bart's business trip. I stayed overnight because my mother took the kids. Rory came back early and there we were."

"This is none of my business," said Lynn, "but I'm glad to know in case I hear rumors or am asked questions." Lynn took Audrey's hands. "I don't know what else to say."

Audrey nodded. "Rory said you would be a good listener and had a sense of fundraising mine fields."

Lynn grimaced. "Do you expect any ugliness?"

"I don't think anything will happen unless my husband gets vocal." She shook her head. "I don't know what's gotten into him lately, but his behavior is so strange." She was silent a moment, then stood. "My marriage problems aren't your concern. I appreciate you listening. I have to get to my office." She wiped a tear that was sliding down her cheek.

Lynn walked her to the office door. "Let me know if you think I can help in some way."

Audrey nodded and left the office, her head down. Lynn moved to the window and watched the woman walk slowly to her car. She was carrying a burden, and Lynn was helpless. Marriage problems, as she had learned, had to be solved by the two partners, not by family or friends.

* * *

It seemed as though Audrey had just left and before Lynn could get to work, someone else was walking into her office. Maybe she needed to return to her home office for privacy. No, that wouldn't work. Her home office seemed to get cluttered with friends and neighbors looking for coffee, snacks, and gossip. She stood at the top of the stairs frowning at the new arrivals.

"Lynn, we have an idea we want you to listen to," said Michelle Grayson. She looked up at Lynn, who appeared to dare anyone to approach her aerie. Penny Rawlings and Trina Healey stood behind Michelle staring up at Lynn as though preparing to charge the castle walls. They were the beautiful people of River Bend. Three young, talented, attractive women with wealthy husbands. What a combination, thought Lynn! Of course, it seemed to Lynn that at any given month at least one of them was pregnant. She squinted. Nope, no one seemed to be pregnant this month.

"You want to invent a new fundraiser for me that will raise millions and allow me to retire." Lynn couldn't imagine why these lovely women had come by without calling or texting or something. She started down the stairs. Her office was too small for this mob.

"I thought we did that already," said Penny. The young women had helped the hospital raise funds through a virtual dinner dance, proving that fundraising didn't stop in a pandemic. In the past they had worked with River Bend Reads on a book fair that raised bundles and thrilled all the local readers with a few very popular authors zooming in for seminars. And before that was a pre-pandemic Christmas house tour that still had everyone talking.

Lynn smiled and said, "Nelda just made some coffee," as she led them into the conference room.

"We need some advice," began Penny, the lawyer in the group. "We want to start a business."

"You can't," cried Lynn, "who'll raise the money for all our nonprofits?" She squinted as she remembered, "But you already have jobs!"

"We can still do our jobs and raise money, too," said Michelle, the CPA. "We have a lot of time on our hands with working from home these days and we've been listening to what Trina tells us about her students." Trina, a former reporter from LA, currently taught journalism and creative writing online at the community college.

"I've got so many talented students that I think we should start a regional magazine," announced Trina.

Penny jumped in. "Since we all seem to be at home and staying in touch through the internet, we thought we could use the internet to help young parents get valuable, factual news for their families." They all nodded because they had all witnessed what news fabricators could do to the public's state of mind. Conspiracy theories seemed to have more believers than facts.

"That's why we want to disseminate information and local news for families," concluded Michelle.

"I've seen such things in larger towns," said Trina. "I think if we stick with a three or four county area, and use community college students as stringers, we can have something great.

And the community college might be interested in maintaining a link to our website to expand student work-study options. I think we can do a really good job and have a great time!"

"Will this be print or online?"

"Both. We'll sell ads for both versions."

"Will this make money?" asked the fundraiser.

"It will after about two years," said the CPA. "I've done the math."

"I'm drawing up the papers," said the attorney.

"And I've gotten started on our business plan," continued the CPA.

"I'll be the editor and recruit writers and staff," said Trina. "I hope I don't have to quit my job at the school." She thought a moment. "I think the community college might support this idea as long as it doesn't require their funds. Things are tight right now."

"So why have you come to me?" asked Lynn.

"We need moral support and we want you to have a monthly column on philanthropy and nonprofit issues. And we want you to help us recruit other women to support us financially and in other ways."

Lynn stared at them. "You're pretty well connected yourselves."

"Our husbands are pretty well connected," Michelle corrected her. "Have you forgotten my background?" Her alcoholic mother had been murdered several years ago.

"And I'm not what some of Nathan's friends thought was an appropriate match for his nephew," said Penny. The attorney had married her husband only a few months before their baby arrived.

"That's only because all those women had daughters they wanted to marry off to Buck," Lynn reminded her. Nelda scurried around the room, pouring coffee and sharing some fudge Rory had brought to the office that morning.

"And people can't seem to forget that I shot Buck's sister and shot a prowler," Trina reminded everyone. Trina had stopped a prowled who was after her children, and had shot Buck's sister protecting Danny Valeri, one of Dusty's detectives.

"And you come from LA," added Michelle with a knowing look.

"So you see," said Penny, "we need someone like you and Piper endorsing our idea."

"Why? Your husbands can just write checks and, ta-da, you're in business."

They looked at one another. "We're not asking.. . .

". . . them for a dime. . .

". . . until we've raised fifty per cent of what we need to start up."

"You're not a nonprofit. So what do you want from me?" asked Lynn.

"Would you bring together a group of women that you think would listen to our proposal and consider us as an investment?"

"But you already know everyone," argued Lynn.

"We know everyone in our role as young and pampered wives," moaned Michelle.

"You still have jobs," Lynn reminded them.

"Be serious, Lynn," Penny chided her. "Everyone thinks our husbands just let us play at our jobs. Even in these times we have to prove ourselves."

Lynn knew they were correct. When she started her job at the Philanthropies, she was viewed as the daughter of a respected community leader who happened to need a job. It had taken some time and some innovative ideas on her part before everyone acknowledged that the Philanthropies' successes - a growing bottom line in the endowed funds, scholarship funds and community funded projects - were a result of her energy and creativity. Lynn's guests were correct: beautiful, young, wealthy women had to work harder.

"Who do you want to meet?" asked Lynn.

"I can tell you who we don't want to meet," said Michelle. "Not my mother-in-law, or Judge Dunn. That's family money for both me and Trina."

"I don't know what to say about Amelia," said Penny. "I don't want to hurt her feelings, but her husband is my father-in-law."

Lynn started writing names on the white board. "Tell me what you think of these people." As she wrote, the young women threw out other names. Finally, they dissected each suggestion.

"This town is too small," moaned Michelle, "Half of those women know my mother-in-law. And they all have dealings with Amelia's company."

"I have a suggestion," said Lynn. "I'll visit Sophie, the judge and Amelia. They have to know about this idea because their friends will ask them what they think about this endeavor. And I'll ask them to encourage their friends if anyone should ask."

The young women nodded. Step One, done!

* * *

The South End Clinic was shiny, clean and smelled great. Mutt Mason, newly credentialed RN, was completing his first week of work. He loved his job. This is what he had worked for. He wanted to serve members of the River Bend African-American community, making certain they received great care. And he wanted to be a good example to other black youngsters who came to the clinic. He wanted them to see a young black man working and succeeding in healthcare. He looked at his reflection in one of the store front windows on his walk along South End's deserted store fronts. Ick! He just wished that the scrubs the clinic provided were a different color, something to enhance his milk chocolate skin tone.

He had finished his shift at the clinic and was returning home. He still lived with his mother, and most of the money Mr. Hennessey had given him was still in the bank. Mutt was never certain what he had done to earn it, but his mother made him save it and work his way through the community college RN program by working nights at a nursing home as a CNA.

His mother worked there as a cook. She had been wise to keep him busy through the years of schooling. He saw what had happened to some of his friends. And now he was an official RN! Employed and proud!

Since the spring time-change had occurred, it was lighter in the evenings for his walk home. He nodded to friends and to patients. Folks waved and smiled. Everyone was proud of the local boy. Lost in thought he barely noticed as a dark-skinned woman began walking beside him. He finally became aware of DeFran Kaiser when she bumped him with her elbow. DeFran, Franky to her friends, was a good-sized woman and the elbow bump almost landed Mutt on his backside.

He moved out of elbow range as he greeted her. "Franky, you doin' ok?" She looked him over. She was probably fifteen years his senior. And she had a reputation for being smart. Of course, Mutt knew that being smart and recognized by the greater community for your brains was not something that happened to black women. He mused on the idea that so many smart folks were ignored because of race or gender. But he was tired and didn't want to take up those challenges on his walk home. "You be the nurse," she scowled, "you know how I am."

"Yes, ma'am." He was smart, too, and decided to act like he had a brain. "You have something to say to me?"

"I do." She continued to walk beside him as they turned down his street.

"I guess you want to talk to me about something important." He knew his dinner would be delayed because Franky was always recruiting for some cause or fighting some injustice.

"I knew you had smarts," she smirked as she followed him into his yard.

"I guess you want this talk to be private."

"Smart again." She followed him past the small flower bed his mother had filled with spring bulbs along with other early blooming flowers toward the front door.

When they were in the house, he said, "Mama is working tonight."

"I know. I want to speak with you." She followed him into the kitchen and watched as he found soft drinks and bag of chips.

He nodded at her to sit and he placed a can of soda in front of her and put chips in a bowl. He sat at the table across from her. "Does Mama know about this?"

Caught

Franky nodded. "She told me she was working tonight. 'Cause this is a private talk." He waited while she sipped her drink. "Do you know I'm on the clinic board?" He shook his head. She sighed. He could see her reordering her explanation. "Because the clinic gets federal funds it has to have patients on its board. And folks to represent diversity." She threw her arms out. "That's me all over."

"That's great news," he said. "You're a smart lady." Franky had long been acknowledged as a quiet leader in the black community.

She shook her head. "They don't think so. They only want me as a patient and for diversity. They don't care if I can think." She chuckled. "They haven't figured me out yet." Then she turned serious. "They put me on the finance committee."

"Who's they?"

"Your director Ms. Eliason and that Mahaffey fellow. They run the board real tight. In fact, that's why I'm here. I don't like the looks of things."

"What things?" He toyed with a chip.

"Let me tell you first how we operate on the committee. Jan Ryan is our treasurer."

"She's ninety." Mutt recognized the name of a reliable home health nurse who had served many in the community until her own health began to fail.

"Well, she doesn't know what's going on no matter how old she is. I think that's why she's in that slot. And then our CFO who does whatever Ms. Eliason tells him. And me and another board member who doesn't speak English well." She frowned. "Another bow to diversity." The change in Franky's voice told Mutt that the smart Franky was ready to get serious about this meeting. She continued, "I think someone is cooking the books. I can't follow some of the money. I think some of the pharmacy numbers are baked. And I think Ms. Eliason uses the clinic credit card for her own private purchases."

Mutt sat up. "You're way out of my league. I don't understand all that finance stuff. Why are you telling me?"

"Because you have to help us." Franky glared at him. "South End needs that clinic. You know how good the care is. You know what the clinic does to help our old folks and pregnant women and babies. Healthcare in South End is a service we all deserve. We need to protect the clinic and I think Margaret Eliason and that Mahaffey fellow can bring it down with their schemes."

"Mahaffey?" Mutt recognized the name from the attorney's work in the community.

"I think he's involved with the money, too. He has a way of directing the financial reports so not much is said and then the full board just accepts our committee report."

Mutt thought over what she had said. He first wondered if Franky's information and suspicions were correct. His conclusion: Franky was no fool. He next wondered what a new RN, a young black man could do? Nothing! He didn't know finance. He didn't know the people involved. He rarely saw the director or the CFO. And he didn't think he had ever seen this Mahaffey fellow. He only knew the name as a big important man in River Bend. Franky stared at him waiting. He owed her an answer. "I have a lot to learn about the way the clinic operates before I can help you. This won't happen overnight."

She nodded. "I know. This is just the beginning. You're my first contact." She frowned. "Maybe my only contact. I don't think my other friends on the staff would get excited about mismanagement. They're just happy to have jobs close to home."

He agreed with that. He tried to understand what Franky wasn't saying. Was she talking with him because he worked at the clinic or for a bigger reason? Did she think he was leadership material in the community? He paused. If she thought he was smart, maybe he was. If she thought he could become a community leader, maybe he could. He heaved a sigh, crumbled a chip in his fingers and said, "I have some ideas. You collect all the finance papers you can. I'll keep my eyes open around the clinic and ask some questions."

She nodded. "Tee LaMont will help us." Teniquia LaMont was a respected black detective working with Dusty Reid in the James County/River Bend Joint Investigation Unit.

Mutt grinned. He had forgotten about Tee. She would at least listen and maybe point them in the right direction if they discovered bad stuff. "We got us a plan. Collect information and then we'll talk to Tee."

Franky reached her hand across the table. "Thank you."

Caught

That was when Mutt realized that Franky thought this was a very big problem. He would have to find out more. He also realized something else. Tonight he had become one of the new leaders in the black community.

CHAPTER SIX

Lynn looked at her calendar. It was only Wednesday and within the last week she had been presented with two ideas that had merit and would take a lot of work. Piper's clinic could be a major project for the Philanthropies. She would have to give some thought to how it was presented to the board. The magazine, on the other hand, was not a Philanthropies project and she could do that in her off-hours.

She snorted. Off-hours? Since the vaccines arrived in River Bend, everyone was waking up, like Brigadoon - sort of rising from a pandemic stupor. Folks were ready to be normal again, on steroids. The summer festivals were gearing up. Restaurants were ready to entertain diners indoors. She expected to see dancing in the streets.

She climbed the stairs to her office lost in memories of the last several months and bumped into Rory who was racing out of his office. "Hey, boss." He had explained to her that at work he would call her 'boss' and after hours she could answer to 'sweetie.' He grabbed her before she tumbled backward down the stairs. As he held her, he asked, "Did you really have a shoot-out up here?"

Lynn sighed at the memory. "Sort of. That Anastasia Brandonhopf woman came to get me because she thought I had figured out that she had killed Mr. Plummer. Tee fought her." Lynn reminded Rory, "You know who she was, the executive director for that big philanthropic foundation?" She nodded to herself remembering how Anastasia sought revenge at the termination of a long affair with Darryl Plummer, husband of popular local pediatrician Dr. Robin Plummer.

Rory grinned, recalling the scandal. "That's what I like about working here. The Philanthropies is always in the thick of murder and mayhem."

She frowned. "What would you think if it was your murder?"

"Why? Do you think there will be other shootouts?" He was oblivious to her threat. "Good thing my office is up here away from the crazy people."

"What do you mean crazy?" Nelda called from the desk downstairs.

"Not you, gorgeous." He pulled Lynn aside and whispered, "She's terrific, but maybe a little crazy."

"I heard that!" echoed up the stairs.

He shouted down the stairs. "We're talking about a grant." Then he dragged Lynn into her office. "We are talking about a grant," he confirmed, "Yolo needs to review her grant for us again." Yolanda Valeri had been given money to use for nonprofits in River Bend. She had awarded a three-year grant for a proposed program to help clients of various agencies learn money management, budgeting and ways to avoid exploitation through loan schemes.

"Is there a problem?"

"Did Audrey stop by the other day?" Rory was finally getting to the point.

Lynn nodded. "She assured me the project will not be hurt." Lynn didn't want to talk about Audrey's confession.

He looked relieved. "Things are going very well. This consultant they're working with has them on track to meet the grant timing. I think we might have to leverage some funds as a bridge until they go from Yolo's money to developing a funding stream - grants and fundraising." He shrugged. "The usual."

The agency committee had been working with the consultant for several months. Lynn was glad to hear they were moving forward and also glad that Rory had replaced her as the grant manager for the funds. "Thanks for all the help you give them, Rory. Salley has told me that they appreciate your input." Salley Connelly was Lynn's sister-in-law and the driving force behind an array of programs helping victims of domestic violence and sexual assault.

"I've worked with agency mergers and redesigns before. This will succeed because everyone involved wants success more than ego enhancement." He moved some papers and sat on the edge of her desk.

Lynn thought about what he had said. "You're right. Salley, Audrey and Bertram want what's best for their clients."

Bertram Luft was the dynamic director of the Hunger Alliance. He had worked to bring the rescue mission, home delivered meals and various church sponsored food pantries under one umbrella. Audrey Decker was the respected and innovative director of Exceptional Children, a program dedicated to serving clients and families of the developmentally delayed. "They do understand working together. What do you think about the consultant?"

Over the length of the grant the committee had struggled to find someone to help guide their work. After one consultant quit because of family issues and another was sidetracked by the pandemic, they had hired James Thurman. "James has them in hand. He knows when to push and when to let them lead." Rory sighed. "James and Audrey both want the project to succeed. I think they will bury the affair."

"I hope so," sighed Lynn. "I don't know her husband well and I don't like learning about people's marital problems."

Rory sort of snarled. "Bart Decker is a creep. I've been over to have dinner with Audrey's family. Cute kids, phony husband. I have a gay man's sixth sense about some people. Bart is sneaky and sly. He's up to something."

"He makes you uncomfortable?" She was trying to understand what Rory was saying but he was being vague.

"I just don't trust him. He's not what we see." Rory stood up straighter. "I'll keep an eye on Audrey. If she needs us, I'll let you know."

Lynn and Rory parted, and each of them thought about what can happen when personal lives intruded into professional lives.

* * *

Franky Kaiser was sitting at her kitchen table using highlighters of various colors to follow funds around the financial reports of the South End clinic. There was a knock at her door. Frustrated that the noise interrupted her thought process, she reluctantly shuffled to the front of the house to respond. Opening the door she was startled to find a skinny white girl trying to look like some cartoon character, all black straight hair, pasty white skin and a few facial piercings. "I ain't buyin' whatever you got."

The stranger held up her phone screen. "I see you got a room to rent."

Caught

Franky worked hard to present her 'accepting diversity' demeanor. Sometimes it was hard, especially when meeting some of the Lord's stranger creations. Channeling peace and serenity she replied, "Yes." Stepping back she allowed the woman to enter her home. "If you take a seat, we can discuss my rental." She nodded toward her sofa.

The stranger pulled an envelope from her bag and handed it to Franky. "My name is Delsey Ledges. I'm a photojournalist and I'm in town to do some work for my friend, Trina Healey." She watched as Franky scanned copies of an email exchange between Trina Healey and Delsey. In the email, Trina invited Delsey to come to River Bend and help her establish a local magazine for parents. Or as Trina wrote, *Bring your camera and take some photos of children and healthcare. You know what to do to make folks smile. I have some journalism students who would like to learn about the power of photojournalism.*

As she read, Franky's eyes grew large. Her visitor was a photojournalist and a friend of Mrs. Healey, married to the detective, Mars Healey. Wheels started turning. "Why do you want to rent here? You can go anywhere." Although, Franky thought to herself, with those piercings and that Goth look, she wouldn't be welcome in some of the pricier places in town.

"I walked through this neighborhood and I felt comfortable." Delsey sat back and sort of smiled. Franky wasn't sure it was a smile because she was distracted by one of the piercings.

"What are you doing for Ms. Healey?"

"Do you know her?"

"I know her husband."

"She's starting a magazine for parents or something. I know her from her days as a Hollywood reporter." Delsey stopped and studied her potential landlady. "What do you know about her husband?"

"He's a fine man."

The reporter accepted that information. "She wants me to do a photo piece on healthcare focusing on children in the community and talk to her journalism students."

Franky let that sink into the spinning wheel of ideas. Journalism, reporter, and maybe an investigator? Had her prayers just been answered? She squinted at the stranger. "Let me ask you something?"

The curious landlady chewed her lips. Delsey nodded. "Do you investigate things?"

"Depends." The little beaded piercing above Delsey's eye quivered with interest.

For the next hour Franky explained her concerns about the clinic and finally she and her new renter came to an agreement. Franky made plans to attend church on Sunday to thank the Lord for his gift - a strange looking white lady investigative reporter.

* * *

Jim and Marianna tumbled into Lynn's kitchen, grinning. Lynn looked at the leftovers she had planned to feed to Dusty. Barely enough for two, not enough for four! "Don't worry," sang out Marianna, "We brought dinner. We're celebrating!"

Lynn waited for the celebration announcement. She knew they had received their vaccines and couldn't be pregnant or getting paroled. She wondered what else was celebratory at their age.

"We've had a nibble on our script proposal!" Marianna grinned and hugged Lynn. Jim put the bags of carryout on the table. Lynn waited to hear more.

Jim said, "We stopped at the Bistro for a special meal." He began unpacking the containers. The dog tried to help. Evidently he liked Bistro carryout, too.

Finally Lynn brightened. "Your script!" Marianna had been encouraged by her Hollywood connected son to spend the lockdown developing script ideas because all the new online TV services were devouring content. "Will you become rich?"

"No, but my colleagues and I will get billing as creators and paid to develop script ideas to keep continuity of characters and storyline." Marianna opened a wine bottle and poured while Jim set the table. "Isn't that great?"

"I guess," said Lynn. "I don't know anything about the industry." She looked over the dinner offering with curiosity.

Dusty walked in and as usual, walked directly to the butler's pantry and placed his gun in the locker and his phone on the charger. He came into the kitchen, kissed Marianna on the cheek, petted the dog and asked, "Dinner?"

"Marianna is telling me about her TV series," Lynn informed him, wondering why Marianna got a kiss and the dog got a pat. What was she, chopped liver?

He looked at the meal Jim was setting out and accepted a glass of wine from Marianna. "We're not eating leftovers tonight?" Lynn shook her head. He gave her a kiss and sipped his wine. Then he helped Jim so he could get a closer look at the meal. She wondered what that meant - a kiss only for new food, no kiss for leftovers? But she was distracted as she caught part of Marianna's explanation.

" - but they insist on making you a woman," she said to Dusty.

"What?"

"My series is based on some of Dusty's cases," she explained to the kitchen audience, "but the producers want the Dusty character to be a woman. They say the name Dusty is gender neutral."

"What?"

Marianna sat at the table and helped pass around the food as she went into detail. "There are a number of well-known actresses ready to segue from movies to TV and currently looking for a series. It will depend on who they cast and how they play off the various ethnicities, you know, Asian or black or Southern."

"They think Southern is an ethnicity?" Lynn's head was drowning in entertainment logic.

Marianna was oblivious. "They want to have a developing relationship with Dusty and Mars."

"What?"

She waved away the concerns. "If Dusty is a woman, she can have a personal relationship with Mars, you know, my character Mars. But it depends on who they cast as Dusty and who looks best with her on screen." She piled the rest of the salad on her plate and grinned her delight. "Don't you think it sounds great?"

Dusty poured himself more wine and tried not to think about River Bend's response to a TV Dusty/Mars relationship.

CHAPTER SEVEN

"You heard the board, Rachel," Lynn said to her board member, Rachel Teague, as she recapped the directives from the Philanthropies board. "Developing a grant proposal idea for Piper's school clinic to include a partnership with the hospital AND with the South End clinic seems to offer an opportunity to create a pilot project that can do a lot of good for South End children and eventually for all children in James County." Piper had submitted her resignation to the Philanthropies' board and followed it with her clinic idea. "And Kip Mahaffey is chair of the clinic board," Lynn added as the final inducement to insure Rachel's leadership in the project.

"Please don't ask me to co-chair that project with Kip," pleaded Rachel Teague.

Lynn was puzzled. "The two of you seem to be good friends. I thought working closely on this project would be no problem." She waited for a response that would offer an explanation.

"I just can't. We just can't." Rachel's eyes pleaded for Lynn to understand.

"I'm sorry if I've caused a problem." She was still confused.

"You haven't." The woman stared out the window of Lynn's office. "Kip and I have been friends for decades and have worked on many community projects together. But," she sighed, "I can't now."

Lynn was bewildered trying to understand Rachel's response. "I'll look for someone else as your co-chair if you're willing to take on this project, because I want you at the head. The Philanthropies needs your leadership and commitment to make this a success. You also have the state legislative contacts if the program requires state funding or legislative directives." She saw the panic and sadness in the woman's face. Reaching out Lynn took her hand. "I'm sorry to have upset you."

Caught

Suddenly there were tears in Rachel's eyes. After the meeting with Kip last week, she had been feeling tense and vulnerable. "It's becoming very difficult for me to work so closely with such a handsome, charming man. Although Kip is always proper and respectful, I feel my power to resist an . . . intimate relationship with him is dissolving." She raised her hand to stop Lynn's comment. "No, he hasn't even suggested anything. It's me. My husband has declared that he's no longer interested in sex. He's flirted with some of the Viagra type drugs but insists that he takes enough drugs and his libido doesn't care what he takes, it's retired." Rachel sighed again. "Kip and I have never been unfaithful, but I can tell you, for my part, if I have to be in contact with him under the intense work of this project, I would tumble. I am so lonely - being in the same house with a man who isn't interested in touching, let alone engaging in sex, is a very stressful existence." The depth of her sorrow was in her eyes.

Lynn's heart broke as she listened to Rachel talk about her marriage. "You don't owe me an explanation," she said, hoping Rachel didn't offer any more insights into her marriage. Then she felt guilty for that thought! This lovely woman was in pain.

"I have to talk with someone," she said, fumbling with a tissue. "Maybe I can exorcise my demons that way." She patted Lynn's hand as an apology. "Last week, Kip asked me to chair his election campaign. I told him I would help but I was too busy to take a lead role. I almost screamed at the emotional tension between us. I don't know what he felt but I . . ." She wiped her eyes. "That day we met in the park. I wondered if he felt as I did. Then I felt like such an old fool. So here I am, a sorry, sad, sex-starved old woman and no place to put that energy." Abruptly she stood. "I have another appointment. Why don't we talk later when I'm more coherent?" She picked up her notes and left Lynn speechless in the Philanthropies office.

* * *

Sitting puzzled and saddened in her office, Lynn pondered Rachel's response to working with Kip on the health clinic project. She would respect Rachel's request and start looking for a topnotch co-chair for this effort. She rolled through her mental rolodex evaluating potential partners. She needed more input. "Rory," she called from her desk. It wasn't a professional way to communicate but he was just across the hall. And he was proving to be a great addition to her thinking process.

"Yes, boss." He appeared like a genie popping out of a lamp.

She said, "We have to get our action plan together on this school clinic project." She outlined the work to be done.

When she was finished he said, "After her presentation, Piper gave me contact information for other school-based clinics in neighboring counties." He was quiet after that statement and Lynn knew that he was already planning for success.

"Rachel has agreed to lead the study and help the pilot project team organize. She's great at getting folks to focus." Lynn thought about what she would say next because she wasn't certain when information became gossip. "Because Kip Mahaffey is board chair at the clinic, I thought he would make a great co-chair. But Rachel said she would prefer a different co-chair." Rory nodded knowingly. She frowned at him. "What?"

"Boss," he said, "I like Rachel. I don't like Mahaffey. He's not a good person."

"Rory, he's a community leader. He and Rachel have chaired several successful projects. And we all read that news story in The Chronicle about his run for mayor." She didn't know why she was arguing. She was still very confused by Rachel's confession. "I'll respect Rachel's request, but I don't understand her reasoning." She stared at her grant manager for clarification.

He scoffed. "She does the work. He takes the credit."

"Really? I thought they were a team." Lynn mentally looked back at past Rachel and Kip projects. "He always shows up for the meetings and makes the presentations."

"But she's the one who probably organized and wrote the work plan and final conclusions. And met with interested people and listened to all viewpoints and lobbied politicians." Rory stopped and took a deep breath.

"Maybe it's because he had to work at his law practice."

"Or maybe it's because he's a creep?" Rory was promoting a recurring theme in this discussion.

"I'm shocked to hear you talk like that."

He closed her office door. "Because I'm a little different," acknowledged the gay man, "I have a developed sense of knowing when someone is real or just giving me a face. Do you know what I mean?"

She nodded. "I think we had this conversation about why you don't like Bart Decker."

"Same reason," huffed Rory. "Rachel's real. Mahaffey gives me face. He also gives her face."

"What do you mean?"

"I think he lets her think he finds her fascinating and smart and hides his true opinions."

"You're confusing me. Is he gay or something?" Lynn wondered if she was drowning in this discussion. And she admitted, "I don't have any negative impressions about Kip. He's pleasant, willing to defer to Rachel at meetings."

He shook his head. "I don't know how to describe my feeling. You've seen them around town. He's charming and considerate of her. His behavior gives the impression that maybe there's more to their relationship. But he's really using her as a smoke screen for his real relationships."

"He's having an affair with Rachel or some guy?" Her mind flipped to last evening's dinner and the TV Dusty/Mars relationship. She pulled herself back to Rory's explanation.

"No, you're not listening! He's using her, touching her, smiling at her in public so we'll think they're having an affair. I bet she goes home to her husband and never even gives a thought to his behavior because she'd never have an affair."

Lynn looked sad. "I have heard a whisper every now and then that there was something between them. But I've ignored it."

Rory gave her a knowledgeable frown. "There are others in the community who have seen them and believe there is fire behind the smoke screen."

"That's evil gossip. That's unfair. That's, that's-"

"Exactly," agreed Rory. "But that's the kind of guy I think he is. I agree with Rachel. Let's find a better co-chair." They were both silent as they mentally ran through potential partners for Rachel.

Finally Lynn said, "I think my father might be a good choice, or Herbie. And we should invite Sherry Vonder and Amelia because they have worked with Piper to move the idea forward. And maybe Zachary because he wants to help with funding. And Piper, of course.

"Take Kip out of the mix and maybe add Doc Noah for healthcare creds and you have a winner of a committee." Rory stood.

"Thank you," said Lynn. "You've given me a lot to think about." She sat back in her chair, thinking about people who aren't what they seem. She had met several folks like that and it seemed the world contained still more.

* * *

Lynn and Dusty sat in the Bistro having a quiet sort of fancy lunch for their private anniversary celebration. They had managed to enjoy this event by lying to everyone they knew. It was glorious. As they sat in the quiet corner they watched several acquaintances come through the dining room for their own lunches, confirming to Lynn that people were struggling to return to pre-lockdown days. As she watched folks gather she said, "Half of these meals are meetings. It looks like business lunches have survived the pandemic." She watched three Chamber of Commerce members wolf down fancy sandwiches as they argued about something. At another table the DA was whispering intently while Judge Dunn listened and nibbled at a quiche. Kip Mahaffey and a young man new to his law offices were sitting at another table where they shared a chuckle and flirted with the waitress. Lynn frowned.

Dusty reached for her hand. "This is a celebration lunch. Why so low?"

She cast her eyes toward Kip. "I had an interesting discussion with Rachel Teague this morning. She told me she doesn't want to work with Kip on any projects. Then I told Rory because we need to find her a co-chair for this new Philanthropies' committee. He said that some folks whisper that Rachel and Kip have had an ongoing affair for several years." She wanted to cry.

Dusty squeezed her fingers. "She's too good for him."

"You don't like Kip?" Lynn was surprised that Dusty's response matched Rory's. Was Dusty's detective sense similar to Rory's gay guy sense?

Caught

"He's not having an affair with Rachel," said Dusty in a whisper. Lynn's eyes almost popped out of her head. Dusty never gossiped. He continued to whisper, "I can't say anything, but trust me." He knew he would be sorry. But he liked Rachel. And he had the evidence that Kip shouldn't be trusted.

Right now, Lynn wanted more. "What do you mean? Are you investigating him? He does too much good work in town. No one will believe you." She looked around making certain there were no spies behind the potted plants. "Tell me!" she hissed.

Dusty chided himself for even mentioning this. He couldn't tell Lynn that Kip had a girlfriend and they met regularly in a cabin near Hank Seymour's cabin. In fact the regional drug task force used Hank's cabin for stakeouts. All they ever caught was Kip and his lady friend. Dusty cleared his throat and lowered his voice more. "I think Kip Mahaffey is a bad person. Over the years, he has used Rachel as a smoke screen, making folks think he is good for the community and hinting that there is more between him and Rachel than there is. During that time he has had sexual affairs with other women and has been able to hide that side of his life from everyone. He's not a nice man." Dusty ended his whispered oration. But later tonight he was certain Lynn would work her own method of interrogation to get more details.

Lynn looked like she would burst with curiosity. Dusty took her hand. "Let's enjoy our lunch. Happy Anniversary!"

* * *

Franky Kaiser had scheduled another meeting with Mutt Mason. Tonight the quiet meeting was at her place. In South End everyone minded their own business, but watched everyone's business, just in case. The neighbors wanted to be ready to hide if guns came out at a party or a drive-by shooting. They also wanted to know what they shouldn't know and could deny accordingly. So Mutt was confident that no one cared that he was going to Franky's – they noticed but didn't care because Franky and Mutt were leaders in the community. And Franky was big enough to punch anyone who got curious.

He knocked politely at the door and waited to be invited in. A white, strange looking woman answered the door. "Yes?" asked Delsey Ledges, photojournalist.

"I'm here to see Franky."

Over her shoulder Delsey called, "Franky, your date's here."

Mutt opened his mouth to deny his status as Franky's date. But Franky was quicker. "That's Mutt, my informant." He opened his mouth to object to being an informant, but Franky continued, "I told you about him, the nurse."

Delsey scanned the nurse. "Why aren't you a doctor?"

"I like being a nurse."

She stepped back and let him into the house. "Franky said you're going to help her with this clinic thing. What do you know?"

Mutt scowled at the pushy white woman with the nose and eyebrow piercings. "Who are you?"

"Delsey. I'm here visiting a friend."

"Franky is your friend?" The nurse sounded curious.

"No, I'm renting a room from her. My friend doesn't have space for me." They stared one another down until Franky interrupted.

"Hey, Mutt. This is Delsey." He nodded. "She wants to listen. She's interested in healthcare."

Mutt was suspicious. Why would this stranger be interested in a local clinic? But he did want to learn what Franky had found out and he had some information to share. "As long as you don't blab," he cautioned Delsey.

"I'm a vault." Her eyes danced. He frowned.

"Let's sit at the table." Franky led them into her kitchen. The table was covered with papers. "I got all the stuff I could. I went over to do some house cleaning for the treasurer, Miz Ryan, and sort of borrowed all the files she had."

"Won't she notice?" asked Mutt.

"No, she just throws it all in a pile on the floor by her desk. I told her I had put it all in a box and stored it in her attic. She said she was glad it was gone because she never understands what they talk about." Franky stared at the mound of papers. "I don't understand it either. I can see where the credit card charges are. But I can't prove Ms. Eliason buys stuff for herself. The CFO does a good job of covering things, you know, expensing charges to routine accounts. And I see funds being given to Mahaffey or being laundered through his law office paying for vague contract services." She looked puzzled and helpless. "We need someone to look at this who knows something. What do you got?" She stared at Mutt.

He looked at his listeners. "Since you mentioned the pharmacy, I've kept an eye on things. I think we get a lot of controlled substances in and I don't see them going out to our patients."

"How'd you learn that?" asked Delsey. His opening statement altered her initial impression of the young man.

"I can access patient records. I just scanned through and didn't find a lot of prescriptions for that stuff. I can't get into the pharmacy inventory. And I don't want to ask questions. But maybe the pharmacist is taking them, not Ms. Eliason."

"That little girl from your high school class works in the pharmacy. I bet you could sweet-talk her and get information." Franky wiggled her eyebrows.

"Hell, Franky," he shouted, "I'm not some soulless spy who seduces innocent women for information."

"It would probably only take one time. She's not that pretty." Franky straightened her extra, extra-large t-shirt.

Mutt's eyes bulged. "I don't treat people like that. She's a sweet girl. She doesn't need me messing with her mind."

Delsey sat and listened as Franky and Mutt bantered and argued for several minutes. She cleared her throat. "I have a suggestion." They looked at her, both ready for a solution to their argument. "I can put some cameras in the pharmacy and we can see if anyone is taking anything."

"Isn't that illegal?" Mutt wondered what this person did to know about cameras. He squinted at her trying to discover who she was.

"Only if you're the police. Regular people use cameras for security every day." She sounded smug. She didn't want them to see her excitement. She had been looking for a good healthcare story. This situation sounded like it had a lot of interesting parts.

Franky smacked her fist on the table. "There we go. You don't have to seduce anyone." They looked at one another and waited to hear the journalist.

Delsey laid out her proposal. That night she texted her friend, Trina. *I'm in town and may have the lead story for your first issue.*

* * *

After lunch Dusty and Lynn had returned to their respective offices. Although this was a special day for them, they were still being paid to work. But it was finally bedtime and Lynn was ready. Dusty stood in the bathroom with his pajama bottoms hugging his hips and with his toothbrush dancing around his molars, lost in thought. Warm hands skimmed his bare back as a threateningly sweet voice asked, "How do you know Rachel and Kip aren't having an affair?" His toothbrush seemed to get stuck in his tonsils.

Finally he got his toothbrush under control, spit, rinsed and said, "Just trust me."

"You can trust me, too," cajoled Lynn. "You know you can tell me things and they will never cross my lips." Dusty started coughing. She slapped him on the back. "That's really rude," she hissed, "you know I only tell Piper the stuff she'll find out anyway." He opened his mouth to begin listing all of Lynn's indiscretions, but she held up her hand. "I know. You think I talk too much."

He nodded, waited for her to say more. He was surprised by her silence and he said so. "I'm surprised you've surrendered."

"I haven't surrendered. I just didn't want to hear the same old song. Why is this information so much different than everything else you've ever told me?"

"It's part of an ongoing investigation."

"Who? Kip? You caught him doing something illegal?" Her voice quivered with excitement.

Oh, the regrets, he thought to himself. He had to say something or they would never get to sleep tonight. "There's an investigation." She looked as though she had a million questions. He placed his hands on her shoulders. He wasn't certain but he thought she might be levitating. "A really important investigation. And sometimes when you are watching for one thing, other people, not related to the investigation, pass through the camera."

Caught

"You caught Kip having an affair with someone, not Rachel!" Triumph! "On camera?" Double-triple triumph!!

How did she guess that, he puzzled? Maybe she really did have a nose for crime-solving. "That's all I can say."

"You haven't said anything."

"I just haven't said anything you can tell Piper."

"How long?" She trailed a finger down his chest.

"How long?" He was losing interest in this conversation.

"Until I can tell her."

He walked over to the bed and pulled the covers back. "A matter of months. This has been going on over a year. It's not us local guys, it's bigger agencies, so I can't say anything else."

She slipped into bed and he pulled the covers over them, wrapping his arm around her and pulling her close. "This is a real heavy-duty investigation. You can't know anything and you have to stay away, stay safe." She raised her head to ask for more details and he put an end to the discussion in his usual manner. She didn't object.

CHAPTER EIGHT

Trina and her magazine partners met in Mars' old bachelor apartment, a loft on the third floor of his Uncle Hutch Dunn's law offices. In Trina's mind it was a perfect place. Space for her imagined crew of magazine staffers, and space otherwise known as the bedroom, for a place to put babies or small, napping children. Because Trina, Michelle, Ronnie and Penny had a total of nine children. Ronnie was Michelle's sister and the wife of Kevin, River Bend's IT mavin. Ronnie's two were the oldest, Kevin, Jr. and Lisa. They were in school. All the others were younger. Yikes! Trina looked around the loft and thought she better find a few cribs for nappers and maybe stock up on disposable diapers and other baby needs. And maybe some toys and things to entertain the older children.

Wait! This was a magazine office. She needed supplies and equipment for her staff. Was her idea too big? Would she raise enough money? She heard the ding. Someone, she hoped her partners, was coming up in the elevator. She heard the door open to the loft. "Grab a seat," Trina called from the bedroom, "I'm putting the baby down." Pasting a confident smile on her face she walked out to greet the ladies.

"This is a great space," marveled Michelle. "I remember coming to a party or two here in the old days."

"Me, too," said Ronnie. "I had my first date with Kevin here."

Penny looked around the big, sunny room. "Isn't this where you slugged Nancy?"

Trina rolled her eyes. "Haven't you forgotten about the girl fight?"

"I don't want to forget. Nancy needed to be slugged." Penny still worried that her sister-in-law would return to River Bend and cause trouble.

"Enough old memories," Ronnie said, calling everyone to order. "I have to pick up kids at three."

Caught

Trina led them to the kitchen island and told them to sit. She opened the grocery bags and put out the drinks and snacks. Michelle groaned as she spied the vegetable tray. "Can't we have cookies or something."

Trina scowled, "I haven't lost my baby weight yet. It's vegetables for everyone."

Moaning and complaining the others took seats on the stools around the counter. "Tell us what to do," said Michelle as she took a carrot stick, "You're the professional reporter."

"I know reporting," said Trina after biting a broccoli head. "I'm relying on you all to help with everything else." Three sets of eyes bugged out. She made a calming gesture with the broccoli stem. "I know what we need. I know how I want to organize. But I need to know what I can spend and in what order."

With that introduction the meeting began, and ideas bounced around the loft. Trina stopped to nurse the baby while Ronnie got IT organized. Michelle opened her laptop and got accounts formed into a budget. "What do I do?" Penny asked.

"Keep your ears open," said Trina, "you're our legal defense."

"I do have some suggestions," Penny began. "I recommend a formal contract or memo of understanding with our stringers. Pay rates, and legal defense if they need protection under the Constitution." Three women stared at her. "You know, free press, free speech, libel."

"Yikes!" cried Michelle. "Will we be sued for something?"

"There may be risks depending on how well we train the reporters," said Trina. "I think we can do it. But as editor I'll have to pay close attention to their stories."

"This is getting complex," said Ronnie coming back from her focus on building their internal network for back-office communications. "Getting the office networked is a piece of cake. I don't have a clue about this legal stuff."

Penny reached for celery. "I think we can do this without any problem. We're talking about a family magazine. We're not a gossip rag and not going to be political or investigative." Ronnie and Michelle felt better with the edict from the attorney. Trina felt uneasy.

Oh-oh, thought the editor as she recalled Delsey's late night text! "Let me tell you what I've done," said Trina and three pairs of eyes looked worried. She gave them a weak smile. "I thought I could offer the students, our stringers, professional help besides me. My plan is to contact some of my old friends and invite them to visit for a few weeks to help with training. A retired editor or two, folks with some magazine or newspaper experience."

"That doesn't sound scary or libelous."

Trina squirmed uneasily. "I've invited my friend Delsey Ledges who's between assignments. She's a world class photojournalist. I thought our magazine could start off with some great photography if she agreed. There are two students who would be interested and learn a lot from her."

"That sounds exciting!" exclaimed Ronnie.

Michelle looked up from her laptop. "She's not in our budget."

Trina hung her head. "We didn't talk money. She's here. I'll cover her living expenses."

"What kind of a person is she?"

"Unique." Trina laughed at her friends. "She's way outside your comfort zones. Sort of Goth, not yet thirty, maybe lesbian, I'm not certain. And afraid of nothing. You've seen her work in newspapers, TV and magazines." Trina enumerated Delsey's prize winning, expressive photos from some of the most dangerous places on earth. "Delsey believes in getting close to her stories. She's already in town living off the land or at some campsite."

"Maybe I can find some funds for her in our budget," said Michelle. The others nodded.

Trina looked at her friends and gave them an apologetic look. "What?" Michelle and Penny asked together.

"Delsey sent me a text last night," Trina finally admitted. "She says she's found our first big story." Three women stared at her. Trina raised a hand before all the questions erupted into the room. "When she's ready we'll hear and we can veto the story." Everyone relaxed.

"We're doing a magazine for parents," observed Penny, "She's probably photographing children at play all over town." Everyone nodded. Just the vibe they wanted for their magazine!

* * *

Caught

Lynn had thought a lot about Rachel's confession concerning her marriage and her relationship with Kip, as well as the interesting fact that both Dusty and Rory disliked Kip. It just proved to her once again that one never knew what really happened within a marriage. On the other hand, she was always interested in how people perceived one another. Dusty and Rory agreeing to dislike the same man, go figure. Putting aside Rachel's problem, Lynn got lost in the reality that she and Dusty were celebrating their fifth anniversary. Finding him had been a surprise. And finding love again had been the biggest surprise.

When he walked into the kitchen, she was lost in marriage thoughts - her and Dusty, Will and Piper, Doyle and Lori, even Jim and Marianna. She was looking forward to a weekend celebrating with the family since she and Dusty had shared their own quiet luncheon the other day.

"I guess you haven't heard," he said jolting her mind back to the kitchen and dinner preparation as he walked through the door, "your friend Rachel Teague was just in a car accident. Before you panic. She'll be fine, but the woman in the other car wasn't so lucky. Mrs. Mahaffey was being taken to a doctor's appointment by her housekeeper when they hit your friend."

"Rachel and Mrs. Mahaffey? I have to get to her, to both of them." Lynn grabbed her purse and keys. "Take the lasagna out of the oven in a half hour." She was gone.

* * *

At the hospital Lynn endured the mask challenge in the visitors' lobby and quickly located Rachel. She had already been assigned to a room. When Lynn got there, she interrupted a conversation. ". . . and I've called the kids."

Owen Teague turned as she entered the room. "Lynn, how did you hear about this?" He stopped, his mask slung under his chin and smiled. "That's right, that husband of yours knows everything."

"He doesn't know everything, he just hears everything. How's your wife?" Lynn pulled down her mask and gave him a warm smile. Owen winked at her as she matched his chin masking option.

"I'm fine, just a little sore." Rachel struggled to sit straighter on the bed and pat her hair at the same time. There was nothing she could do about the hospital gown. "They want to keep me overnight. I told Owen that he'll have a quiet night, I won't be snoring." She moved stiffly, suggesting that a soreness was moving into her joints.

"I've told you that you don't snore." Owen took her hand. "That phone call really frightened me. I don't like to think of you leaving me behind."

"He's afraid he'll have to cook and do laundry," she said and patted his hand.

Lynn listened to the relaxed banter between these two people and tried to find the sad woman and the unloving husband. Perplexed she joined the friendly chatter for a few minutes then excused herself. "I think I should also visit Mrs. Mahaffey." She wrinkled her brow. "I don't know her very well, but I have met her."

"I don't know her well, either," admitted Rachel. "What a terrible way for us to get acquainted! I'll try to visit her later. I think she's in worse shape than me."

With that Lynn said good-bye and pulling up her mask ventured out to find Mrs. Mahaffey. After stumbling through some misdirection she found the lady several rooms down the hall from Rachel. The woman was all alone in a dimly lit room watching the evening news.

"Mrs. Mahaffey?" Lynn rapt softly on the open door, pulling down her mask. "May I come in?"

The woman stared out at her from the bed. "Ms. Powers? Please call me Anita. Thank you for stopping by." Anita Mahaffey was a bit overweight. Her hair was dark with gray scattered throughout. She looked sad and tired as though she had lost an important battle but was trying to maintain her dignity.

Lynn stood at the foot of the bed and toyed with her mask ready to slip it back up if a nurse popped in. "My husband told me that you were here. Can I do anything for you?"

Anita didn't try to sit up straight. She spoke from the semi-reclining position her bed allowed. "I'm fine. My housekeeper is bringing over things I'll need." With that information Lynn asked a few questions and again offered help and assistance which was declined.

Caught

After the brief visit Lynn returned to her car, thoughtful. Owen Teague was at his wife's side. Maybe the Teague marriage wasn't as lost as Rachel thought. On the other hand, after all that she had heard about Kip Mahaffey recently, Lynn understood why Anita Mahaffey was alone in her room. Kip had called Anita while she was there and told his wife he would drop in to see her tomorrow. Anita had repeated the message to Lynn, remarking, "He's always so busy."

Lynn sped from the hospital parking lot, angry at the man she had once thought so charming and kind. And now she was more curious. What was Dusty investigating that intersected with Kip's life? And with whom had he been caught on camera?

The worst part about this gnawing curiosity was that she couldn't share it with anyone. Piper might know who the woman was. She had spies everywhere. Or Rory! He was slowly becoming her gossip addiction. Rory knew and Rory always shared!

She reached home and hoped Dusty had taken the lasagna out of the oven. Walking into the kitchen she was shocked to see that he had and that Piper, Will, Bryce and Jeff had joined him to eat it all. "Anything left?" She was hungry and not happy.

"There are those leftovers from the other night that we didn't eat," offered Dusty.

"Or my leftovers," chimed in Piper. "If we hadn't found Dusty alone with this lasagna we would have had to eat last Wednesday's Chinese carryout." Lynn had purchased the family sized lasagna from the gourmet grocery store. It was to have provided leftover meals throughout the weekend for her and Dusty.

"You had Chinese carryout and didn't tell us?" Dusty stared at her.

"You probably had something better," countered Piper.

"No, we didn't. I would have remembered."

"Stop it both of you," Lynn growled, "What's left for me to eat?"

"Leftovers."

CHAPTER NINE

By noon Saturday Rachel was released from the hospital. After setting a time for Owen to collect her, she decided to walk down the hall and visit Anita Mahaffey, a woman she hardly knew. She entered the room and slipped down her mask.

"You have nerve walking in here," the bed-bound woman snapped at her visitor.

Rachel was shocked at the hostility. "I just came to see if you're comfortable or need something." She had no idea what else to say.

Anita struggled to sit up, stabbing at the bed controls. "You've been having an affair with my husband for years. Are you here to make certain I'm incapacitated for a while so you can take another trip together?" The woman in the hospital bed was very angry.

Rachel gasped. "I am not having an affair with your husband," she whispered once she found her voice. "Who told you such a lie?"

"He did." Anita Mahaffey scowled at her visitor.

"He did? Why would he lie to you?" Rachel felt off balance and confused. Was this some sort of karma punishment for her lustful thoughts about Kip?

"Or why would you lie?" challenged the woman. They stared at one another. The woman in the bed, dropped her gaze first and fussed with her bedsheets. "He never really said you two were having an affair, but you both worked on so many community projects together and traveled to conferences together. My friends noticed things."

"We've never traveled together." Rachel took a seat on the bedside chair before her knees gave out.

"You both went to Atlanta last year for that fundraising conference," Anita pointed out.

"He was there and I was there for the conference. But I was there with my husband. We took off after the meeting to visit some relatives for a week. They lived about three hours away in Aiken, South Carolina." Rachel finished her statement with a puzzled frown on her face.

The woman in bed had a panicked look - then gave a deep sad blink which finally turned into a tragic stare. "I always thought it was you," she whispered. "I knew I couldn't compete with a woman as beautiful and poised as you. Everyone knew you and liked you. Even I like you! I was just grateful you kept sending him home." She was crying now. Rachel reached out but withdrew her hand, not knowing if Anita would appreciate a consoling gesture.

After Anita's tears subsided, she gave one last sniff then said, "All these years, when he's come home late, supposedly after meeting with you, he always smelled of alcohol, was always chipper. He'd be surprised that I was still awake and make up a story about someone at the meeting wanting to talk. I finally began to pretend I was asleep on those nights, so I wouldn't have to listen to his lies."

"But that doesn't mean he was with a woman," argued Rachel. "He could have been meeting with anyone, having a late drink." The Kip Mahaffey she was attracted to was not a liar or a womanizer.

Anita shook her head. "If I asked who he was with, he always said, 'someone you don't know.' Or he'd say, 'checking up on me?' Like I had no right to be curious. If I pursued, he always changed the subject by saying, Rachel this or Rachel that, you know, silly comments or observations that always left me wondering if you and he were having late night drinks at least once a week or more often. This last year, he often seemed to be busy on weekend evenings, too. I've had a difficult bout with this virus and have been slow to recover. I think that he has taken advantage to have drinks . . . and things Fridays and Saturdays."

"We never have late night drinks," said Rachel. She was drawn to this sad woman who appeared very lost and heartbroken. "We almost always meet during the day, in committee meetings, but we do meet for lunch sometimes, alone. We always seem to have a lot to talk about. Nothing very personal. He never said you had this virus." Rachel shook her head capturing a memory. "He did once ask me about the kinds of gifts he might buy for you. I told him no appliances, always something intimate."

"I've never gotten anything intimate, not even a piece of jewelry."

"You're kidding," gasped Rachel, "He showed me a beautiful necklace once, pearls with a large gold clasp. I even asked how you liked it and he said that the reward met his expectations."

"I never received a gift like that." Anita held the bed sheet adjusting a bandaged broken finger atop the bedding. The car accident had given her several bruises and a broken finger.

Rachel gripped the arms of the chair. "I'm speechless." So much whirled through her head. Last week she had been ready to finally let surface what she thought was a mutual passion between herself and Kip Mahaffey. What a fool! "Are you certain? I've worked with your husband for almost twenty years in this community and have never heard a hint of another woman."

Anita stared at her visitor. "You were the other woman!" She smirked, "My friends have warned me for years sharing the gossip floating around you and Kip. These last years based on his overt behavior I have finally believed them. And here you are making statements that suggest he's a liar." Rachel opened her mouth to argue. Anita shook her head. "I believe you because I have known Kip to lie to me many other times." Her eyes sort of flashed with satisfaction or vengeance. The lighting in the room made it difficult to tell. "You must know who she is!"

"I have no idea." Rachel shook her head.

"He's used you," stated Anita in a bitter apologetic voice. "Just like he uses everyone."

"You make it sound like I'm his fake girlfriend." Anita nodded. "Why? Is he using me to cover another life?" The other woman nodded again. Rachel sat up in the chair, reality dawning. She thought about her years working with Kip. He often came to the meetings at the last minute, usually sending her an email the night before begging that she help out because of his clients' demands. In recent years she had just taken over the planning of agendas, note taking and almost complete management of any project they chaired. He was always there to receive the praise. This was a new thought for her. Hmmm.

Anita nodded as the truth became evident to both of them. "I think he's purposely misled both of us. He had to keep you friendly and eager to work with him to provide cover for his other relationship. He always let his behavior toward you fuel gossip about you both. That's what my friends saw, what the community saw."

Rachel stood and took Anita's hand. "I'm so sorry to have caused you so much pain all these years. Is there anything I can do?" Rachel was sick to her stomach wondering just what others in the community thought about her and Kip.

They talked for a bit more until Owen interrupted. "Here you are. I accused the nurse of losing you." He walked into the room. He slipped his obligatory hospital required mask down to his chin with the loops still around his ears. A mask wearing method becoming common.

Rachel turned to introduce him. "Owen, this is Anita Mahaffey. The other half of my accident." Owen visibly gulped and Rachel wondered if he had heard the same gossip as Anita. "I told her you were coming but I would be back to visit her." They heard a rap at the door as a nurse chirped a greeting and came around the curtain. Three guilty people raised their masks quickly.

"Mrs. Teague, I thought we misplaced you," she chuckled through her mask.

"I was visiting with my friend, Anita, until my husband arrived." Rachel smiled but remembered she was wearing a mask. "We were just leaving." She blew a masked kiss to Anita, nodded to the nurse and took her husband's arm as they left the room.

* * *

Lynn walked out of the laundry room and was surprised to be pulled into Will's arms. He nuzzled her hair. Leaning back he gave her a kiss on the forehead. "I think we should have an anniversary, too." She smiled at her half-brother as they cuddled in her kitchen. "It was about this time of year that Jim surprised you with me." Will was the product of Jim's sexual indiscretion - a weak moment as Will's mother had offered her gratitude for Jim's legal defense of her brother.

She nodded. "I remember. I was so confused. I was recently widowed, Dad was sick and I had Jason and a new job to deal with. You seemed like a burden that eclipsed all of those concerns."

"Wow!" He released her and walked to the kitchen drink refrigerator. "That's all negative."

She nodded. "You were more than the last straw. You were a whole bale!"

"Yeah, I remember that vibe. You always seemed to give me a great death-ray stare." He handed her a beer, then asked, "Why did you change your mind?"

"Dad liked you. So did Jason and Piper." She laughed. "Well, Piper more than liked you." Will laughed. Then he became serious. "What did change your mind?"

Lynn sipped her beer in thought. "One day I looked in your eyes and noticed that they were my eyes. The same color. The same as Dad and Jason." Putting her beer down, she wrapped her arms around his waist and hugged him. "And with all the turmoil of Dad's illness and my widowhood, I liked the idea of a big brother to share my worries."

"Here, here," called Jim as he walked into the kitchen smiling at his children as they embraced. "I'm glad I brought you two together." His eyes twinkled. "More people to look after me in my old age." He insinuated himself between them savoring the moment.

* * *

Rachel walked into her house deep in thought. Throughout the drive home she reflected on all the years she had worked with Kip, had been used by Kip. His own wife was a victim of some horrible sham of a marriage. And she shuddered to think how close she had come to making the mythical affair real. Struggling with those thoughts, she hadn't realized she was standing in her kitchen until Owen spoke.

"Can I get you anything?" asked her husband interrupting her bleak deliberations. "Are you still sore?" He had carried her small bag into the kitchen.

"I could use a drink." It was a small lifeless voice.

"Something's wrong," he concluded as he pulled a bottle of wine from the wine rack. He had been surprised to find Rachel and Mrs. Mahaffey together. "Do you want to talk about it?"

"That's a strange question," she replied, "you've always ignored my dramas." She took the glass of wine and sat at the kitchen table knowing she sounded a little snippy.

Caught

Owen sat across from her with his own glass. "I guess you're right. But seeing you in the hospital frightened me. And you and Mrs. Mahaffey looked, I don't know, like you both had resolved something." He sipped his wine. The kitchen was silent.

At that moment she knew Owen had heard the same gossip. "This is certainly a day for," she emptied her wine glass and continued, "for strange conversations."

"Are we discussing my comment?" He refilled her glass.

Without answering she got up and found some crackers to munch with her wine. "I haven't had anything to eat. It's been a long time since my hospital breakfast." She ate two crackers and sipped her wine. Taking a deep breath she said, "Anita Mahaffey accused me of having a long-term affair with her husband." Owen stared at her as she explained, "We had an enlightening discussion in that hospital room. I learned that she and many of her friends had thought Kip and I were an item." Another long silence.

Finally, "I've thought the same thing," he whispered, refilling his own glass.

His comment confirmed her suspicions. She drank more wine. He refilled her glass, again. "I'm not! We're not! And that's what I told her. She said that Kip hinted we took a trip together. Remember when we went to that conference last year? You and I went to visit your sister afterward. Evidently Kip stayed away as long as we did and hinted, or something, that I was the woman that kept him away. I didn't understand at first until she explained what she suspected. We had a very fruitful discussion. And we both concluded that he has manufactured a very public friendship with me to act as a smoke screen for his relationship with some unnamed woman, or women." She sipped again. "And what do you mean you thought I was being unfaithful, too?" Her eyes flashed.

"All those years of working on projects with him." Owen gripped the stem of his glass at a loss as to how to hold a conversation that should have happened years ago. "I've never been interested in the community work you do. I always took it as a sign that you were bored at home. When I began to hear the gossip about you and Mahaffey, I surrendered and accepted that I was correct, you were bored. Working on your community projects with him filled your life." He gulped his wine.

"That's why I ignored your talk about your community work. I didn't want to know what you and he were doing. I never wanted to talk about that life."

"Do you remember what you said the first time I chaired a fundraiser?" He shook his head. "You said, 'when you bring home a salary, I'll get excited.' That's why I never talk to you. I feel as though I'm two people, Owen, the respected woman in the community who knows everyone and gets things done and your empty-souled wife who's always faithful and always home wondering what I have to do to attract your attention." She finished her wine and walked out of the room.

He followed her. "Empty souled? You're putting words in my mouth. I never said that."

"I don't want to talk about it," she said, stopping at the foot of the stairs, turning back to face him, trembling in anger and frustration.

"You're always like that," he mimicked the tone of her reply. "You act so aloof and judgmental. No wonder I thought you were fooling around."

"Is that the reason you're AWOL from our bed?" She took a deep breath, deciding that today she would throw all her frustrations at him. "You thought I was unfaithful so you, what, you found your own girlfriend?"

He blanched. "I never . . ."

"So, what's your explanation for the last five years, you were being a martyr? You were punishing me? You never had any interest in sex and my assumed infidelity saved you from any pretense?" This conversation surprised both of them. All the things that should have been said years ago spewed out.

"We have sex." He couldn't look her in the eye.

"When you have an overwhelming need. Did we ever make love?" Her eyes were flashing.

"That's what this is all about, love? That's just the stuff in books. This is real life. You women think life should be romantic." He scoffed. "Life is hard work!"

"Let me sum up this conversation." She cleared her throat as if preparing to address a crowd. "For several years you've thought I was an unfaithful wife and now you admit that it may not have been of real interest to you because you don't love me anyway and continue to have no interest in my activities, or presumably, my life." She glared at him. "I'll sleep in the guest room tonight." She ran up the stairs and he heard a door slam.

* * *

"You, sit!" ordered Marianna pointing to Lynn then waved to Piper and Harriette. "We've organized this party so you and Dusty can just sit and enjoy." Tonight was the family celebration of Lynn's marriage to Dusty.

Lynn looked around the yard. No food! Her spring plants were blooming in celebration. The azaleas were trying to outshine the bulbs - daffodils, tulips and narcissus. But no food. No one had fired up the grill. She did note that the usual coolers, filled with beer and soft drinks were in place. She turned at a noise. And there was the food! Her clever friends had brought in a food truck, one of the favorites usually parked at River Dog Brewery. Soon the table was covered with trays of her favorites. Gyros, Greek salad, crispy onions along with Dusty's favorites - Buffalo wings and nachos.

Piper whispered to her, "And wait until you see the dessert tray." Lynn almost swooned in anticipation.

It looked like a lot of food for just the family, so she was not surprised when others started to drop in. Emily Jacobs and her grandchildren, from next door, were first to arrive. As she stated, "The kids need to be in bed early." She twinkled her engaging smile, "So we came early."

Dusty's unit and families added more mouths and eager youngsters to the mix. And then Lynn's two-person Philanthropies' staff made an appearance along with a few of her favorite donors. Since the college crowd was preparing for end of semester exams, they were AWOL. Bryce, Piper's son, came saying, "I told the guys I would eat for them."

Of course, all of Dusty's brothers drifted in and out. His mother had declined but asked that one of her sons bring dessert back to the farm. Lynn received a text from Jason: *Sorry to miss the party. Three weeks to graduation!*

To top off the evening everyone applauded when Danny unveiled the desserts - chocolate lava cake, big macadamia nut cookies and three different cheesecakes - caramel raspberry chocolate cheesecake, pecan pie cheesecake and almond amaretto cheesecake.

As the evening came to a close, Dusty stood before their friends and family, raised his bottle of beer and said, "I've told you before, Lynn, but I'll say it in front of everyone. You're the only one I ever proposed to, because you're the only one I wanted to say yes."

Hugs, kisses, applause. It was a great time in a chilly spring evening.

* * *

Rachel rested on the bed in the guest room, staring at the ceiling. I could have been such a fool, she thought as she reviewed her discussions with Anita and with Owen, and her temptation to have an affair with Kip. She thought about all those years working with him. The secret smiles he gave her, innocent email that sometimes suggested more than the message itself - and the thrill she experienced each time.

In fact, the secret looks weren't very secret. Rachel remembered a comment about three years ago. A woman said, "That guy is really into you."

"What do you mean?" Rachel had asked.

"The way he looked at you," explained the woman.

"He's not into me. He has a wife and family and so do I."

"Excuse me," the women had said. "All I'm saying is if a man looked at me like that I'd follow him home."

"He's just grateful we accomplished so much at our meeting today." Rachel remembered feeling very uncomfortable with the discussion. The woman had shrugged and walked away.

Rachel thought over that discussion, and then recalled all the other looks Kip had given her - the smiles, the winks, the small touches on her hand, her arm. When she added it up and considered it with her new information, she realized that he had been sending signals to everyone in town that they were a couple - a secret couple. How many people had assumed she and Kip were in a long-term affair? Certainly his wife and Owen thought so. Who else?

How would she ever find out and how could she ever endure the embarrassment? Get a grip, she told herself. You never did anything. And he can't use you anymore. Anita has his number - she'll make

Caught

discovering his secret life her challenge. Anita had been a surprise in many ways. One of those ways, Rachel was certain, was the steel she suspected in that very quiet, long-suffering woman.

But Rachel still felt violated, still felt foolish and as of this evening she felt betrayed by her husband. What would happen between them? What did she want to happen? Could she, a healthy middle-aged woman, live the rest of her life with no affection, no touching, and virtually no dialogue with the man she shared a home?

She tossed and turned all night. And when the sky brightened she had a solution.

CHAPTER TEN

Lynn yawned as she waited at the courthouse coffee shop for the judge to arrive. Judge Athena Dunn liked her community meetings to occur before court. Sophie Grayson, attorney H. Lawrence Grayson's mother, and Amelia Rawlings, owner of Amelia's Maids, were already in line grabbing coffee and muffins.

The judge came breezing in, waved to Lynn and squinted at a table that some deputies immediately vacated. "See how I scare everyone. They'd rather drink coffee in a stairwell than sit near me," she laughed. The judge was in her late-fifties, looking every bit her age. She refused to color her hair as many of her friends did. She wore make-up only when she remembered and she always wore sneakers on court days, because she said no one saw her feet behind the bench. Even with that, her complexion had a healthy glow because she spent weekends outdoors fishing or hunting. She wore her gray hair in a subdued bun at the base of her neck, a very dignified look that she said was easy to care for and required no hairdressing talent. Lynn enjoyed every encounter she had with the judge.

"Isn't this great," chirped Sophie Grayson. "This vaccine has us all back together." She was older than the judge but believed in makeup and stylish clothing.

The judge smirked, "There are a few assholes around this courthouse that continue to call the virus a hoax." She looked around the room, "There's no vaccine against stupidity." They all nodded agreement, then collected drinks, napkins and an extra chair.

Once the women were seated, Lynn began, "I wanted to bring you in on a project - -"

"The girls are starting that magazine," said Sophie. She was Michelle Grayson's mother-in-law.

"You know?" gasped Lynn, "They only told me a few days ago."

"Herbert," said Sophie, referring to her son, "suggested that I invest in this project to support women in the community. He said he didn't think a husband should interfere."

"My father," said the judge, referring to Mr. Hutch Dunn, a venerable attorney in town, "says that the family should support family. He has a crush on his new niece, Trina." The woman was married to Mars, the Dunn family heir.

Lynn looked at Amelia who laughed as she said, "Zachary says give her money, but act like it's my money, not family money." Zachary Rawlings was Penny's father-in-law and Amelia's husband.

"We can also raise money from our friends," said Sophie. "I want to be a part of this. It sounds exciting. I don't know much about magazines, but they should get someone who knows the older demographic involved also. We need factual news, too."

"That sounds like you know more than you're letting on," teased Lynn.

"I've done a little research."

"So what do I tell the girls?" asked Lynn.

The judge looked at her friends. "Just tell them you've convinced us to be silent supporters." She winked and sipped her coffee. Step Two - done.

* * *

Bryce Hanby sat on an old bench in the cemetery abutting Dancing Creek studying the evening shadows. He had been invited for a private discussion with a new acquaintance, Rory Prentiss, who lived in a carriage house on one of the old estates. Dancing Creek was a neighborhood of the homes built by the wealthy of River Bend over a century ago. Several years ago, locals, dismayed at the condition of some of the historic mansions, began purchasing and reclaiming them. The Palmer Mansion was the oldest. Nathan Taft and his family had spent time and money rehabilitating the oldest estate. It was now a lovely, up-to-date home enjoyed by Nathan and his nephew Buck and his young family.

Bryce looked around the cemetery. Over the weekend he had met Rory at Lynn's anniversary party. The older man had suggested they meet in the cemetery, that he enter through the main gateway, park at a quiet spot, and hike over to the oldest part and wait. Rory had been secretive, and had cautioned, "Sweetie, you need me, but no one needs to know."

The young man smiled to himself. Rory knew. His best friend Beth had guessed he was gay and Bryce had only told his mother. That had been several months ago. Did everyone else know? Had Piper told anyone? He was certain she hadn't because she had said to him, "When you're ready, we'll tell the family." He had been so relieved to share his secret with her. Now Rory wanted to talk? I guess, thought Bryce ruefully, one gay guy can always recognize another.

A twig snapped and Rory came walking through the forest that was the old cemetery. "Can you believe how big these trees have grown?" He smiled at Bryce. "I hope a tree grows beside my grave when they finally plant me. Do you think I should leave instructions?"

Bryce smiled at the man and moved over to make room on the bench. "No, sweetie," advised the older man. "Men like us don't sit together on a bench. We walk where everyone can see us." He tilted his head. "Come on, we can walk and talk."

"You mean gay men?"

"At least you're not in denial." Rory gestured him to follow as he stepped around a tumbling headstone.

Bryce rose and began walking along the narrow grass pathway winding through the grave field. He didn't know what he was supposed to say. So he asked, "Why are we here?"

"Oh, sweetie," sighed Rory, "that's a big, existential question. All I want to do is give you some pointers for surviving in a small town." They walked in silence until Rory finally asked, "Who knows?"

"My mom. She said she'd be with me when I'm ready to tell the family." More silence. "How did you know?"

Rory gave him a sidelong glance. "How long have I lived in this town?" Bryce shrugged. "I watched you, and some others, grow up. I knew probably before you did. And now I want to help." A longer silence. "I'm not propositioning you. I'm not recruiting you. I just know from experience that you will need a friend to advise you. And sometimes a friend to have your back."

Caught

Bryce laughed. "I can't see you fighting for my virtue." A sigh. "I left that on Broadway with my career." Those were melancholy memories for the young man.

"I have seen you around town with that attorney." Rory sounded confused.

"Beth?" Bryce grabbed a leaf from a low hanging branch. "She figured me out, too. She's the one who made me tell my mom. I helped her move to Raleigh for a new job. And I visit often. I stay at her place and explore dating options there."

"Any luck?"

"Nothing. I've decided to keep my job here until the world gets normal again. Then I'll look for something in a bigger city." More silence as they walked. "Any advice?"

"I want you to be safe," admitted Rory. "You sound sensible. My advice is that you tell your family sooner rather than later. Your life will be less complicated. They'll be curious, but they won't ask questions. I've watched your family over the years. They're all good and accepting people. Some of my friends would give an arm to have a family like yours."

"What about a social life here?" Bryce was admitting that his life in River Bend was sterile.

Rory sighed. "As much as I think your family will be understanding, I have learned that living your real life has to happen away from home. I suspect that within a few years, when you have developed a long-term relationship they'll adjust and accept. You could even live here as a couple, but all of you will feel more comfortable to start if there is sort of a veil over . . . . things."

"I thought the world was changing," argued Bryce.

"Not always and not everywhere." Rory gave him a sad truth. "And not aways in the ways we would hope." They walked along the pathway, sometimes stopping to read the old inscriptions and marvel at the dates.

Bryce finally asked, "How do I tell them?"

"I'd tell your brothers first." Rory smiled at him. "Then when you talk with anyone else, they'll have your back." He poked Bryce in the arm. "And they will fight for you. My brothers did."

* * *

"You're home," said Owen in a delighted voice. Rachel had spent the weekend working in the yard and cleaning the house. She hadn't found any time to speak with Owen or return to their bed. Monday evening he was happy to smell dinner and find her in the kitchen.

"Dinner will be ready, soon. We have to be at bridge at seven." She was surprised that she sounded so normal to herself. Had she been pretending so long that it had become natural to act as though she and Owen were in a loving relationship? He left the kitchen and she heard him whistle as he ran upstairs to wash and change for the evening.

At dinner he said, "I didn't know what to expect after this weekend." He shoveled casserole onto his plate.

"Nothing's changed," she said. "I'm too old to leave and taking my share of our investments and property would leave us two old poor people. I have to get ready." She left the kitchen.

Returning from an evening of bridge, Rachel watched her husband flop on his recliner in the den and flick on the TV. She climbed sadly to her room and washed for bed.

She was startled awake as her husband shook her. "I thought you said nothing's changed. Why are you sleeping in the guest room?"

"Nothing's changed," she replied. "We came home, the TV captured your attention and I went to bed."

"But you're in here," he argued, his eyes scanning the guest room.

"Nothing's changed," she replied again, "I still cook and clean and wash your dirty underwear. Good night." She pulled the covers up to her ears and turned her back to him.

"I'm not playing your little game," he muttered as he left the room.

* * *

To get Delsey into the clinic, Mutt volunteered to close the clinic on one of the late evenings of operation. The clinic usually stayed open late on Monday and Thursday with an open dental clinic attracting many patients. It was usually a busy and confusing night. He saw a masked Delsey come into the waiting area. He stepped out, called her name as though she were a patient and then ushered her back to his examining room. She followed him with her big purse slung over her shoulder. No one seemed to notice one more masked person.

"Where's your director?" Delsey asked slipping down her mask as he closed the exam room door.

"She never stays for these late nights. We don't do medical exams tonight. The dental clinic operates in another wing."

"Where's the pharmacy?"

"Around the corner, but it's locked I can't get us in."

"Show me."

They both scanned the hallway before slipping on masks and stepping out of the exam room. Mutt grabbed a folder to look official as he directed his fake patient through the clinic. Walking into the pharmacy hallway from the 'staff only' door, Delsey studied and paced the area. "What rooms are on either side of the pharmacy?"

Mutt studied the hall and all the closed doors. "An examining room on either side, but behind on the back hall is a maintenance closet and the director's office, some storage and other offices." He took her to one of those fire exit floor plans and pointed out the various rooms.

"Yes!" She walked up to the pharmacy door which was half glass and studied the back wall. She paced and pulled a pad out to do a quick sketch then tapped the pencil against the diagram. "Take me to the storage closet."

Mutt led her through the clinic, away from the hubbub of the dental rooms toward the quiet back hallway. He opened the closet door. Delsey stepped around him and flicked on the light. She studied the space, paced, studied her sketch, then pulled him inside and closed the door.

"Hey!"

"Shut up." She clapped her hand over his masked mouth. "No one saw us come in." She sloughed off her bag and walked toward the back wall. "I need a ladder and an extension cord." Mutt pulled a tarp back and showed her a ladder. They searched the shelves and found a cord.

Aligning the ladder to the back wall, she climbed, removed a ceiling tile, and standing on the top of the ladder, stretched herself up into the ceiling. After more stretching and fidgeting she called down, "I got a tile loose. I can put a camera in here and we can watch the action over the course of a week." She scrambled down the ladder, rummaged through her bag and scurried back up the ladder, disappearing into the ceiling. She dropped an electrical cord to him. "Plug this into power."

He attached it to the extension cord and found an outlet. Soon he heard the sound of a drill. Next came sounds of a small hammer and some shuffling. Her feet came out of the ceiling. She handed down her tools, the extension line, and a small sack of leavings. "I think I caught most of the dust from the drill." Back on the floor, she grinned at him.

He began to remove the ladder. "Wait," she said, "Where is the director's office?" She nodded to the walls on either side of the closet.

"That's the wall of the director's office and the other wall is part of the pharmacy storage room." He pointed to each of the side walls as he spoke.

She grinned. "Two good places for more cameras." He gasped. She patted his arm. "Be calm. I brought enough. We might as well use them." He shook his head, probably in despair, and moved the ladder.

"You better be fast, because you have to leave before the clinic closes." He frowned. "I don't know how I would explain you leaving with me when I lock up." He frowned at her. "We have security cameras outside the building." He shrugged. "Drugs." He thought that explained the cameras. She nodded because it did.

"I'll blend in with the patients when I leave." She traced a finger along his cheek, winked, then scramble up the ladder. She proceeded to place cameras in locations she thought useful to address Franky's concerns.

When she finished, the dental clinic was still busy. Mutt sent Delsey back to Franky's, reminding her he would check in with Franky later. He watched her leave the waiting area with a practiced nonchalance. He wondered what she was in real life - a spy, a bank robber? And it dawned on him that he had never asked about her work or how she knew about cameras. Maybe Franky knew.

CHAPTER ELEVEN

At breakfast Owen asked, "So what do we do when we travel? Will you demand separate motel rooms? And what about when we stay with friends and family?" It had been three nights since Rachel moved to the guest room. He felt at sea.

"We haven't taken a trip for over a year. We'll sleep in the same bed if the circumstances require it." She placed scrambled eggs in front of him. "Under this new system, I want you to tell me if you can see that anything has changed."

"I can tell you right now. . . You're sleeping in the guest room!"

"You haven't touched me for two months. What difference does it make to you?" She held his gaze.

"We must have had sex in the last two months." Owen didn't shy away from sex talk. He was becoming stronger as a sparring partner.

"I don't just mean we haven't had sex for two months. You misunderstand. I mean you haven't touched me in two months. No hug, no kiss, no arm around me as we crossed the street or climbed out of the car. I can't remember our last sexual encounter. Whether I sleep in the guest room should make no difference in your life." She sat at the table to eat her own eggs.

"So, I guess this means you think you can have an affair with that guy?"

"Why would I do that? I'm not interested in men. You've admitted that for many years you thought I was unfaithful and you couldn't be bothered to discuss it, and he has demonstrated for many years that he found me a perfect tool for his secret life. Both of you have used me without regard for my feelings. And right now I think you're the bigger villain." She poured them both more coffee.

"I don't like this," he pouted. "Do you want me to go to counseling or something to get us back to normal?"

"Do you think you need counseling?" She gave him a hard look. "Or do you think I need counseling?" He raised his brow and looked as though he might agree with that statement.

He asked, "Are you coming back to our bed?"

"Why?" she asked, "Have you been inconvenienced or found the services wanting? I haven't missed a meal. I still clean, cook, and do the laundry. What difference does it make where I sleep?"

"The kids'll be visiting in a few weeks. What will you do then?"

"Cook, clean, launder and I guess I'll sleep in your bed unless you would prefer some other arrangement."

"I guess I can cope," he said. He threw a crumpled napkin across the kitchen table and stood.

Before he could leave the room she announced, "I've accepted a two-week assignment with a consulting firm." Surprised, he sat back down staring at her. "I'm going to Milwaukee on Thursday to work with a nonprofit to consult on strategic planning."

"Alone?"

"No, I'll be traveling with a woman I met a few months ago. She attended my workshop at a philanthropy conference and invited me to join her team." He looked so lost sitting at the table, his hands seemed frozen around his coffee cup.

She was touched by his silent, confused response, and in a soft, kind voice she said, "You're not a bad man, Owen. You're a successful businessman. You supported me and the children comfortably. The only problem is where our lives intersect. For me it's no life. For you it's, well, I don't know what it is."

"I thought it was a marriage." His voice softened, too.

"I guess it is, and maybe as a marriage, it's more common than we know." With that she felt her heart break.

"So this is our life from now on?" he asked. Was his heart breaking, too?

"What's different than it was two weeks ago?" She began to clean the breakfast dishes.

He shrugged.

"What's different," she answered her own question, "is that we acknowledged the quality of our life together. Now it has to be faced."

"What if I change . . ."

"Whatever you do will be too little, too late. And even at that it will only last until football season when your attention will be pulled to the TV every minute that you're home." She finished putting dishes in the dishwasher and wiped her hands. "When I return from my trip, we can talk about this more. Maybe we'll see some other path."

"That sounds so touchy-feely," he scoffed.

"And that may be part of our problem," she sighed.

"What do you mean?"

"We define marriage differently. You see it as some comfortable non-interactive existence. You know, I'm as handy as a pet but don't have to be walked in the evening and I help you feel as though you're not alone. I, on the other hand, would like to be touched, or even just acknowledged, and have my interaction with you be a cut above care for a pet."

"You always talk as though you know every one of my thoughts and intentions," he challenged.

"This is a conversation. You should be saying things you want to say." She waited.

"I've never understood you. I provide for you. We have a comfortable house, we have friends. I could never understand why you had to be out in the community. If I were the wife, I'd stay home. You don't need to be out getting beat up by the world."

"I'm not beat up, I'm challenged. I'm an intelligent woman who enjoys working on problems and organizing things. I like the praise I receive." She straightened the chairs at the breakfast table. "I'm glad I've finally said all the things on my mind. I'm sorry you find them upsetting. But to learn you thought I was having an affair while I was being a faithful wife is depressing, it suggests to me that our marriage is false, and I have no idea who you are."

"I'm the guy you married."

"I know that now. A quiet hard-working man focused on his career and providing for the family. And defining his family time as meals and TV now that the kids are gone - sort of your reward for all your work."

He frowned at her. "I've got to get to work." He walked out to the garage.

She stood in the kitchen and listened to the automatic garage door open, Owen's car leave, and with a final thump, the garage door close. Rachel leaned against the kitchen counter and stared out the window.

* * *

Father Nick had asked Lutheran minister Tilson Butler to accompany him to John Gillespie's home. "What have you got me into, Nick?" teased Tilly. "We going to break up some satanic cult?"

Father John Gillespie had been buried in the rites of his church. Now it was time for Nick to address the man's final requests. Nick chuckled to himself as he guided his car around the steep, curvy mountain road. Tilly was an interesting choice for this adventure. In fact, Nick had wondered several times over the last days just why he had turned to the Lutheran minister. He thought it was because, as clergy, they had more in common with one another than they did with their own congregations. He also knew that venturing into the deep western North Carolina coves as a Roman Catholic priest might be challenging. Tilly, a native of the region, could be helpful, you know, have his back.

Per Tilly's instruction their dress for the day was un-clergy. He was in jeans, a sweatshirt and hiking boots. Nick was dressed the same. "I told you," the priest answered the question for the tenth time, "John was my old professor and he asked me to clean out his place."

It was a two-hour drive to the outskirts of Murphy. Tilly was navigating. "When we get to the gas mart, it says here the house is up and behind." He looked at Nick. "Are we gonna have to bushwhack to this place?"

"I don't think so." Nick slowed in the curve. "There it is." The gas mart was a rundown brick building with two gas pumps and a rack of propane tanks snug against the side of the building. The parking pavement was losing its fight with weeds. Next to the mart was a small garage advertising car repairs. Across the road was a tumbledown vegetable stand. Nothing was ready for sale this early in the season.

"And there's a house right behind," observed Tilly. He studied the three fellows in front of the mart. "I suggest we stop here and introduce ourselves." The men stood in a line blocking double entry glass doors. "Let me talk," warned Tilly. "I grew up in these parts."

Caught

The two men were scrutinized by the gas mart trio. After looking them over, one man nodded to Tilly's sweatshirt that claimed him as a Tarheel. Then he studied Nick's Notre Dame sweatshirt. After some thought and a quick spit into the dirt, he said, "At least that there's an ACC school."

Nick smiled. Now he understood why his friend had snorted at the sight of the sweatshirt as he climbed into the car. Tilly, in his role as native, greeted the men and got a tepid response. He finally got to the point. "My friend came here looking after a fellow, John, that worked here."

"He dead?" asked one of the men.

"Yes." Nick stepped forward.

"You Nick?" asked another of the men.

"Yes."

The spokesman nodded. "He had Bundy here," another fellow nodded, "drive him to River Bend. He said he'd be back, but if not, then his friend, Nick, would come for his things." The man sighed. "He was a good fellow. Sorry he passed." The others nodded. The spokesman continued, "This here is Bundy and that's Mickey." Each man nodded. "And I'm Lucas." Once they had names the trio looked less threatening. Mickey was the oldest, maybe late thirties early forties. He appeared to be a farmer. Lucas had a trim haircut suggesting recent military service. He was neat and might be the gas mart clerk.

Bundy was a young man in his mid-twenties who, as suggested by his clothing, was the mechanic at the garage. He cleared his throat. "He took good care of my aunt for years. It was the least I could do. They never asked for much." He moved toward Nick. "C'mon, I'll show you the house. We ain't touched nothing."

Bundy led Nick and Tilly behind the mart and up the walkway to the small, neat house. "It's locked."

"I've got the key," Nick assured the man. He unlocked the door and they stepped into the house. The living room was lined with bookshelves, an old sofa sagged against one wall and a wheelchair stood at the window as though it had spent years looking out toward the mountains. Nick looked at Bundy. "Can you tell me something about your aunt?"

Bundy grinned. "That there chair didn't stop her. She was a nurse. She got herself a job in a big hospital in Charlotte where she got real sick and we thought she was dead. When we all trouped down to see her, she said goodbye and sent the family home. Then one day she comes back here with John and that there wheelchair. She'd say her heavenly father saved her." He shrugged. "I was a young'un. That's all I remember. John, he moved in and took care of her. She helped us all with her nursing advice. He worked at the mart and fixed up this place. They stayed to themselves. You could see them on the porch of an evening sittin' and holdin' hands." Bundy shifted uncomfortably. "I gotta get back. I have that repair shop beside the mart."

"Could you drive the car up here for us so we can pack his things?"

"I'll have Mickey do it. Lucas is the day manager at the mart."

"Thank you."

When Bundy left, Nick pulled out the other key. "We're looking for a closet or something where John said I would find his gear." Nick shrugged. "I don't know what I'm looking for."

Tilly held up a delicate ink sketch of a priest kneeling in prayer that he had found on a side table. "Is this John?" Nick nodded. "He wanted you to collect his priest gear. It's locked up here some place." Tilly spoke with such confidence that Nick believed him. They walked through the little house and Tilly called, "Here."

In the bedroom he was jiggling a knob on a locked door. Nick inserted the other key. They found a very small windowless room with an altar and several priestly vestments, ironed and with patches in some places. Nick sighed, "John told me he never stopped being a priest." He looked through the supplies. "This is what an Army chaplain would use for a quick service." He found a bottle of red wine and chuckled. "I guess he improvised. He told me that living here made him sympathetic to missionaries in the field in places like Africa. I guess they improvise, too."

Tilly laughed and slapped Nick on the back. "Only another preacher would understand." And Nick was glad he had invited his friend along. "So what are we doing?"

As Tilly asked, Nick spied an envelope on the little altar. Opening it, he pulled out two documents. He scanned the first and read it aloud, *"Nick, you found it. Take my gear. Take my books, keep them or spread them around. They were good friends over the years. And take Anna's artwork. When you go through the papers here you will see that I owe a lot of money to the owner*

of the mart. He knows; I didn't embezzle. Hope you can pay him back. And I'd like to make some bequests if you can find the funds. My will explains it all. Only tell folks if you can manage the funds. In God, Father John Gillespie."
Nick stared at the letter while Tilly scanned the second document.

"Shit, Nick," Tilly gasped, "this adds up to about three hundred thousand."

He waved the sheets under Nick's nose.

"That's how much he owes to the mart owner?" Nick was puzzled.

"No, for everything."

"What do you mean for everything?"

"Listen to this," said Tilly. "He lists all the merchandise he gave away at the gas mart. Diapers, soup, aspirin. Then he's got a list of bequests." Tilly rattled the pages. "He wants to give people cars and houses and glasses." The preacher was puzzled. "Did he leave a bankbook or some cash with you?" Nick shook his head. "Then how did he expect you to come up with the money for all this sh-, I mean stuff?"

Nick shook his head. "Three hundred thousand? Are you sure?"

"It's just a rough estimate," grinned Tilly. "You know how we preachers can eyeball a collection plate?"

Nick looked back at John's note. "He says," reported the priest, "that I shouldn't mention any bequests unless I can find the money." They looked at one another understanding the challenge of two preachers trying to find money for needs not related to their own congregations. How could they ask for money to provide cars and houses and eye-glasses to a mysterious group of folks? It probably made more sense to a congregation to send money to foreign missions than for him and Tilly to solicit funds for a gaggle of folks in a hidden North Carolina cove. The little house was quiet. Sunshine danced along the spokes of the wheelchair, the sketch of the priest in prayer fluttered in some invisible breeze and they said together, "Sean." When any of the clergy in Nick's rectory poker group needed quick funds, they always turned to Sean Hennessey, multimillionaire and poker player.

"We can at least ask," said Nick. "John said not to say anything unless we got the money." Tilly nodded. Nick scanned the house. "Let's pack up some of these things. And get back home."

Nick packed up John's priestly paraphernalia while Tilly looked over the books and collected the art work. He called to Nick, "Look at this.

His Anna was quite an artist." Tilly held out another ink sketch of a priest saying Mass in the little closet and under the drawing was, "My heavenly Father." Tilly waved the paper, "She knew he was a priest."

"I believe she did," agreed Nick. "Someone kept his garb neat and mended after all these years. John told me God used Anna as a channel for His love. He told me that sometimes God loves us through another person."

Tilly hung his head. "I understand. That's why I haven't remarried. My wife was my love, my life. When she died I couldn't imagine anyone filling me with the love I received from her."

Nick patted his friend on the back. "And that's why you're here today. You understand."

They packed all John's priest gear, as much artwork as they could find, and some of the books. Driving back to the mart, they parked and walked over to Bundy's garage. "You fellas done?" asked the mechanic.

"Bundy," said Nick, "John left a will and we'd like to return in a week or so to read it and give out some bequests." A voice niggled at the priest, *You haven't asked Sean yet!* Nick smiled to himself, remembering he was in the faith business, believing was a big part!

"Money?"

"Some." Nick didn't want to say too much. He had to ask Sean for the money first. He handed Bundy a list. "These are the folks mentioned. Could they all be here? Would they all fit in the house? What time would be good?"

Bundy rubbed a knuckle under his jaw as he studied the list. "We might could all be here at lunch time." He shuffled his shoe in the gravel. "If you give us enough notice."

"It's a date," agreed Nick. "We'll be here one day at noon as soon as we clear things up." Nick chided himself for speaking up so soon without even asking Sean. But he wanted to give something back to the people whom John had loved. He'd pray, and trust.

* * *

All the way back to River Bend the two men planned their approach to Sean Hennessey. Three hundred thousand was a lot of money and the need was for folks two hours west of River Bend, for a bunch of strangers.

Not only that, but they also had to talk with someone about the legalities. John had written his will but had no money for the bequests. He had relied on Nick to find the money! Was that a real will? How did they disburse the funds when some bequests were to children for future education and other matters. And how did you bequest funds that didn't exist?

Tilly slapped his knee. "Let's call. I got a signal." He waved his cell phone, "Tell Sean we're having a game tonight and we really need him because ..." He ran out of reason.

"What if we say we need help?"

"Naw, he'll know we want money."

"What if we tell him to drop in for a visit and bring his wife?"

"Maybe she isn't as loose with the purse strings as he is," suggested Tilly.

Nick was frustrated. There was a lot to investigate before they understood all the implications of John's wishes. But Sean had to be asked. "Just call him and ask him to meet us at my place."

Tilly checked his phone once more to make certain of a signal in the mountains then initiated the call. "Sean, this is Tilly .... Can you meet me and Nick at his place?" Tilly frowned into the phone. "Let me put you on speaker." His fussed with his phone, then asked, "Would you repeat your question. Sean?"

"How much?" echoed through the car.

They looked at one another, Nick swallowed and said, "Three hundred thousand."

"This better be good," replied Sean. "You there now?"

"We're about an hour away."

"See you then." He ended the call.

"Was that yes or no?" They debated the question all the way back to River Bend.

* * *

Sean and his wife, Lee, were waiting on the rectory's back stoop when the preachers arrived. They could see that the car was filled with books and papers. Nick stretched around gathering the relevant documents.

Tilley searched the floor in front because he had slipped off his boots. They finally got out of the car.

"Lee?" Nick and Tilly were surprised that she had accompanied her husband to meet with the preachers.

Sean threw an arm over her shoulders and pulled her close. "We're a team. We promised to agree on spending our money."

Nick had a sinking feeling. He didn't know Lee well. Was she as giving as Sean? Would she laugh at his proposal and take Sean home? Gulp! He rushed to unlock the door. "Welcome." The priest brought his guests into the rectory kitchen. "I don't know if I have much to offer."

"Beer," muttered Sean as he offered Lee a chair at the table.

"Yeah, I got that." Nick put the papers on the table. At the refrigerator he raised an eyebrow to Lee.

She smiled, "I'll have a beer, too." He pulled four beers from the refrigerator and flung a bag of chips on the table.

Sean looked at Tilly. "You involved in this, too?"

"No, I'm here for the entertainment." He sat at the table and drank his beer.

Nick took a long swallow. "I don't know if you heard that a man died in the church a week or so ago of this virus. He was an old seminary professor of mine who left the priesthood a long time back. He moved in with a lady." Tilly slipped some of the sketches onto the table. "She was wheelchair bound and an artist. She drew sketches of John and their life together." Sean picked up the sketches - sketches of children, pets, mountain scenery - and passed them to Lee while Nick continued. "She died of this virus a few months ago and he came to me to carry out his wishes and to die in the church."

"Three hundred thousand?" asked Sean.

"What was her name?" Lee asked an unexpected question.

"Anna Pace." Nick tried to remember what little information he had. "We met her nephew today. She had been a nurse in Charlotte and got some disease and told the family to let her die." He shrugged. "Her nephew had been young at the time and wasn't clear about details. He said they respected her wishes and left her in Charlotte. After some time she returned home with my friend John." Nick drank his beer, continued. "It's unclear to me if they were married, but she and John lived together until she died of covid a few months ago."

Caught

Both Lee and Sean talked over one another to ask more questions. Finally, Sean said, "You first."

She nodded. "Was Anna the artist?" Nick nodded and indicated the sketches strewn across the table. Lee pulled a tissue from her pocket and wiped a tear. Then she began a story. "I knew an Anna Pace once who was a nurse and artist in Charlotte. I was at the hospital doing an in-service training. I was affiliated with a university program and traveled around doing trainings." She took a drink. "The Anna I knew was a dedicated nurse. One day she was treating a woman who had survived a terrible beating from her husband. The man came into the room and began shouting and threatening his wife. Anna attacked him. I only heard the story. I wasn't a witness.

"They told me she jumped on his back and pounded on him. He picked her up, punched her, and threw her against the windows. She didn't fall the four stories to the ground but got caught on the broken glass of the window frame. Her injuries were severe. I suspect she didn't want her family to know the truth and explained she had a disease."

Sean took his wife's hand and caressed it. "What do you know about Nick's friend?"

She said, "Nothing. I heard during my next visit for a training that she had returned home and she had met a fellow and was married."

The men were silent for a time sipping beer and thinking. Finally Sean asked Nick, "How are you involved in all this?"

"John was an old seminary professor. He came to St. Bridget's to ask my help with his death and aftermath."

"Aftermath?"

"He asked me to clear out his priest gear and take Anna's artwork and some of his books. He also left his will. He wants some debts paid and he wants to make some bequests. He told me to keep quiet about the will unless I get the money."

"Debts?"

Nick handed Sean a summary of the money owed the mart owner. The list included: Mrs. Rice, $10 for medicine, Mrs. Allen, two packages of diapers for the new baby. It was a diary of John's charity to his customers. Sean looked up and raised an eyebrow, passing the pages to Lee. Nick volunteered, "He was night clerk at a gas mart. He said the boss knew what he was giving away. John saw it as a loan."

Sean was curious. "Bequests?"

Tilly spread the will out in front of Sean and pointed, "Tuition for Jeanie and Drake, glasses for Amber, car repairs for Lucas. It goes on to the next page." Tilly nodded. "It adds up."

"Why'd he leave the priesthood?"

"He didn't," said Nick. Tilly placed Anna's drawings of the priest on the table. "He told me that he never stopped being a priest and that a lot of folks needed a priest late at night at a gas mart. He also had a small altar set up with his old vestments and all the things he needed for saying Mass. I think he said Mass every day." Nick looked at his friends. "He told me that sometimes God loves us through another person. He told me that Anna was God's love to him."

Sean was silent. He understood that concept. He knew that his wife was a physical love but also an undefined all-encompassing emotion. Was it God's love? He shook his head. He tried to stay at arm's length from religion and it kept coming into his life. He decided he would wrestle with that thought another day.

Before Sean could speak, Lee said, "We'll give you the money."

Both men held their breath waiting for Sean's agreement. "You heard the lady." Both men relaxed in a gusty sigh. "But, let me study this will. We might set up a fund for this John to help his friends for years instead of one payout. If you need glasses you need them more than once."

Nick gasped. "An endowed fund?"

Sean shrugged. "Something like that. Let's talk to Herbie and Lynn. We might do something fine in your friend's memory."

Nick was speechless. Tilly grinned and finished his beer and said, "You're getting pretty sophisticated about giving away money, Sean."

"I have to with you bandits always trying to pull some scheme."

Nick handed around more beer, still reeling from Lee and Sean's generosity.

CHAPTER TWELVE

When the alarm went off, Rachel reached over her husband and turned it off. "You came back," Owen smiled.

"I was in this bed last night. You never noticed. I've proved my point. Please quit whining that I sleep in the guest room. You just proved you have no idea where I sleep." She got out of bed to get ready for the day. "I'll get breakfast."

Owen settled at the table and Rachel placed a plate of eggs and sausages in front of him. "My plane leaves at noon. I'll text you that I'm okay."

His eggs looked unappetizing, but he tried to act as an adult - whatever that was when your wife confused you - while he buttered his toast. "What if I bring in a woman while you're away?" He took a bite of sausage.

"It will just confirm what I've suggested. You have no desire or love for me, but as you've just acknowledged you can see yourself with some other woman. Have fun." She collected dishes from the table. "I'll be back before the kids come to visit. Just have her things out of the house."

"I want you to stop this. I want things like they were."

"What has changed?"

"You sleep in the guest room!"

It was sounding like the chorus to an old song.

She ignored him. "I'll fly out from Asheville. You can track me on your phone. I activated the app. You'll always know where I am." She finished cleaning the breakfast dishes. "I have to get to the airport." She left him alone to finish his coffee.

Rachel finished packing and listened as Owen left for work. She was as confused as he seemed to be. She'd give their marriage some thought while she was away. Maybe there was a solution she hadn't considered.

* * *

"I'm black," muttered the angry woman through clenched teeth. "How can you say I look pale?" Teniquia LaMont, detective with the James County/River Bend Joint Investigation Unit clutched her examination gown closer.

Dr. Rita Rutherford blew out her breath. "Your blood cells, blood count and sleepy eyes tell me, a trained medical examiner, that you need to rest. If you were white, you'd look like a ghost."

"Gimme some pills," ordered the detective, "I've got work to do and kids to pick up."

"You've got to take some time and rest."

"I don't have time to rest. I have three kids and a husband, online schooling and a job."

"All the more reason," said the very reasonably sounding doctor. "Get dressed. I'll be back." And she left the examining room.

When she returned she had her prescription pad and began jotting. "Here're my instructions. Lonzo and you are going to Hank's cabin for five days. Your mother and Moneek will handle the kids." She handed the note to Teniquia. "I talked to everyone."

Tee sputtered. Her mother couldn't handle the kids. Moneek, Lonzo's sister, was looking for a job. And she remembered the cabin. She had spent time there a year or so ago on a stakeout with Mars and some state guys. It was not some restful getaway.

"This virus? Mama?"

"You don't have the virus. Your mother and Moneek have had shots. Your kids are healthy. You are the problem." Dr. Rita wasn't listening to any argument. "I've even told Dusty."

"You can't. That violates HIPAA." She referred to federal regulations to preserve patient confidentiality.

"I told him I was isolating you for a few days per CDC rules."

"You just said I didn't have a virus."

"Yes, but I can't tell Dusty the truth. That would violate HIPAA." Medical logic!

If Tee had the energy she would have banged her head against the examining table in disgust. "You aren't making any sense."

"I am. You need rest. It's this or a week in one of the nursing centers."

Caught

"They have sick people."

"You're sick. You need rest. So what will it be, five days in Hank's cabin or a week in a nursing home or the hospital?"

"Okay, I'll talk to Lonzo."

"He's already packing the car." Dr. Rita paused a moment, trying to form the appropriate words. There was no other way to say it. "When I told Dusty, he just asked that you do some surveillance while you're there." She shrugged. "Was he teasing?"

Tee nodded because she didn't want to talk about the history of using Hank's cabin for intermittent surveillance on one of the neighboring cabins. Dusty's unit and the regional drug task force had been watching a cabin near Hank's place on and off for over a year. Great, she thought, a week with my husband and local drug dealers.

* * *

Dusty walked into the kitchen and sniffed to see if there was a dinner being prepared. He put away his weapon and placed his phone on the charger. Walking to the under counter drink refrigerator, he pulled out two beers. Lynn was standing at the stove stirring something. "I don't want a beer this evening."

"They're both for me." He flopped in a chair and popped the first cap.

Lynn came over to him dripping sauce on the floor from the spoon she carried. "Poor baby." She gave him a kiss, grabbed a towel and wiped the floor following the drips back to the stove where she dropped the spoon in the pan.

He sniffed again. "What are you cooking?" She had developed a new interest - finding recipes on the internet and following the video of the preparation. She had her iPad propped up by the stove and was listening to some chef tell her how to make something.

"I'm making chicken paillard." She squinted at the iPad and read, "It's a super easy refreshing spring dinner. The lemon," she reached for a lemon and dropped it on the floor. Recovering it she continued, "adds a fresh taste."

"Whatever." He opened the second beer. He stared into space while she rattled around the kitchen tossing salad greens onto a plate, quickly frying some pounded flat chicken breasts in a hot skillet and getting everything to the table as the video ended.

"Ta-da!"

He applauded and finished his second beer. "This looks nice," he said as he took the bottle of wine she had placed on the table and filled the wine glasses.

She looked at the empty bottles on the counter behind him. "Tough day?"

He nodded as he attacked the chicken. Swallow. "Sheriff has covid." More food. "Tee is sick." Gulp of wine. "Office is a mess."

"Tee is sick?" gasped Lynn. "Has she got the virus?"

"No, Dr. Rita says she's rundown, but I'm supposed to say she had covid because if I know she's rundown it violates Rita's doctor oath, or something. Lonzo took her to Hank's cabin for three or four days. Rita set it all up."

"Hank's cabin?" The mysterious cabin. "Why don't you ever take me there?"

"Next time there's a stakeout, I will." More wine because his chicken paillard had disappeared.

"What about the sheriff?"

Dusty shrugged as he sat back. "We're waiting to hear. He tried to be a tough guy and ignore the vaccines and masking mandates."

"How did a cure become so political?" Lynn seemed to ask the air because Dusty had no clue. "Did Sheriff Dunwoody think avoiding the vaccine would get him re-elected?"

"I think a certain segment of voters would be impressed," replied Dusty. "We're all just waiting to see how serious his illness is."

Lynn shook her head, puzzled. "I've listened to the various national news outlets speak of this reluctance. I didn't think that misinformation would influence River Bend. What are people thinking?"

"Who knows?" Dusty carried his plate to the sink. "It has become a political issue whether to be vaccinated or not and cautious about this virus." He laughed. "Bergy called me when he heard about Dunwoody and said no one talked like this when the polio vaccine was ready. Bergy said he remembers his mother dragging him to get a shot."

"So what's different now?"

"I don't know. Maybe we've gotten too suspicious of government?"

"And we'll put our health at risk?"

"If you don't trust the information, you don't think you're putting yourself at risk." He pulled her to her feet and hugged her. "We'll just take care of our friends and family. And just like everyone talks about herd immunity, maybe the immunity will protect the vaccinated and stupidity will pass from the herd DNA as the unvaccinated pass on."

"That's a little harsh."

* * *

"You got plans for this weekend?" Bart Decker asked his wife as they sat watching the late-night news. The kids were asleep. Bart had spent another day working from home monitoring their toddler daughter because the two boys had returned to school.

Audrey didn't like the tone of his question. It was a sickeningly sweet request. "No," she replied, "We've almost finished with these weekend meetings. We're almost ready to present our proposal to the Philanthropies."

"Yeah, yeah," he snickered. "Weekend meetings for the Philanthropies. Is that what they call having an affair?"

She blanched but said nothing. He may only suspect. "As I said," she summed up, "I have no plans for the weekend. Will you be tied up?" She glanced up at him from her crocheting.

He stood and continued to sneer. "I got plans. You got the kids. I've been doing more than my share."

"And I appreciate your efforts. I'm concerned about the summer. When school is out, I don't know what we'll do. The boys are getting too big to be happy in daycare." She was talking about the challenges all parents were facing with the outfall of the pandemic. Daycare had almost dried up.

"I won't be the summer daycare. I got things to do." Now he sounded angry. "I gotta return to my office."

She didn't want to argue because she knew the discussion would return to Bart's suspicion that she was having an affair. Well, it was over. James had understood. She wondered how many marriages were as hostile and sterile as hers. Watching as he turned off the TV and turned out the lights, she said, "I'll speak to Mom and Dad this weekend about their help with daycare this summer."

He nodded and climbed the stairs to bed. She sat alone in the dark waiting him out as usual, hoping he was asleep when she finally went bed.

CHAPTER THIRTEEN

It was soon no secret in the community that Sheriff Dunwoody was very ill. He had succumbed to the virus and it had earned him a bed in the hospital. "I'm going to need to take a leave of absence while I get this here treatment done," he explained to his two faithful minions who were wrapped up in germ protective gear. "I think we should make Fiore interim sheriff. He did a great job with that fiasco about the airplane and that LaMont woman chasing murderers all over the country." Here Dunwoody winked. "Fiore will look good as the interim and I can claim all his success and leadership and beat that asshole, Dusty Reid, come next election." He coughed. "I told the county manager and he's handling the paperwork with the department attorney."

Doug Fiore had resigned from the Highway Patrol and been hired by the sheriff as the community relations person for the department. During the short time he had been in the job, Doug, a friend of Dusty's, managed the news on both Teniquia's assistance in solving a twenty-year-old murder in Des Moines and Dusty's staff protecting folks from a local jail escapee. He had crafted his news reports with an acknowledgement that Sheriff Dunwoody had been guiding the success of his staff. The sheriff was delighted, but the rest of the community knew better.

"But, Sheriff," moaned the taller masked and wrapped minion. "I thought I could be interim."

"I'm trusting you two to keep an eye on Fiore while I'm here. Remember I have to get reelected if you want to keep these jobs." Two minions nodded.

* * *

"This is a great place," said Lonzo, Tee's husband, as he assessed Hank's cabin. "Look at the big screen TV. He must have satellite. He must have a generator. Where's the remote?"

Tee dropped her small overnight bag on the floor. "I thought we were here to rest and relax."

"Baby, you rest and I can watch basketball." He wrapped her in his big, warm arms. "Then at night after you rest we can relax together." He chuckled and it made his chest rumble. "Now you get some rest. I'll get the cooler. I brought enough food so we don't have to cook."

And that's what she did. The tired mother-detective found a bed and was soon asleep.

Tee awoke a few hours later and it was dusk. Walking into the great room of the cabin she expected to find Lonzo enjoying the big screen TV. The room was silent and empty. She heard a sound overhead. The loft?

"Lonzo?" she called. "Are you up there?"

"Baby, you should see this equipment." He looked down over the railing.

"I know. We use it when we do our stakeout here. There's a persistent rumor that the cabin across the way is a drug drop or supply center or something. We never find anything."

Lonzo rolled his eyes, "Except Margaret Eliason and Kip Mahaffey having sex."

"You watched them having sex?"

"I took a pass on that entertainment. But I've watched them concoct some medication."

"What?" She raced up the stairs. "You've seen a drug buy or something?"

"No, I just saw her give Mahaffey a shot after she mixed some things together. I suspect it was one of those shots high priced docs give to their high-priced patients to keep them on the cusp of a high."

"What are you talking about?"

"You know how some Hollywood types and politicians get some type of drug maintenance from their physicians to keep up their energy and their edge?"

"How can you tell what she gave to Kip?"

"It's just a suspicion. I can go look in her trash."

"No, you can't, we don't have a warrant. Besides we've been watching this place for a year and we've never seen shots." She glanced out the window toward the cabin.

"He isn't the only one."

"What?" Her eyes popped. A voice in the back of her mind cautioned, *you should be relaxing*. Another voice reminded her that Dusty had encouraged her to keep watching the cabin. That's why she was tired, too many conflicting instructions and demands. Kids, Dusty, motherhood and career.

"Some other guy came by and put down some cash, got his fix and left."

"Who?"

"I don't know his name. One of those country club types."

This conversation had Tee excited, curious and on edge herself. She was supposed to be resting and relaxing, but her cop-gut was all atingle. "How could this be so obvious to you while the drug investigators have never spotted anything?"

"Maybe it's a new operation."

"Or maybe they had a warning that we would be watching." Innate detective suspicion tugged at her.

"Wow, babe! You went right to conspiracy. You think it's someone on your team warning the perps?"

She smirked, "That's how I'm trained to think. I know it's not one of my guys. But maybe someone on the regional task force is warning the drug suppliers." Tee sat on the stairs and thought through the situation.

"Just arrest the cabin owner," suggested Lonzo. "It must be that Mahaffey guy."

She began walking around the cabin lost in thought. Her husband watched. He could almost see the ideas running through her mind. She finally gave a huff and said, "We've tried for months to find the owners." She nodded. "Not my team, but one of the other agency teams. They keep telling us, er, the rest of the task force that ownership is deep in forestry records. The forestry and wildlife guys haven't found anything yet."

"The team member giving that bad information must be the bad guy," concluded Lonzo.

She smiled at him. "That would be too easy. All the reports from the forestry guys are emails sent to the account the overall task force uses to receive data. Someone could be fooling with the email or asking the wrong question and we wouldn't know who because we never thought to look." She flopped onto the couch. "We trusted everyone we were working with and never challenged information."

"Why are they using the cabin this weekend?"

"They can see our car so they know we're not DEA. During a stakeout the guys are dropped off down the road and hike in. We don't use any lights in here at night. So if they see our car today they'll think we're just a friend of Hank's." She climbed to the loft, peered through the equipment and said, "If you see anything through this, this is how you take a photo." She demonstrated and Lonzo nodded. "I'm here on ordered rest, but if you see something, we'll tell Dusty when we're back in town." Her eyes narrowed. "And nobody else." Lonzo nodded.

* * *

Dusty's cell pinged warning of an incoming text. *Sheriff to appoint Fiore interim.* He studied the text. It was from the county manager. He immediately called. "What's going on?"

The county manager whispered, "I'm giving you a heads up. Dunwoody is really sick. He wants Fiore to be the interim sheriff. His doctors are telling him he hasn't even started recovery yet. They expect him to get sicker. They anticipate a few months stay. I'm crafting a contract for the county attorney to have Fiore sign. He's an okay guy, right?"

"God, yes!" Dusty's enthusiasm leaped through the phone.

"Be quiet," came another whispered caution. "No one knows yet."

"Thanks." Dusty slipped his phone back in his pocket and smiled. What a day! The sun was shining and birds were singing. He hoped he didn't have to wait too long before the news was public.

* * *

Owen Teague walked into his empty house. His wife had gone on some consulting job. She emailed him this morning and said she would send him a daily note so he would know she was still alive. The message was dull - nothing about the town and nothing about the work she would be directing. He stared out the kitchen window. She was right, he didn't care. He thought about her work in Milwaukee and didn't feel left out. He didn't want to know.

The phone rang. "Is Rachel there?" asked a woman's voice.

"No, she's out of town for a few days."

"Is this you, Owen?"

"Yeah." Caution.

"Maybe you can help me. This is Camille Stein, I need volunteers to help tomorrow with the cancer fundraiser at the football field. Everyone is happy to be unmasking and we expect a mob."

He hesitated. The caller charged right on. "It'll only be for the morning. We need bodies. No decisions to make. I'll even have hot coffee."

Owen looked around the quiet, empty house, maybe he should get out. He laughed. "What time?"

* * *

Sean and Lee Hennessey had only been married a few months but had slipped into many loving habits suggestive of long-time marrieds. One was to sit on their porch in the evening, gossiping and waving to neighbors. They watched a baby toddle in the grass. She was the baby Lee and Sean had helped deliver on his living room floor during an electrical blackout and blizzard. The siblings waved at them as the baby unceremoniously plopped on the grass.

"Our baby is growing up," Sean teased.

"That was a lovely experience," replied Lee. "And she is healthy and happy. Have you told her parents that you have set aside a small gift for her college tuition?"

Sean shrugged. "I thought we could wait until she graduated from high school."

Lee laughed. "What happened at your meeting today about John and Anna's fund?"

"It's all set," he explained. "Lynn told me she has two big projects pending and wanted my little problem solved and off her desk. So,

Herbie got the paperwork done and Nick has invited me to go with him to read the will. Tuesday. Wanna come?"

"I can't," she moaned. "I promised my niece I would babysit and then I want to visit my hospice patient." She leaned against him on the glider. "I told you we were too busy to be married."

He laughed and kissed her. "And I told you. You could be as busy as you liked all day as long as you were in my bed at night." She laughed but didn't reply because one of the neighbors bounced onto the porch to share some gossip.

CHAPTER FOURTEEN

"Are you Rachel's husband?" asked one woman as they handed out brochures. The tented booth was crowded with morning volunteers and folks interested in cancer information.

"I didn't even know she had a husband," said another. They looked at Owen.

"We've been married for almost thirty years and have three kids." He had to speak after that comment. He didn't know what else to say. It didn't matter, the conversation continued without him.

"I thought she was involved with Kip Mahaffey," said a third. Then blushed as she realized what she had said.

"No," whispered a fourth, "he's been having an affair with some woman for years but Anita won't tell me her name. And before her it was someone else. He's always had someone on the side. He's such a cad." Owen was surprised at the hostility in the gossip and at how much the ladies seemed to know.

"Why does everyone think he's so cool?" Another women rasped the question.

"Who knows? It'll be harder this time. He's secret sex life is starting to unravel."

"How do you know? And what do you know about the other women?" The volunteers gathered around the speaker, almost ignoring the folks seeking health information.

"His wife isn't talking or sharing information she's getting from a private detective," replied the lady with the most knowledge, then she turned to Owen. "With your wife out of town, he doesn't have an alibi." She gave him a knowing nod.

"What do you mean?" Owen asked, trying to look mystified, hoping he was signaling that he and Rachel had no challenges in their marriage. The conversation swirled around Owen and he tried to stay busy with the visitors to the booth and keep an ear on the gossip. The ladies in the booth knew all the details. They brought him up to date on the pending Mahaffey downfall as they were naming it. Rachel had been telling the truth. She was a faithful wife. Had he really doubted her? Or, as she had suggested, had he just not cared?

"I heard Rachel visited Anita in the hospital," one woman offered, looking at Owen.

A short woman gulped. "That's right. Rachel put her in the hospital."

Owen shook his head. "Anita's driver caused the accident. Rachel and I talked to Anita the other day." He hoped that morsel told everyone that he, Rachel and Anita Mahaffey were all friends. What should he say when Rachel returned, after learning all this information?

A women, wearing a lot of makeup, tilted her head, calling the booth workers close, indicating she had the latest. "I talked to Anita last night." Another woman with information. Owen suspected Anita was spreading information as fast as she could. The woman continued, "She's saying Kip has used Rachel as a smoke screen for his many affairs." She winked at Owen. "Many of us thought they were having an affair for years." She patted his cheek. "But she has you and you look like such a good guy." She turned back to the other listeners. "Anita says Rachel and she are on the same page." All the women looked at Owen, letting him understand that he was one of the insiders. He sort of nodded.

Activity ramped up in the booth as visitors stopped by to purchase cookies and get free handouts. As the bustle ebbed, the women were feeling more relaxed around Owen and began to tell him about their personal associations with Rachel. Someone recapped her work as the former chair of the Hospice board as she organized the million-dollar budget.

Another woman talked about working with Rachel at the Hunger Alliance and a third said, "And she's been on the Philanthropies board for years. She helps that Lynn Powers raise boodles."

"And we're all reading Rachel's blog about her experiences in nonprofit work. She uses so many local examples that we all enjoy it. Don't you?" They all looked at Owen. He nodded as he sipped his coffee waiting for the conversation to continue. Blog?

When he got home, Owen poured a drink and stared out into the back yard. He had learned a lot today about his wife. Several people stopped by to thank him for all her community work. They all assumed that he had been supporting her efforts in the background, like some perfect husband. He was shocked when he learned that she chaired the board of a nonprofit that had a multimillion-dollar budget. He was stunned to learn that she had spent time in Raleigh lobbying the legislature and participating in statewide studies on children's issues. He had never wanted to hear about her community work. Today the information dam had burst.

What a dilemma! He was impressed with her work. Although it didn't put food on the table, her work had made a difference to many in River Bend and possibly in the entire state. Did his job have that impact? But his work provided the resources for their comfortable life. He felt, what - both pride in his wife and frustration with their recent marriage upheaval? He tried to find the balance. He wondered if she would be back to herself when she returned next week.

The house felt empty.

* * *

Lynn and Piper scurried around Lynn's kitchen setting out drinks and snacks in the dining room and moving furniture in the living room to accommodate all the expected guests. Or should they be called investors, wondered Lynn? Her foray into big business had developed into a major success. A number of local businesswomen and reliable community volunteers had gotten wind of the project and wanted to be a part. Lynn had been clear that the business partners were looking for investors, not people with more ideas. As Trina said, "Let them start their own magazine. We know what we want to do."

This afternoon the magazine team would present their ideas to potential investors, twelve guests. The crashing and thumping at the kitchen door told Lynn that one of the magazine staff was dragging the presentation paraphernalia into the house. Ronnie, Michelle's sister and magazine IT director, as Penny called her, lugged in a large container of electronics.

"This will be a hi-tech presentation," Ronnie announced as she slammed the door. A trailing electric chord got caught in the jamb and yanked Ronnie and the container backward. Piper rushed to help. With some assistance, the magazine IT director got her equipment into the living room.

"Let's put my screen in front of the fireplace," she suggested to Lynn. "I want to put my projector here." Ronnie patted a tall plant stand in the foyer.

"Anything you need," said Lynn as she grabbed the fern off of the stand and stashed it on the desk in Dusty's office.

Then Ronnie spied Lynn's prized Taft Tea Table. "I can use this to hold the computer." Soon she was running wires and adjusting her screen.

Lynn was distracted by Penny coming in the front door with Amelia. They were each carrying trays of cookies. "We have Nathan's silver service in the car. He insisted," said Amelia.

Sophie Grayson was pounding on the kitchen door. Piper opened it and helped her carry in more food and several bottles of wine.

Lynn looked at the women gathered for the presentation. It was quite an eclectic group. Marge, Sophie Grayson's sister, had insisted on being included and had made the trip from the retirement community near Winston-Salem, a four-hour drive away; Emily Jacobs, Lynn's neighbor, sat closest to the wine; Bev, a county commissioner, Camille Stein, active community volunteer, Millie O'Hara, the widow of Jim's law partner, Marianna, Dr. Rita, and Piper's mother, Glenda. The IT partners Janet Bergman and Sara Margolin were some of the younger investors invited. They had a very successful consulting business and were certain as young mothers to be interested in the new venture. Michelle's sister Beth, in town from her new job in Raleigh, was assigned to pass cookies and pour wine.

Trina and Michelle delivered the presentation. The women asked savvy questions and offered names of others who might be interested in this project, either as content contributors or investors. It was a heady afternoon.

* * *

Caught

Will and Piper sat in Lynn's kitchen finishing the leftovers from the afternoon investment meeting. "How did it go?" asked Will. He popped another cookie into his mouth.

Piper swallowed a piece of asparagus wrapped in something delicious. "Very well. Penny had prepared some documents with investment information. Some of the ladies said they needed to talk to their finance people before saying anything."

"I remember when I was looking for initial money for my plant," reminisced Will. "I had the ideas but no money. Jim helped me a lot because he knew who had money. They didn't all understand what I had invented, but they trusted Jim." Years ago Will had invented a small gadget that soon became necessary to automakers as they worked to improve gas mileage. The small piece continued to be the backbone of his manufacturing facility, but he had expanded into specific pieces for trucks and some specialized vehicles, and even for some very specific auto manufacturers. "It was shaky in those early days," he admitted.

Piper gave him a kiss as she scored the last cookie on the plate. "That's because you're brilliant. I think this magazine will be a hit, too. And the girls don't need as much money as you did." She wandered the kitchen looking for something more to eat. She brought a half-eaten tray of fruit skewers to the table, along with a cream cheese fruit dip.

"Save some for me," called Dusty as he thundered down the stairs and into the kitchen. "I knew I shouldn't have left you two alone with the leftovers." He scanned the kitchen. Not a cookie in sight. He reluctantly took one of the wrapped asparagus. "Lynn says they got over half the money and think Millie and Emily will come in with the rest." He grabbed a fruit skewer.

"Marianna said she invested something, too," said Lynn as she came into the room. "Rita said that Hank is torn because he's already helping Beth purchase an airplane. Sophie told Rita not to worry because Herbie would give Michelle whatever money she needed." Hank had two daughters involved in the magazine, Michelle and Ronnie. "According to Rita he has promised to buy ads every month as his show of support."

"When do they start publishing?"

Lynn shrugged. "I'm not sure, but Trina did say that their financial concerns have been eased with the investors today. She also hinted that they had a reporter friend of Trina's already in town." She watched Dusty eat the last fruit skewer. "Hey, there's no more food!"

As if on cue, Bryce and his grandparents thundered into the kitchen with bags of Chinese carryout.

Glenda, Piper's mother, bubbled, "I knew you girls would have no time for dinner after that investors' meeting."

Will hugged his mother-in-law while relieving her of one of the carryout bags. "Isn't she brilliant?" Everyone agreed as they unpacked dinner.

CHAPTER FIFTEEN

The sheriff called Doug Fiore into his hospital room and explained the transition. "Fiore, you got a lot of experience. I want you to be acting sheriff while I'm here. These folks don't like us to have many visitors so I can't do my job from this damned bed." Doug nodded around his mask and other protective gear. The sheriff continued, "They're putting me in an ICU bed soon." He labored to breathe. "I told my boys you would be in charge. They'll work for you just like they worked for me." A dry hacking cough. "You take care of them while I'm gone. I'll see you get a raise when I get out of here."

"I'll do my best, sir." Doug was glad to be in all the required protective gear because he wasn't certain if the sheriff would read his reaction to the news. Minefield was his first thought. How could he work with those two assistants the sheriff had groomed? And what freedom would he have to direct operations if he was interim? He needed a discussion with the county manager and then a very private one with Dusty.

"I hope so," short, labored breath. "I expect to hear only good things about your work and have my reputation grow." The sheriff tried to wink, but he was drifting off.

"You have to leave, deputy," barked a nurse, "his bed is ready. We'll be putting him on a ventilator soon. The doc told us to get him ready."

Doug watched as the hospital bed was pushed into an ICU room. Through the glass he watched as things were attached to the patient. "Sir, you have to leave." A nurse pushed him toward the elevators.

Once outside Doug removed all the protective gear. He looked around and saw the sheriff's two administrative officers coming toward him across the parking lot. He nodded to the men. "I met with Sheriff Dunwoody. They were getting ready to put him on a ventilator. I also heard from the county manager. I have to go in and sign some papers."

The two men nodded. The taller one said, "We're here to work for you and represent the sheriff."

"Thank you," said Doug. He had worked with these men for several weeks. They were professional lightweights with little substantive law enforcement experience. "Gentlemen, since you were so close to the sheriff, I want you to take two weeks with pay and go into quarantine." Doug used his concerned face. "I don't want you both sick with this stuff. Take time off and get that vaccine if you haven't already."

"Sheriff Dunwoody said that there cure was a joke," sputtered the shorter man.

"And look who's hospitalized," Doug pointed out. "The man is very sick and you two spent a lot of time with him. Please at least take time to quarantine to stay healthy." They both looked suspicious. Doug had an idea. "Look, my aunt has a place in Hilton Head. You can take your wives and go there. Or girlfriends. It has a pool and it's on the ocean. A cleaning crew comes in once a week. You fellows just go relax and stay healthy."

Two deputies, delighted at their good fortune, grinned at him. "She won't mind?"

"She's elderly and is happy when my friends use the place." Doug made a mental note to warn Aunt Emily Jacobs what he was doing. "Go on home and get packed. Here's the address and number for the security folks. They'll let you in." He scribbled on his notepad, handed the notes to the taller deputy and slapped them both on the back. "You go and rest up."

* * *

Dusty got into his office with the news about Doug burning a hole in his psyche. The county manager had texted, *All papers signed!* He wanted to tell everyone, then sing and dance around the office. Even a few weeks without Dunwoody's meddling would be a relief. Instead he walked in and got down to business. "Tee is on medical leave." Both detectives had been out of the office for a few days - Mars, working from home in his new house, while Danny had been in Charlotte cleaning up some details on an old case. Both Mars and Danny gasped. "It's not this virus," Dusty went on to explain, "Dr. Rita says she's rundown. Lonzo is to keep her at Hank's cabin for three or four days." He looked at his calendar. "They got there on Thursday."

"Working from home is easier than coming into the office," observed Mars. "Why is she rundown?"

"That's because you don't also cook and clean and watch the kids while you work from home." Dusty had gotten an earful from Dr. Rita even as she said she shouldn't say these things because of confidentiality. "I'm working with the county manager on the sheriff's budget today and tomorrow. What else is pending?"

Danny scanned the calendar on his computer. "I'll tell the regional drug task force that the cabin is in use for a week. Not much else listed," he shrugged, "a couple of online trainings."

Mars was staring at his own computer when he shouted, "Listen to this!" He looked at Dusty and Danny. "It's a message from the county manager to all staff. Doug Fiore is the interim sheriff because Dunwoody is in ICU for an unknown length of time." He grinned into the office.

Danny crowed, "I feel like dancing!" He did a little rhythmic hustle around his desk.

"Calm down." Dusty knew how Danny felt. "It will only be for a short time. But I admit it will make our lives more pleasant."

Mars snorted. "Pleasant? It'll be like coming to a party every day Doug's in charge."

"Just don't let it show," cautioned Dusty. "If Dunwoody and his guys think we're happy, we could sink Doug's appointment."

The two men nodded as Mars suggested, "We should tell Tee. That'll help her get better quicker."

* * *

By prearrangement Mutt again worked late during the evening of the dental clinic. The waiting room was jammed with folks needing extractions and other dental attention. He noted Delsey's text: *In waiting room.*

He slipped out from the 'staff only' door along a wall of the lobby and nodded. She was standing close and slipped in. They walked quietly down the corridor to the janitor's closet. Mutt already had the ladder in place. "What do you think we'll find?" He had been curious all week.

"We'll see a lot of activity during working hours. I'll work through all the digital hours and I'll call you when I think we've got something out of the ordinary."

"Have you done this before?" He wondered just what gave her the experience to know what was not ordinary. He had tried interrogating Franky but he still had no idea of Delsey's skills, motive or interest.

She smiled at him. "Trust me."

He rolled his eyes. "Will I lose my job?"

"Let's get the camera chips and leave. We can talk at Franky's." She scrambled up the ladder, switched out the camera chip. It looked more like a big throat lozenge.

"That's a big chip," he said as she handed it down from the ceiling.

"That's a battery. Hand me the one in the bag. The chip's in my pocket." She dealt with the other cameras, replaced the ceiling tiles and scampered down the ladder. "We're all set. The equipment will collect information for another week. Let's get to Franky's."

"I'm closing tonight. I'll be there later."

When he arrived at Franky's, Delsey was sipping a soft drink. "Can you tell me what you do that you're an expert in spying on people?" He wasn't certain what he had gotten into and he was curious about her spy-like knowledge. "How come you know about these things?"

Delsey kept her eyes forward, deciding to tease him. "That's me, a spy. The CIA taught me everything."

"You're undercover here?" He squinted at her trying to find a dangerous femme fatale. "We had some terrorists here a few years ago. They tried to kidnap some lady who worked for the government." He pulled up a chair. "I was never sure what happened, but the police or FBI or someone raided a house round here and found stuff."

"Really? Terrorists?" She'd have to ask Trina about that. Her detective husband might have been involved. Delsey hadn't met Mars yet. In fact, she hadn't seen Trina face-to-face yet. The initial conversations with Franky and Mutt about suspected clinic shenanigans had piqued her interest in a story bigger and more dangerous than the photo series on local healthcare Trina had suggested. She hoped her suspicions panned out. It would be a great coup for Trina's new magazine.

Franky walked into the kitchen. "What you got?"

Caught

Delsey smiled. "We got five days of digital twaddle that I'll boil down to digital art."

Mutt huffed and the two women stared at him. He addressed his question to Franky. "How come you got her involved? She had all these cameras. How do we know she's not looking for a drug supply or something?" His body language was saying that this had gone far enough until he knew more!

"I googled her," said Franky. Mutt raised his head, alert.

"What'd you find?" he asked.

"She's famous. She's got awards for her work." They looked at Delsey as Franky took a beer from her refrigerator. "Now talk."

Delsey got her own beer. "Yeah, I've got awards. I'm good at my job. I don't have a current assignment so I'm here to help my friend start a new magazine. Trina -

"Healey?" barked Mutt.

"Didn't I tell you that?" asked Franky feigning surprise."

"No," came the thick sarcasm. "You just told me to take her to the clinic to spy. Now you tell me Mars Healey is involved!" He hadn't realized the detective was indirectly connected to Delsey's work. Mutt had some memories of his teen years and interactions with the detective and Mr. Dusty. He had to admit, the experience had been more positive then threatening. He smiled. He'd like to meet up with the detective now that he was a successful and proud RN.

Mutt turned to Delsey. "I knew you were a spy," he frowned refocusing on the discussion.

Delsey laughed at her friends. "I'm between assignments so Trina invited me to do some photography for her new magazine. She and some of her friends are starting a local magazine for parents. That's why I'm doing a healthcare spread." She rubbed her fingers on the condensation of the drink can. "I came into town early because I like to get a feel for a place. And I met you guys and," she grinned, "my reporter nose tells me we may have a more interesting story here than child healthcare."

"There's something bad at the clinic." Franky gripped her bottle, nodding knowingly.

"I have to review my film. Let's meet tomorrow night." She turned to Mutt, "You bring dinner, about six?" He nodded. She finished her drink. "Now, let me get to work." Pushing back from the table, she headed up stairs to her room.

Franky looked at Mutt. "What do you think?"

He shrugged. "If it's anything, at least Ms. Healey can show her husband and he can investigate."

Franky was thoughtful. "Salley over at the shelter always told me that a good director should always have a solution when she presents a problem to the board."

"What's that mean?"

"That means," explained Franky, "if this reporter has found something bad, like a clinic mismanagement, folks will expect me and the other board members to think our way out of the problem." Franky finished her beer. "I better get thinking."

CHAPTER SIXTEEN

Father Nick had sent word to Bundy to confirm the date they would return to John's house. Herbie had made sense of John's last wishes. Payment had been sent to the gas mart owner, some fellow in Chattanooga who owned a half dozen marts in the region.

When Nick had contacted him the man had said, "Hell, I knew he was good for the money. He managed the most profitable of my places. He made me carry baby supplies and school supplies and over the counter medications." The man snorted. "He refused to carry prepackaged muffins and had some lady baking them fresh every day or so. He cut back on the soft drinks, but increased baby formula." Now he was laughing. "He hired an older couple to serve food instead of the prepackaged sandwiches like my other sites. They sold tomato sandwiches in the summer and fried bologna in the winter. If that place was a town, he woudda been mayor."

Here they were today returning to John's place. Sean was driving his double cab truck, navigating the steep climbs with ease. Tilly sat in the front directing while Nick sat in the back seat, reviewing his notes. "What do you think these folks expect? Do you think they have assumptions about what they'll be getting or should be getting?" Nick had spent hours haggling with Herbie and Sean and Lynn about an endowed fund and conditions and recipients.

"They'll take it like good mountain folk," said Tilly. "Your friend, John, built a community in this cove. They'll appreciate whatever he left them."

When they arrived at the gas mart, Nick could see the crowd gathered at John's front porch up behind the store. He gulped. These were suddenly real people. Bundy came forward as Sean pulled the truck to a stop near the house.

"Mr. Nick," he nodded to the priest, "we're all here like you asked." He pointed to a table with two chairs placed under an old poplar and several other chairs arranged in a semi-circle in front. "We thought it would be more comfortable to gather here."

Nick shook hands with Bundy. "Thank you. I brought my friends. You met Tilly and this fellow is Sean. He's . . ah, ah . . . the attorney's representative, in case you have questions." Nick and Sean sat at the table at Tilly's insistence. He found a chair at the back of the crowd, waiting to be entertained.

Once the crowd settled Nick cleared his throat and began his presentation. "Let me begin by telling you that John was an old friend of mine. He came to me as this virus ate at him. He asked that I take care of his estate and Anna's and give some bequests to you folks who had made their life so filled with love." He heard some sniffs and marveled that his Sunday homilies were never this difficult. "I guess I should introduce us." He glanced at Tilly who nodded. They had talked about explaining John to these people. Nick wanted his old mentor celebrated. "Tilly is a Lutheran minister in River Bend." The pastor waved from under a tree at the back. "Sean works as a machinist and he's retired from the Coast Guard." Sean nodded from his chair beside Nick. "And I, like John, am a Roman Catholic priest." He heard a collective gasp and hoped no one was expecting lightning to strike. "John was my seminary instructor. In his last days he came to me to help him close out his life. I didn't need to help him return to God. He never left God. He lived his life here with all of you, serving Him every day through his care and love for Anna. And for all of you." Nick didn't know what he expected to see in the eyes of his listeners, but he saw acceptance around the tears. And then he knew, these people had loved John and Anna.

"We knew he was a man of God," said an elderly lady. "Don't never mind what church. He was a man of God." Everyone nodded.

"Then I'll get on with the reason why we're here today." Nick ran a quick hanky under his nose. "John wanted me to close out his estate and to pass on gifts for some of you." He pressed the papers on the table in front of him. "First, Bundy?" He looked around. The mechanic stood. "John says you are Anna's nephew and you get the house here that had belonged to her parents, keeping it in the family."

A women cried as she clutched two toddlers. "Bundy, no more trailer!" The crowd clapped.

Sean looked behind him at the house and ahead at the excited family and scribbled a note to Nick while the crowd was distracted congratulating Bundy and his wife. Nick scanned Sean's note. *This house isn't big enough for that family. He needs money for an addition.* Nick cleared his throat. "As I said, Bundy, the house is yours and John and Anna included money for additional space for your growing family." More clapping. Bundy's wife sobbed and laughed and hugged her husband.

Nick held up the papers and folks were quiet. "Mickey?" A sinewy man in farmer's garb, waved. Nick thought of him as one of the welcoming Magi. "John says you run a fair produce stand but you would run a great stand with more produce, so he's giving you some land." Nick marveled at how Sean and Herbie had found land close by Mickey's homestead. John had been sketchy in his instruction, only suggesting he wished he could help Mickey expand his farm. The priest handed Mickey a deed. The crowd was stunned. Their faces asked, 'What next?'

And Nick continued, "Lucas?" A man, the third welcoming Magi, with a buzz cut looked wary. Nick smiled. "John says you were a medic in the Army and you take care of your parents. He said you need a new car and tuition to attend UT - Chattanooga to become a nurse practitioner. Taking one class a semester won't do. So he wants you to have a car or truck and tuition and expenses until you finish." Nick looked over the edge of the paper. "He expects you to concentrate and finish in a few years because the cove needs a nurse." Folks whistled in agreement. Lucas hugged his father.

"Where's Amber?" Nick called out. The crowd whispered with curiosity and excitement.

A little girl about five with thick glasses came forward. She smiled at Nick and Sean. "That's me. I like ice cream." Amber had figured this out, thought Nick. Everyone seemed to be getting what they wanted. She'd put in her preference.

Sean cleared his throat and Nick looked down at a new note. *What's her problem?*

Nick asked, "Are your parents here, Amber?"

"I'm here," said a young woman at the back of the crowd. "She don't have no daddy."

"Can you tell me her problem?" Nick smiled at the little girl.

"She needs some operation. Anna tried to get her to Duke but I don't have no car or money enough." Sean coughed.

Nick rattled the papers. "You do now. John and Anna wanted to make sure Amber gets her care." The young mother sobbed. Bundy's wife ran to hug her.

Nick looked at the crowd. "That's all the special bequests. But John and Anna loved all of you. They have set up a fund to guarantee tuition and schooling needed for you and your children. The first two scholars are Jeanie and Drake." Two teens popped up from the crowd. Cheers ruffled the leaves of the poplar. "And the fund will also help with healthcare. As you see Amber will be the first patient to receive care. And finally, John and Anna set up a revolving loan fund to help you folks when needs come up. They knew you are people who don't take charity but work hard for what you need." He looked at the folks. "Any questions?" The crowd erupted with questions. Nick was glad that Herbie and Lynn had helped outline the parameters of the fund. He handed out a brochure that explained conditions and contact information. Sean walked through the audience shaking hands and exchanging greetings. Tilly did the same because he owed Nick for the entertainment.

* * *

Mutt stumbled into Franky's kitchen with bags of food from Uncle Chicken hanging on one arm and two six packs in the other. He was still in his work scrubs from a hard day.

"Get those germs out of my house," screeched Franky as she saw the stains on his clothing.

He dropped the food. "I'll be right back." He raced from the yard to his house for a quick shower and change. Franky was laying out the food when he returned.

"Where'd you change, in a phone booth like Superman?" She licked Uncle Chicken's special sauce off her fingers. "Delsey said to wait for her; she's taking a quick shower." Franky lowered her voice. "I think she worked all night. Couple a times I heard her cheer, like she saw something good."

Delsey came into the kitchen. Mutt stared at the almost stranger. She had removed her piercings and had not applied her Goth make-up or clothing. She looked cute and almost normal in a t-shirt and pair of sweats. Her hair was still that dyed Goth black, but for a white girl she wasn't bad looking. He ignored the tats on her arms.

"That smells great," Delsey said as she pulled out a chair and took a plate from Franky. She looked at each of her friends. "I think we got something. But I don't know these people so maybe they're being normal." Franky and Mutt both pushed their plates aside and stared. "Eat," ordered the reporter. "I need energy. I worked most of the night and all day today." She nodded at the papers and laptop she had placed on the counter. Franky attacked the chicken wrap while Mutt took a slice of one of Uncle Chicken's new specials, a Greek pizza advertised with lamb and feta cheese. Delsey talked around her food. "Remember, there's no sound so we don't know if someone is saying 'kill him,' or 'pass the mustard.' We'll have to be careful about our conclusions. But some stuff is obvious."

After dinner Delsey set her laptop on the counter and the three of them clustered on one side of the table. She lowered the lighting, keeping only the stove nightlight. "I need to see my notes and we need to see the screen." She began the video and her narrative. "We'll watch life in the exec's office first. It's mostly routine but I pulled out a few scenes." They watched as Margaret Eliason and Kip Mahaffey greeted one another, hotly.

"They're having sex!" gasped Franky.

"In her office?" Mutt was stunned.

"I cut out all the action, just wanted you to see the intro moves." Delsey shrugged. "Same old act." She smiled to herself as her friends intellectually grappled with the scene. "They do this several times over the week." They watched as she ran the aftermath showing Kip readjusting his clothing and Margaret Eliason in her private executive washroom combing her hair and reapplying make-up. Delsey continued the narrative. "I made a quick album of shots of others coming into her office. You have to tell me if any of the visitors shouldn't be there."

"What do you mean?"

"I don't know." She frowned, thinking. "Maybe someone who suggests the boss lady has a conflict of interest. Or someone with a criminal background."

"Criminal?"

"Just look at my photo album."

As the slideshow progressed, Mutt or Franky added identifiers. "Board member." "Medical director." "CFO." "Don't know." Delsey made notes on a prepared sheet, adding names to match slide numbers.

"Let me show you the scenes from the other cameras." She moved to the counter and tapped the keyboard. Soon the scene was the pharmacy. "This s a busy place. But after I saw the other tape, I watched for the director. Here she is, coming into the pharmacy. She doesn't come after hours because there's security on that door." They looked at Mutt.

He nodded. "Everyone is real careful about controlled substances. They require security and a lot of paperwork."

"Watch," directed Delsey. Three pair of eyes saw Margaret Eliason come into the pharmacy, chat with the personnel, sift through some papers, ask some questions which seemed to send everyone scurrying to find answers. While she waited she seemed to say something to the pharmacy director. He nodded. She took a box and read labels as he checked the inventory. During the process pharmacy workers walked through the scene, answered questions or gave reports. Margaret nodded and continued helping with the inventory and the pharmacist continued to check his list. At a distracting point, they watched as Margaret Eliason slipped two small vials into her pocket, then continued reading labels and placing boxes and bottles on a shelf. The pharmacist continued his list checking. Mutt and Franky didn't need a neon sign to note the pill palming.

"Now watch." Delsey turned to Mutt. "This segment looks like a tour or something."

"It's an inspection by one of the federal government funders. Mr. Mahaffey had to be there as board chair."

"Pay attention." They all watched as Kip stood behind Margaret Eliason and patted her behind. She took the two vials from her pocket and slipped them into his hand. He put his hand into his jacket pocket. The viewers could see smirks on both their faces as they pretended to be listening to something said by one of the examiners.

"He walked out with something," Franky said in a voice full of suspicion.

"Here's a close up of a label." Delsey flashed a still shot up on the screen.

"That's a controlled substance all right," stated Mutt, obviously disgusted with what he had seen.

"Now what?" asked Franky.

Delsey turned off the laptop and sat back at the table. "It's up to you folks. Police? DEA? Lawless posse?"

"Did you show this to Ms. Healey?" asked Mutt.

Delsey closed the computer and moved her chair so that she faced her new friends around the table. "I don't know what to do. This magazine she plans doesn't include drug-busting. Her vision was a benign, upbeat forum for parents on kid issues and other things related to current life. You know, online learning, finding daycare." She stared over their heads seeming to look into Franky's microwave for an answer. Finally, she said, "Trina is a great reporter and I think if she sees what we have she won't flip her magazine idea to a crimefighting rag." She looked at her friends with a smile. "But I think she'll jump on breaking this story because she brought me in and suggested my topic." She sort of preened in her chair. "She wanted something to set off her first issue or she wouldn't have asked me."

Franky nodded. "Yeah, we know you do award winning shit."

Mutt shook his head. "She didn't expect to find this action at the clinic. So what was she thinking you would do?"

"She may have wanted photographs showing a need for better healthcare for children."

"She wanted you to find something big! And this is it!" Franky finally chuckled, proud of the work Delsey and Mutt had delivered. "Her husband has to know, too. I don't want us to put her in danger if these folks have mean friends."

Mutt gasped, "Danger?"

Franky smacked his arm. "What do you think? These folks are breaking the law. They ain't some book club."

Delsey nodded. "My experience suggests that this operation is part of some bigger operation. Your clinic folks might not know how big. This Kip fellow and Margaret Eliason are just some cog in a bigger organization. I bet they don't know anything about the overall organization but deliver some drugs and collect money." She got very serious as she said, "I bet they just like the money and don't care that they're at the bottom of some illegal drugs food chain."

"The clinic?"

"The clinic isn't involved," said Delsey. "There are too many reports for all the federal and state funds that must be filed and reviewed. I think Margaret Eliason has set up an internal system to cover her small part in this drug operation, and probably doing things to cover her personal expenses on a clinic credit card, but nothing more."

Both Franky and Mutt looked relieved at that statement. Mutt sat up straighter in his chair. "What now? Do we tell Trina and Mars?"

"Mars?" Delsey was puzzled.

"Her husband, the cop."

Delsey smiled at them. "If you're both ready to become a posse, I think it's time we report to my boss."

CHAPTER SEVENTEEN

Lonzo sat at the table in the cabin, checking over some jottings. "I think I have all my notes." His rumbling chuckle filled the room. "This was fun. You detectives just sit around waiting for crime."

His wife scowled at him. "It took you five days of watching to get enough information to be of interest. You didn't sit around."

He nodded as he stood and gave her a hug. "I did get a fair idea of your work. It was boring and interesting." He nibble her ear. "This was a great plan. We haven't had this much alone time since we adopted our babies."

She smiled into his chest. "It is what I needed. A little Lonzo magic." She moved away to finish cleaning the cabin and packing the car. "But I do miss those kids. Let's take them to the park for some play time when we get home. I want to see them run and hear them make noise."

"When are you talking to Dusty?" They both knew that they had done some great detective work during their cabin stay.

Tee wiped the last crumbs from the kitchen counter. "I'll meet with him first thing tomorrow. He may call you in, especially to explain the syringe you saw and other medical observations."

They finished packing their car and locked the cabin. Driving back through the forest, they talked about their private time together and the impact a major drug investigation would have on their family. "I'd be happy if you didn't get involved in any shootings," stated Lonzo.

"Any big bust is months off," Tee told her husband. "We've got a lot of facts to verify first and more issues to investigate. Maybe I'll need more rest by then."

He chuckled as he guided the car around the curve and River Bend came into view.

* * *

Lynn didn't understand why she had been asked to join this Chamber of Commerce ad hoc committee. It had been formed at the beginning of lockdown as businesses tried to understand health restrictions and staying in business. But over time, working together the local business community began to make sense of health regulations. Nonprofits were facing the same challenges as for-profit businesses. Lynn thought they had helped one another and understood one another better.

Walter Varney walked into the Chamber of Commerce conference room. "Hello, folks! Life is certainly looking up." Everyone cheered in agreement. He shook hands all around, even Lynn's. He had gotten used to seeing her at this committee meeting. The wife of a local detective, the thought made Varney shiver.

"Walter," she smiled, "You look like you've been golfing."

He twitched his red nose. "I forgot to use sunscreen. But I came in only five over par." The other five golfers present had comments to add and then the chair gaveled them to order.

"We're here to wrap up the report for the dinner at the end of the month." He held up a sheaf a papers. Thank you, Lev for putting this together. It's a good assessment of local business status. And Lynn, thanks for your piece on nonprofits."

Several members nodded. One man said, "I was sorry to see the Arts Council fold. But I understand why their board made the decision."

Another man commented, "But I was impressed with the actions others took and the visionary thinking that went into some of their response to the pandemic."

Lynn said, "I was proud of them, too."

The chair asked, "Any other information anyone wants to add?"

Someone chuckled. "Walter, I saw that your little barge stayed busy through everything."

He nodded. "My trucks weren't always in demand, but that barge is in demand. Ferrying goods across the river saves some folks time and transportation costs in a tight budget."

"What kind of jobs?" asked a man at the end of the table.

Varney chuckled again. "Shit, you . . . sorry, Lynn . . . . stuff you wouldn't believe. Beekeepers like the barge to take hives to orchards. The barge can carry more hives than a pickup. We drop them near

Portage or Hanging Oak and the keepers have the farmers pick up hives and they all help set them out." He could see several questions on the faces of the seven committee members. "Don't ask me any more. That's all I know about bees. And I deliver free-range eggs and chickens from the Beaumont farm. They do this organic sh . . . . . . stuff. There's a small organic group downstream before the river goes off the escarpment. They collect eggs and chicken from the Beaumonts, honey from the bees and do some business with the botanical gardens."

"The gardens?" Lynn was surprised. "That's one of our successful nonprofits."

"They help the organic growers by starting plants or something. It brings in income." Varney raised an eyebrow. "So you nonprofits are muscling in," he teased her.

"I'm impressed with the niche you fill."

Walter almost blushed. He only kept the barge working because it helped him move contraband without using his trucks all the time. "It's seasonal, but I keep two old guys employed and we keep the river's history alive." What a pile of shit, he thought. But Lynn looked pleased.

* * *

"I don't know what Delsey wants," Trina explained as she finished diapering the baby. "She just asked if she and some friends could meet with us."

"Remind me again who this woman is." Mars pulled Brian off his ankles. The youngster seemed to be using them as tree stumps. "Have I met her?" He reached down and lifted one of the cats out of the wet baby towel. He wondered how he had ever lived as a bachelor. They had been living in the large, renovated Victorian for a few months. The house had never been a home when he lived there with his parents, but life was different now. Three kids, six cats and, as of last week, a rescue puppy - Mars loved every minute of his life.

Trina handed the baby to him as she cleaned up the changing table and wiped her hands with sanitizer. "Delsey Ledges is an award-winning photojournalist. I met her years ago. We started out in the gossip rag business but she scored a few great pieces that moved from gossip to investigative journalism. She's a little unconventional, but very skilled in her craft."

"Unconventional?" He patted the baby's back and chuckled at the tiny burp.

"You'll see."

"Who's coming with her? Did she bring a team to River Bend?"

There was a knock at the door. Trina pulled Brian out from under the changing table. "I guess we'll soon have the answer to your questions." They could hear Holly and the puppy racing to the door as Brian scrambled to his feet to join the greeting party.

Mars handed off the baby and was right behind the children as the door opened. "Mutt?" Mars allowed everyone to enter as he slapped the young man on the back and shook his hand.

"Heard you graduated and got a great job! Congratulations!" He turned to the next caller. "Franky?" He gave her a hug. "How's everything? Come on in."

The final visitor stood at the door. Brian and Holly were mesmerized. They had never met a Goth. Mars took one look and asked, "Delsey?" And the word 'unconventional' echoed in his mind. "Come on in. I see you know our friends Mutt and Franky." Behind his back, Franky and Mutt grinned at her. They had assured the Goth journalist that Mars was a great guy.

Trina came up to the group. "Delsey?" She handed the baby to Mutt and gave her friend a hug. She turned to Mars. "She's been in town a while but this is the first face-to-face we've had." Then she spied Franky and held out her hand. "I'm Trina."

"Sorry," apologized Mars. "I thought you knew her. This is Franky Kaiser." He turned to the other guest. "And Mutt." The young man grinned over the baby's head.

"I rent a room to Delsey," explained the large black woman. That statement explained nothing. "She and Mutt have been looking into healthcare." Mars raised an eyebrow as his detective sense whispered to him.

Trina's reporter sense nudged her as she exchanged a glance with her husband. She turned back to Delsey. "Are you settled in? Have you been doing background?"

Delsey shrugged. "Yeah." From experience working with her, Trina knew when Delsey presented that nonchalant attitude something was happening.

"You have a report?" Taking the baby from Mutt, Trina looked at the reporter who nodded. "Everyone?" Another Goth nod. Trina smiled. "Let's get started." Her reporter sense was now galloping. Handing the baby back to Mars, she led her guests into the dining room with its big table and antique sideboard. She had prepared some snacks and drinks. Well, she had sent Mars to the bakery for the snacks and had carried drinks from the refrigerator. "Everyone get comfortable." Brian and Holly climbed onto their booster chairs, ready to be fed and entertained.

Franky, a friend of Mars since he had been a tween, served the children each a sippy cup of juice and a big cookie. "I know Mars got these snacks. He could never resist Umberto's cookies."

To defend himself Mars said, "I got a few pepperoni rolls just in case."

Holly added, "Roll," as she stretched a small arm in the direction of the food. Franky cut a roll in half and added one half to her plate and to Brian's along with a big cookie.

Mutt took a seat beside Brian and helped him get control of the sippy cup. Mars sat at the table with the baby on his shoulder while Trina took drink orders from her guests. Franky gave the three children each a kiss on the forehead and sat down. Delsey watched the activity in the family tableau, lost in thought.

Once everyone was settled, Trina said, "Go ahead. The kids want to hear everything before bedtime." Holly nodded.

Delsey took a sip of her soft drink. "I got into town about a week ago and found Franky's rental ad. I had your concept for healthcare and talked with Franky about services in town. She mentioned the South End clinic because she's on the board. She sent me to do some background and asked Mutt to show me around." She glanced at Franky and waited.

They all looked at Franky who seemed reluctant to speak. With a big sigh she began, "I had told Mutt I was worried about the clinic budget. Kip Mahaffey asked me to be on the finance committee and I felt over my head looking at all the money and how things flow, you know, where the income comes from and where it goes." She nodded.

"And regulations and insurance and co-pays and things. I worried that I wasn't qualified." Mars snorted. She rolled her eyes. "I know. I have a money knack but these accounts are like following a line of string in a ball of yarn." Another sigh and a taste of her pepperoni roll. "I've been studying the reports and started to feel something wasn't right. I told Mutt." She looked at him.

He took the cue. "I told Franky I would start keeping my eyes and ears open. It's only been a few weeks so I haven't seen much. And I have my patients to see." He was proud to say that and grinned. "I hadn't seen anything until Delsey came along."

Delsey moved into the spotlight. "When I asked Franky about renting from her, we talked about my background and the topic Trina had suggested, healthcare for children. I guess she thought it set itself up for some great, warm and cuddly photography and maybe exposure to the critical needs of some children in the community." She glanced at Trina.

"Hey," challenged Trina, "I want to make a splash with the magazine."

"You will," muttered Franky. Mars looked at her, alerted. "I told Delsey about my money concerns with the clinic. I had already told Mutt. So they got together one evening."

"Dental clinic night," interrupted Mutt. "The clinic is open two nights for a dental clinic. I stayed late." He looked at Delsey and she nodded encouragement. "So Delsey came. I showed her around and we talked about seeing how things run during business hours."

"I thought we could set up some cameras and see what a week's activity looked like." The three visitors now looked guilty as they sat silently at Mars' dining table.

"And you found more than you expected." Mars was a detective twenty-four/seven. They nodded. He looked at Trina. "Bedtime?" She nodded. She and Franky each took a child as Mars followed with the baby.

Soon they returned. "We rushed them. They were sleepy anyway," announced Trina. "Now tell me before I burst with curiosity."

Delsey opened her laptop and set it on the sideboard next to the big cookies. "First is an edited look at life in the director's office. I have all the hours saved but you don't need to see everything." She hit the buttons and brought the eight-minute video to life. As Kip Mahaffey and the director embrace, Delsey announced, "I cut the sex. It's on the master." She then showed the album of other visitors to the office. I don't know these folks and I don't know who should and shouldn't be there. Franky and Mutt knew some of the folks."

"Any sound?" asked Mars.

"No, just video."

He asked her to run the album again. "I can think of reasons for most of those folks to meet with the director." Between Mars, Franky and Mutt, they were able to put names to most of the visitors.

"Let me show you the other video then we can talk. I had two cameras set to view the pharmacy." She hit the buttons and the scenes played out including the director slipping purloined vials of drugs to Kip. "Any questions?"

Trina laughed in delight. "My magazine will be a success!"

"Not so fast," cautioned Mars. "This is explosive. Dusty has to see this."

Trina weighed in and the negotiation began.

* * *

Dusty seemed to be brushing his teeth with unusual vigor this evening. Lynn stood behind him and watched him in the mirror. Swish. Spit. "What?" he asked as he sprayed toothpaste bubbles across the sink with his question.

"I was just wondering if your enthusiasm tonight is for me?"

He grabbed her and gave her a toothpasty kiss. "It's always for you." He released her and grabbed a towel. "But tomorrow Tee returns and Dunwoody is in the hospital and Doug is the interim sheriff." He tossed the towel somewhere near the hamper.

She laughed at him. "I hope Tee got enough rest because you sound like you have piles of work for her to do." Lynn followed him into the bedroom. "I hope you let her know how much she was missed." They each grabbed an edge and pulled the bedspread to the foot of the bed.

"She was missed. I've had Sherry Steiner working to keep the paperwork flowing. I've had to listen to Danny and Mars complain about the pressure."

"What pressure?"

He shrugged. "I'm not certain. Either the pressure of me finally noticing that she does all the work and they do nothing, or the pressure of her returning to scrutinize all the work we did in her absence that was done wrong."

Lynn flopped back on her pillow laughing. "It's obvious she needs a raise."

Now Dusty scowled. "I've recommended that for three years. Dunwoody has always found reasons to only give my staff raises at the annual county personnel rate, not higher increases for exceptional work." He took Lynn in his arms. "Sometimes I worry Danny and Tee will have to leave the department for better paying jobs." He kissed her. "But now's not the time to discuss employee retention. I think we should discuss wife retention."

She bit his earlobe. "I'm not going anywhere. If there's any retention discussion, you're the one to worry. This is still my house!"

He pulled her tighter. "I guess I'll have to demonstrate why you should keep me around."

And he did.

CHAPTER EIGHTTEEN

"Really? Doug?" Tee spun around in her desk chair.

Dusty walked in and interrupted the conversation. "Yes, really Doug!" He checked that the door was closed and then he grinned. "Just try to act like we're not impressed." But he was always business first. "What have we got?"

Mars and Tee both jumped up like eager fifth graders trying to get the teacher's attention. "Chief!"

He raised an eyebrow at their response to his question. He looked at Danny, who shrugged. Dusty walked to his desk and sat down, throwing out his hand as though giving them both the floor. They looked at one another. "Ladies first." Mars bowed to his partner.

Tee picked up a folder from her desk and placed it on Dusty's. "Lonzo and I did a little stakeout at the cabin." She squinted at her boss. "Did Dr. Rita tell me that you expected me to work while I was there?"

"I wasn't sure you would have energy for anything else." The other guys snorted. Had her skin been lighter they would have seen her blush.

She cleared her throat. "While I rested, Lonzo played with the equipment the regional guys left there." She opened the file and spread photos across the desk. "He collected a gallery of photos and said he watched this Eliason woman mix drugs and give out shots to some folks while Kip Mahaffey collected the money."

"Shots?"

"Lonzo got a close-up of the vials and says they are some powerful drugs. He figured these guys were on some sort of maintenance to keep up an edge." She shrugged. "I'm not certain, but he listed the drugs with a little description of what they might do. Anyway after watching all the activity -

"Any sex?"

"Oh, yeah, Lonzo watched but didn't photograph." The guys laughed. "Anyway, I have a theory." She waited for their full attention. "We've been doing these stakeouts for over a year and all we ever see is the sex. I think someone in the task force warns the clients and Mahaffey and Eliason."

They all looked at one another. Mars was ready to burst. Dusty gave him the floor. "Chief, you would think we planned this. Or maybe we're just this good."

He pulled two thumb drives from his shirt pocket. "Trina has a friend who set up a camera at Eliason's clinic." He put one drive in Dusty's computer. "And we got this." The opening scene was Eliason greeting Mahaffey in her office. "We have hours of office activity including the sex, but the drive has only eight minutes and an album of faces. The other drive records activity in the clinic pharmacy."

"Stop," ordered Dusty. "Get that out of my computer. Let me think a minute." He walked over to make certain no one was in the hall and that the door was closed. "We should keep this discussion restricted for now." He poured himself some coffee and sat at his desk. The three detectives were puzzled but followed his lead and found quiet work at their desks until he was ready to talk.

With all this startling information, Dusty became dedicated to maintaining secrecy and giving thought to his next steps. Tee's implication that someone was warned about their stakeouts was troubling, but to have evidence surface that implicated the same suspects under different conditions was breathtaking. All sorts of warnings were flashing in Dusty's head. He finally placed one phone call, then said to his unit, "Meet me at my mother's in an hour. Danny, bring some food." He gathered all the information, videos and photos that his staff had presented, stuffed it into a briefcase and left. It was the signal that there would be no more conversation on this topic in the office. Everyone scattered.

Later, sitting at his mother's kitchen table with crumbs from the food Danny had supplied scattered over the surface, Dusty asked, "What are our options?"

"Don't trust anyone and go it alone," stated Mars. The others nodded in agreement.

"What is your wife going to expect? This is her property," Danny asked Mars.

"I think she'll want the exclusive if we take any action."

Dusty nodded. "I'll do what I can."

"What about up the food chain?" asked Danny. "Would this interest the FBI? DEA? SBI?"

"Who knows? We haven't heard from the FBI since the bank robbery." Three detectives snorted. "I don't want us to even think about that operation." Two old, early release felons designed a bank robbery to get themselves returned to prison, claiming a need for healthcare and support with aging challenges. With the unit's help, they ended up back in a federal prison. "And the other two agencies are on the regional drug task force."

"You think one of them is the leak?"

Dusty shrugged. "I'm only certain it's not one of us."

* * *

Dusty walked into the kitchen after the long afternoon at the farm and stopped. There, sitting on a bar stool sipping wine at the kitchen counter while Lynn cooked, was FBI Special Agent Claire Conti, currently Agent-in-Charge at the Charlotte office. "Hey, handsome," she greeted the detective.

"What are you doing here?"

"Just catching up on life in this crazy little town. Any more bank robberies?"

He rolled his eyes as a greeting and walked into the small pantry to put away his side arm and place his phone on the charger. Returning to the kitchen, he stared at his guest, waiting.

Claire gave him a teasing grin. "I was in the neighborhood and stopped in to see what was for dinner and catch up on local gossip."

Lynn waved a spoon, while she stood at the stove. "She has news about those bank robbers." Dusty looked at the agent.

"That guy, Sparky, who had cancer, died a few months ago. But he was kept comfortable. His friend, the guy that looks like Yoda, is in a minimum-security prison, aging. He has some health issues and may last the year. He's getting care and using his carpentry skills to build things." Claire paused and gave them a soft smile. "The staff enjoys him and his stories. They also appreciate his skill. They pretty much let him build what he wants. The warden finds the money somewhere."

Dusty nodded. "Two old career criminals." He snorted. "They have nothing in common with the current crop of criminals. Just two guys who were trying to survive. I'm glad they ended up where they wanted and got the care they needed."

The whole episode of a statewide early release program had delivered three convicts to River Bend. Dusty had been appointed to the local committee to deal with the mandate. The two fellows Claire mentioned had orchestrated a bank robbery to get returned to prison, hopefully a federal prison where they could receive healthcare and spend their old age. They had succeeded with the help of Dusty, Claire and local attorney H. Lawrence Grayson.

"That whole story has gone down as folklore in my department." Claire laughed. "Kidnapping, robbery and those other two eloping or something. Whatever happened to them?"

"I can tell you," offered Lynn pouring more wine for Claire and a glass for herself. Dusty grabbed a beer and sat at the counter to listen. "Letitia still has family here. So I've heard that she is happily living in sin, as her mother tells everyone. Her boyfriend was that big guy and he took her to Kentucky where his family and friends accepted her." Lynn sipped her wine. "I think she's very happy and in love." Dusty snorted again, remembering the very large woman and her very, very large felon boyfriend. Lynn gave him a squinty-eyed look. "She sent me a card several months after she left town. She thanked me for understanding and helping her find a good man."

"What did you have to do with it?" Dusty was mystified.

Lynn shrugged. "I just encouraged her to follow her heart." He choked on his beer.

Claire laughed. "I love this town!" She looked around the kitchen. "I'm staying for dinner. Is it just us?" With that comment they knew they would soon know the real reason for Claire's visit.

Lynn noted the agent's serious attitude. "I can serve dinner and leave you two alone."

"Thank you," said Claire. "And I'm not here." Lynn and Dusty nodded.

Caught

After dinner Lynn shooed them into Dusty's office while she cleaned up and prepared to go for a walk.

Once in Dusty's office with the door shut and the drapes closed, Dusty said, "I didn't see a car."

"I'm not here," repeated Claire. "A truck is coming by in the morning to clean your dryer duct and to pick me up." She chuckled, "So you folks have to give me a bed tonight."

"No problem. Did you tell Lynn?"

"Yes. She figured things out. I think that's why she's so agreeable. She knows I'm here on serious business." The agent got comfortable on the small sofa and Dusty sat behind his desk. "We've been working on a drug operation. I think it has connections with the operation your regional task force is investigating. We've been monitoring and exchanging information with other task forces around the state." She looked at him as her introductory statement settled in.

Dusty sat back in his chair and stared at the ceiling. After several minutes he began, "You must be a witch. The task force popped up for discussion with two of my staff today. Let me brief you." He stood and started to pace the office while he spoke. "We use a cabin for our stakeouts. Tee and her husband just spent a few days there under doctor's orders." Claire looked concerned. Dusty raised a hand. "She's fine, just needed a few days of R and R away from the kids and work. Anyway, she and Lonzo managed to take some photos of interesting activity. All our stakeouts have netted zilch. She returned to work with photos and a theory that someone on the task force is dirty." He looked at Claire as she nodded confirming Tee's conclusions.

Dusty continued, "At the same time, Mars' wife Trina and some friends have started a regional parents' magazine or something. Trina used to be a reporter in LA and she teaches journalism at the community college. To make a splash with her first issue, she invited a photojournalist to take some photos relating to child healthcare." Claire squinted, puzzled at what seemed to be a diversion. Dusty nodded. "Stay with me. This is a strange series of events. Anyway, Trina invited her friend Delsey -"

"Not Delsey Ledges?" Claire was really interested in his explanation now.

"Yeah, she's the one." Dusty shrugged. "I never heard of her, but I guess you have." Claire nodded. He continued, "Anyway she comes to town, finds a room to rent with a lady, Franky, who sits on the board of the South End Health Clinic. Franky had just complained to Mutt about her suspicions of the finances of the clinic."

"Mutt?"

Dusty nodded. "Nice young fellow, friend of Jason's who just graduated as a nurse and works at the clinic."

"I'm starting to get a picture." Claire sat back on the small sofa, her mind beginning to construct scenarios.

"Yes," agreed Dusty. "Franky brought Mutt and Delsey together and they set up some cameras in the clinic, the pharmacy and the director's office." He sat back at his desk.

"Come on, handsome, don't tease!"

He chuckled. "Like I said, you're a witch. Today Mars brings me Delsey's videos and Tee returns from her R and R and brings me photos and we all spent the afternoon hiding, trying to figure out what we had, who we could trust and what to do next."

"Where did you go?" Claire had been to River Bend often enough to know that local law enforcement operated differently than the Bureau.

"My mother's house." He almost blushed. "She got vaccinated and jumped right back into her old life of church meetings and ladies clubs. The house was empty."

"What did you decide?" The agent could only enjoy stories about hometown law enforcement for a second. She had business with this man.

"I don't think we decided anything. We talked about doing our own operation. Gave some thought to you, but we figured you would find us too small to bother with."

"I came here tonight because we agree with your findings. Someone in your regional group is dirty. Information has been leaving our office and finding its way to the bad guys. I hadn't heard anything about the health clinic." She gave him a questioning look.

"It's an interesting layer to this case." He stood and began pacing again. "On all our stakeouts, we've always caught a local attorney and the clinic director at the suspect cabin. It led us all to believe that it was just some love nest. But," he wiggled his eyebrows, "when we saw Delsey's videos, it confirmed the drug connection."

"And the love-nest?"

"We got all that lovin' on tape, too. In her office, in the cabin." Dusty finished pacing and leaned against the book shelves.

Claire went to his desk and took a seat. She opened a notepad and began jotting. Finishing, she reviewed her notes. "If I understand you, we suspect several things. A dirty cop, a love-nest/drug connection, and possibly a connection with a health clinic. Does this clinic receive federal funds?"

"Yes, Franky was real clear and there were some federal inspectors on the videos."

"That means I can finagle DOJ authority and request a warrant with your videos."

"Does that solve a regional distribution set up?" he asked. "Will it shut them down?"

She shook her head. "No. I think you may have enough evidence to close this cog. I don't think it will help us find the informant or the head of the regional operation."

"So how do we play this?"

Claire blew out her breath as she thought. "This becomes my operation. I take down the director of the clinic and her boyfriend. You stay in the sandbox with the regional task force and just stand on the sidelines and complain that the FBI always oversteps. And I'm going to have to work out an undercover op for everything else."

"Can we help?"

"Yes, act like you're angry that we overstepped. Our story is going to focus on the clinic and its federal funding. And that tangles up with DOJ, NIH, Medicare, Medicaid and all the rest of the alphabet."

"Even though it's my evidence?" He didn't have to act angry. He was!

"Yes." Claire was emphatic. "When I get the undercover op going we'll talk again if I see a role for you."

"Do you have a timeframe?"

"As soon as I see your evidence, we can be ready with a warrant. I don't want this to hang around. As for the undercover op? That'll take time to set up."

"I brought all the evidence home with me. We can review it tonight."

She texted on her phone, read the reply, typed more information. Finally she said, "The duct cleaners will be here early and download all your data and take me back to Charlotte." She smiled, "Tell Lynn it'll be me and two others for breakfast."

"Will we get the dryer duct cleaned?"

She smirked.

CHAPTER NINETEEN

Lynn had gotten the word to expect guests for breakfast. So when two uniformed duct cleaners walked into her kitchen, she was prepared. "Special Agent Anselm?" She hugged the young woman and said, "I hoped you were coming. I had Danny deliver those pastries you like." She moved on to her next guest. "Special Agent Wilson?" She hugged the young man and he blushed. "I didn't forget you. I hope you still like eggs over easy with sausage."

"Oh, for the love of," Dusty moaned. Claire walked into the kitchen also dressed as a duct worker and laughed.

"It's good to see you again, Lynn," said Special Agent Anselm. "I thought we agreed I was Leah."

Special Agent Wilson poured himself some coffee and said, "And I'm Gil, remember?"

"Of course." Lynn placed pastries on the table and popped two eggs in a skillet. "Sit down. Breakfast will be ready in a minute. Claire, what are you having?"

"You didn't get my favorite pastries?" she teased.

The toaster popped and Lynn slid eggs on a plate, two slices of toast and three sausage links. Putting the plate in front of Gil, she said to Claire, "I got the bear claws. Right?"

Special Agent Claire Conti almost swooned. "Could use a few eggs, too. It's going to be a long day."

Lynn handed Dusty his eggs and said, "Coming right up." She gave Claire an innocent look. "Don't worry, you can talk while I cook. I won't hear a thing."

As Lynn placed eggs in front of Claire, Piper walked into the kitchen. "I want my dryer duct cleaned, too." She looked around at the familiar FBI faces. "Claire!"

"Shit," said Claire. "I should have remembered the neighborhood menace."

"I guess my ducts won't be cleaned," assumed Piper as she sat at the table. "Bear claws!" Lynn handed her a small plate and a cup of coffee. "Thanks."

"You remember Gil and Leah?" Lynn pointed to the other agents.

"How's your wife? And the baby?" asked Piper as she eyed her bear claw.

Gil pulled out his phone and scanned to some photos, sharing them with Lynn and Piper. "He's almost two."

"Has it been that long?" puzzled Lynn, in a time-flies voice.

"We've got work to do," Claire reminded her staff. They concentrated on finishing breakfast.

Piper, burning with curiosity, asked, "Can -

And Claire said, "No! And if you tell anyone you saw us, remember I wear a gun!"

The agents finished breakfast and followed Dusty into his office.

Again Piper tried, "Why-

"I can't say," said Lynn. "It's something very secret. Dusty won't tell me because he thinks I'll tell you."

"Of course you would." Piper was confident. "So what do you know?"

Lynn gave her a very serious look. "This is real, Piper. When we can know, Dusty will tell us."

And Piper knew by the sound of Lynn's voice that that was that. She ate a second bear claw, wondering about the FBI and real crime in River Bend.

* * *

While Rachel was out of town, she managed to chair two online meetings with her school-based clinic committee. Lynn had been the organizing facilitator behind the meetings, using the Philanthropies Zoom account. At the first meeting, Rachel got acquainted with everyone and got a feel for the committee's potential. Jim Hoefler had agreed to co-chair. Margaret Eliason, director of South End Clinic joined and seemed to be excited about the potential partnership with the schools. Rachel had to admit she was happy that Kip was not involved. However, the other committee members were very enthusiastic - Sherry Vonder along with Zachary and Amelia Rawlings with medical support from Dr. Noah Pflug and, of course, Piper. She was delighted.

At the first meeting Lynn had outlined the Philanthropies role and the proposed planning grant. Margaret had explained the clinic role as opposed to the responsibilities in state law assigned to the public health nurses. It became easy for the committee to see that the idea of a school-based clinic would be possible, and because of private insurance and Medicaid, possibly self-supporting.

The second meeting was as exciting and fruitful as the first. Each member had delivered on his or her assignment. Rachel's had been the most challenging task. But she had managed to get Lowell Lentz, US House of Representative for River Bend's congressional district to agree to a luncheon meeting. When she returned from this consulting job, he promised he would meet her and her friends at the country club to discuss this idea.

"What can he do for us?" Piper had asked. She suspected politicians of not being interested in children who were, by definition, too young to vote.

On the Zoom meeting screen, Margaret had raised her hand icon and Rachel acknowledged her. Margaret had stated, "You all know the clinic receives federal funds. It will be helpful to have our congressman on our side when we ask to add new services to our contract. It will also be helpful to have his staff review available federal grants that might help provide funds to furnish the school clinic with necessary equipment." All the Zoom screen participants had nodded.

"Will you join us for this luncheon?" Rachel had asked Margaret.

"I think you and the others have a closer relationship with the man," demurred the clinic director. She had known that she and Kip would be getting ready for that coming weekend to service customers. She was already planning to appropriate some of the drugs from her pharmacy. Who the hell had time to toady to some local pol?

After a lot of discussion about the best members to attend the lunch, it was decided that Rachel, Piper, and Lynn would meet the congressman. Amelia suggested that they also invite her husband Zachary because he had a long-time friendship with the congressman.

Rachel had again been reminded about the importance of having all the right people at the table to move a project forward.

* * *

It had taken a few days working with everyone's calendar to schedule a meeting at the Philanthropies office to bring Lynn and Herbie up to date on the reading of John Gillespie's will. Tilly had arrived early and was entertaining Lynn with his personal version, "Every time Sean cleared his throat or coughed it cost him another few thousand." Tilly laughed. "He couldn't resist that little Amber with her bottle thick glasses all smudged and held together on one side with a paperclip."

Lynn laughed with him. She knew that children were Sean's weakness, recalling all the gifts and supplies he had given to the children at Piper's school. "So that's what Father Nick's note meant about a car for Amber?"

"Yeah." Tilly sat back in his chair. "Her mother needed a car to take the little girl to Duke for treatment."

"I thought Amber just needed glasses?"

Tilly shrugged. "I don't think John understood her vision problem. Anna had been corresponding with someone at Duke just before she got the virus." He chuckled. "Sean convinced that young mother, a woman named Chelsea, that she needed an SUV to travel all the way to Duke and keep Amber safe. She thought she only needed a small compact car. He told her to trust him; he'd pick out the kind of car John and Anna would think was safe enough."

They were sitting in the conference room and heard the others enter the office. "We're in here," called Lynn. She stuck her head out the door. "Grab a seat. Wine, coffee, soft drinks?"

Father Nick entered with two other men who were carrying on a dispute. Herbie was arguing with Sean, "Two SUVs?" He turned to Lynn, "Scotch, if you got it. This man is crazy. We set up a trust and he keeps spending beyond the agreed amounts."

Sean said, "Beer." Then continued arguing with the attorney. "It's my money! Lucas needs a good car to drive over those mountains and get to school. Besides the dealer gave me a good deal. He had two cars all tricked out with extras just sitting there."

Caught

"That was no deal."

"Yes, it was. They were demos."

Father Nick seated himself away from the bluster. "Beer for me, too." He quickly checked his notes. "Chelsea needs a carseat for Amber. And Lucas couldn't stop smiling when we delivered the cars. He had the tuition bill ready for approval." Nick looked at Sean. "Did you really give both of them a credit card?" They had to wait for an answer because Herbie was close to strangling Sean.

Sean blushed. "They both have expenses, and it seemed more efficient than Lynn getting calls to release money."

"But -"

"I told both of them that Lynn would review the charges and not pay unacceptable or unrelated fees." Sean sipped the beer Lynn had placed on the table. "I think Chelsea will over spend. I told her that the card would only last until Amber's operation was complete and that it had a spending limit. Then it would be closed out and she could get funds for Amber's eyeglasses every year if the little girl needs them." He looked around the room at his friends. "She will be tempted. She's probably never had any extra money to spend. Lucas, on the other hand, is scrupulous. He'll never charge more than he thinks is acceptable. We'll have to watch and make certain we're fair with him."

"We better get down to business, then," said Lynn. "I can see that the John Gillespie fund is going to take time to manage," she glanced at Sean as she added, "efficiently." Someone snickered!

Sean gave her a sheepish smile. "Sorry, I guess I'm giving you more than was in our original vision of this fund."

"Not to worry," she smiled back at her friend, "that's why I hired Rory. He's responsible for managing our accounts."

"I heard that," came a shout from the outer office. Rory walked into the conference room, placing the bottle of scotch on the table. He passed an ice filled tumbler to Herbie and took another for himself. "I'm ready."

* * *

Dusty sat at his desk in his home office, scanning through photos. Tee and Lonzo had managed to grab shots of about fifteen people over the weekend. They never saw cars to catch a tag. Lonzo had explored and found the small parking area and well-tended path to the cabin. Customers drove past the cabin, around a bend and cut into a small private drive that deposited them about 100 feet from the back door. Further exploration pointed to the obvious, customers came into the forest and took the right branch of the old road. They never came near Hank's cabin. The more Dusty thought, the more he agreed with Tee; there was someone in the regional team working against the drug task force and for the distributor.

Lynn walked into the room. "Dinner," she announced. He was startled out of his thoughts. She walked behind him and looked down at his screen. "Suspects?"

He reached up to close the laptop when she asked, "Do you suspect Audrey Decker's husband of something?"

"Who?"

She lifted the laptop screen and pointed. "Him."

Dusty glanced back at her, gave some thought to confidentiality, more thought to how long he had been staring at these strangers and asked, "Know any of these others?" He ran a slow slide show.

"Who are they?"

"I can't talk about it."

"That's Kip! And that's Margaret from the clinic. She's been working with us on Piper's school clinic." Dusty flipped more photos. "That's Bart Decker again and that next fellow looks familiar. Hmmm? Wait, wait, he's one of the new attorneys in town." More photos. "That's all I recognize." She walked around the desk and plopped on the couch, giving Dusty a curious, yet satisfied, stare.

He marveled again at how she could draw correct conclusions from a little evidence. "I can't talk about it," he repeated. "And please don't mention this to anyone."

She curled her feet up under her as she got comfortable, or as Dusty thought, got ready for the kill shot. She smiled. "That's why you told me Kip wasn't having an affair with Rachel. You knew about him and Margaret. Are you going to arrest them?"

He walked over to the couch and sat beside her taking her in his arms. "This isn't going to be pleasant. Kip and his lady friend are in real trouble. There are others who will slide by with misdemeanors and probation."

Caught

"Is that why Claire has been sneaking into town?"

He nodded. "Please don't say anything." He hugged her tightly wishing he could hold all the evils in the world at bay.

CHAPTER TWENTY

Piper had called it the weekend from hell. But it was over; the boys had graduated. They would all be moving back home today. Lynn glanced at the pile of dirty laundry. As she and Dusty left the university they had filled the car with Jason's things. Because, he had argued, he'd never get everything into his car. There had been laundry bags of dirty clothes and some text books Dusty swore had never been opened. But her son was a college graduate and already enrolled in law school.

As a graduation present, Jim and Marianna had bought a small condo for Jason. He would live in the place during law school. There was even space for him to take in a roommate. Lynn was still reeling at her father's generosity. But Jim had said, "In three years, I'll sell it. There are always new students looking for a place to live."

Piper wandered into the kitchen, stepping over the laundry bags. "Jason home yet?"

"He texted he'd be home for dinner."

"Good, my boys will be hungry then." Piper pulled out her phone and began texting. She looked up at Lynn. "I love this curbside pick-up. I just ordered burgers and buns and some sides from the grocery store." She scanned her list. "I also got regular food. Now that Doyle's home, food will disappear." She looked at Lynn and started to cry. "He'll be married next month!"

"Ah, honey, don't cry." Lynn hugged her best friend. "We should all be happy."

"I am happy," she sobbed, "but he's still a baby."

Lynn thought about Doyle. He was Piper's biggest son, over six feet, husky with unruly blonde curls, and an open, winning blue-eyed smile. "I think everything will be fine. Lori is a marvelous young woman and they'll live here in town. You'll see. Everything will be great."

Piper wiped her tears and went off to her curbside grocery rendezvous. In no time it seemed Lynn's yard was filled with Jason and the other boys, along with Dusty and Will cooking burgers and drinking beer. Lynn was surprised to see Patti Ann arrive with Dusty's nephew, Way.

"What are you doing home?"

"This is my break," explained the young medical student. "I managed to score some time for Doyle's wedding, too. But it looks like my time is pretty much organized for the next several years." She looked around the yard, formerly the mask-free zone. "I'll miss all the gatherings."

"Things are changing," Lynn reminded her. "You in med school. Jason in law school. Doyle married. Way is a deputy." She hugged the young woman. "We'll be here when you all finish."

Piper joined the hug, then sent Patti Ann to enjoy her friends. "Lynn and I have to plan the engagement-graduation party," was her explanation.

Patti Ann looked wistful. "I can't be here. But the guys said they would send photos." She moved off.

"I thought we had our party planned," Lynn groused.

"I've thought of a few more folks to invite and some more things we need." Lynn scowled but followed Piper into the house to begin making more lists, hoping this wasn't another opportunity for Piper to cry about her baby getting married!

* * *

"She's gone," whispered Mars. He, Trina and the children were sprawled around their living room like deflated balloons. And the 'she' who was gone was Mars' mother. Palmer Dunn Healey Nolan had finally gotten through quarantine and positive tests and more quarantine to finally arrive in River Bend to meet her new grandchild, Mars' first born.

Trina could only nod. Nursing a baby and starting a magazine were easy-peasy compared to a few days with a whirlwind like Palmer. "When do you think she'll be back?"

"Gamma?" Little Holly was so exhausted she could hardly speak. But she had enjoyed every minute of Palmer's visit. Although Holly and her brother Brian were Mars' stepchildren Palmer had embraced them as her own from the start. When she had walked into the house and been greeted by Holly's 'Gamma' greeting, she had cried and hugged and kissed the children.

Mars chuckled, starting to revive. "She does love these kids. But she won't be back for a while. US quarantine for entry then British quarantine to get back to her place in London will dampen her interest in frequent visits." A routine flight from London to Charlotte to River Bend had turned into an almost month-long odyssey.

"Do you think she'll leave her husband and move back here to be with the children?"

"Marshall is a good man. I think she'll ask him to explore returning to the US."

"Grammy!" Young Brian seemed to second that motion. He was ready for Palmer to return. Every day during her visit was a day of fun and hugs and cookies.

Trina leaned over and kissed Mars. "Your mother is another good reason to be your wife. She is so good to my children and so kind to me." Palmer had given Trina funds toward the magazine. She had even offered to send along some travel stories for the magazine.

Mars stood and pulled Trina to her feet. Hugging her tightly he asked, "What about a pizza dinner, gang?" With that the two kids found the energy to do their pizza dance in anticipation. One more hug for his wife and Mars found his phone to place the family pizza order.

* * *

After eating Dusty's burgers the gang of young friends organized an evening, as Jason remarked, "Like old times." Jason would be returning to his summer job working for Jim. Ricky and Jeff had finished college semesters by attending college transfer classes at the community college. Patti Ann had completed her first year of medical school. Way Reid stopped by to show off his gear as a new deputy in Henderson County. They were playing their version of dusk soccer in the open field behind Lynn's barn. It reminded Bryce that they were all still silly and fun to be with because Patti Ann was the goalie and the guys always faked great sobs when she stopped a goal. He laughed at their antics and he hoped they would be understanding. Because tonight was the night.

He whistled for attention as he carried a cooler out behind the barn. "Let's take a break." He flipped open the cooler and tossed a beer to Doyle.

The soon-to-be groom saw something in his brother's eyes because he grabbed the beer and tumbled on the grass at his feet on full alert. "What's wrong?" Doyle gave his brother radar-like scrutiny.

Bryce looked at the young man, all blonde and big and solid. "I have to talk to you guys." That statement made everyone curious. Bryce was the quiet guy. Soon everyone was sprawled at his feet. He sat on the cooler, rested his clasped hands on his knees and took a deep breath. "I have to say something. Please listen and then you can ask questions or hit me or whatever."

Doyle sat up. "We won't hit you." His voice was mature and serious. "We're your posse." Bryce wondered if his brother suspected something.

Giving Doyle a soft, almost grateful smile, Bryce said, "Let me tell you, first. You might change your mind about being my posse." He looked at each one, even Patti Ann. "I'm gay." A beat.

"So?" Jeff, his younger brother asked as he, too, sat up. Was he daring the others to scoff or sneer?

Patti Ann stood and walked to Bryce. She pulled him to his feet and hugged him then gave him a kiss on the cheek. "You're brave, too."

Bryce scanned his posse. "That's all? No one has any other comment?"

"I'm not surprised," offered Ricky. "You never went after Patti Ann and she's beautiful." He blushed when Patti Ann gave him a juicy kiss on the cheek.

"What about you?" Bryce looked at Jason.

Jason looked at him thoughtfully. "I know this wasn't easy for you. Who else knows? What do you want us to do?"

Bryce wanted to cry. All his worries were for naught. "Mom knows. Now you guys know. I guess I'll tell the old folks next."

"Are you dating someone?"

He laughed. "No." The guys, curious and somewhat confused, spent the rest of the evening asking questions. Some made Bryce laugh and some made him aware of the trials that would be coming with his alternate way of life. It made him wonder if he should have remained silent. But no, that meant he would have no life, or only a life when he spent time in Raleigh using a visit to Beth Seymour as an excuse to have a social life out of town.

There was so much to consider and taking family response into the mix was one of the biggest considerations. The discussion, or as Bryce thought, the great reveal, finally wound down. No one was certain about what would happen next, but for now Bryce had explained himself to his brothers and closest friends. And his world seemed to still be on its axis, turning as usual.

"Does this mean you're leaving River Bend?" His brother Jeff yawned his question as everyone seemed to decide the evening was at an end.

"No." Bryce nodded toward Patti Ann. "I've got a great job working for your father. I want to get back into entertainment, but things are still quiet. But I will leave River Bend someday." He thought about all the talks he had had with Beth. "I'll keep looking for a place that fits me. But you'll all still be my posse."

"Well, be careful," said Way who had been silent until now. "I'll give you a list of places to avoid. Places where you might get beat up or something." He threw an arm across Bryce's shoulder. "There's a lot of meanness around. Dusty and me don't want to scrape you off some barroom floor."

That dash of reality ended the discussion, giving everyone a lot to think about.

CHAPTER TWENTY-ONE

Tuesday when Rachel returned home, Owen was at the airport. He hugged her and grabbed her bag from the luggage carousel. "Good to see you," he said, "the kids are coming a day early. I think I have the house ready." She smiled and climbed into the car. Neither one of them talked on the drive back to River Bend.

Walking into the house she noticed everything was cleaned, and she told him so. "I got it ready for the kids. I made up the beds for them, too." he explained. "Do you want dinner? I can pick something up."

"Thank you. I think I want to take a nap. Don't let me sleep past five." She climbed the stairs and he watched her walk into their bedroom and smiled to himself.

* * *

Dusty drove back from the farm. He was paranoid that others would learn about the FBI plans for a cabin raid. He had gone to his mother's place to talk with Claire on the landline. He and his team were working hard to keep information tight. But his conscience bothered him. What should he do about Doug? In the past Dusty would have acted without informing the sheriff until the last minute and would have only offered minimal information. But Doug was now the acting sheriff, and a friend.

Dusty and the unit were delighted to have Doug in charge, but how much should he know? Dusty wrestled with himself - tell or not tell, too little or all that Doug should know? If I were sheriff, thought Dusty, what would I expect? And the answer was - respect. He knew he never acted as though he respected Sheriff Dunwoody. Was Dusty's attitude part of the problem he had with the sheriff? He shook his head. This was not the time to examine his role in the hostility that had developed between the two men. This was an examination of his relationship with Doug. And it came down to respect.

He placed a call on his cellphone. "This is Dusty. Can we meet someplace private?"

Doug laughed into his phone. "Not you, too. I've had this job a week and everyone wants to complain. They all start just like you did." He mimicked, "Can we meet someplace private?"

"I don't want to complain."

Doug was silent for a moment, suspecting that this was a serious request. "I'm in my office but can be where you are in a few minutes."

"I'll pick up some coffee and meet you in my back yard."

Dusty coasted into his yard and saw that Doug had parked at his Aunt Emily Jacobs' place and walked over. He handed Doug a cup of coffee and a bag. Doug looked in the bag then looked back at Dusty.

The detective shrugged. "Sorry. I just called Umberto and said surprise me." He grimaced. "What did he send?"

"Looks like four cannoli and some broken cookies." Doug emptied the bag onto the clothe Dusty had spread on the table. "I'm new at this sheriff stuff, but are broken cookies the required food for secret meetings?"

Dusty gave his old friend a rueful look. "Doug, I don't know what's required. But I work for you now and I owe it to you to bring you in on a project."

By the sound of his voice Doug knew this was more than a complaint. "I'm sorry for being flippant. So far I haven't heard anything that sounds like a professional law enforcement discussion. Folks only want to complain. You said this isn't a complaint." He waited.

"Correct." Dusty sat and unlidded his coffee cup. "Let me tell you about the fun you could be having this weekend." And he proceeded to tell Doug everything - Tee and Mars' findings, the FBI's interest, and Claire's plan for the raid.

"Whew, this job just turned into law enforcement!" Doug took a piece of broken cookie. He wasn't certain a cannoli would sit well on Dusty's news. "You really believe there's a leak somewhere?"

"Yeah, so me and Claire have kept things close." Dusty shook his head. "But I had to tell you. It would be wrong to do this and you not know."

"I appreciate that," said Doug. "Do you want anything from the department?" He sipped his coffee. "Because I don't know everyone well enough to make assignments. And I don't know who to trust."

"If you don't mind, I know who I want to include on my team." Doug nodded agreement. "I might suggest that you tour the jail and make certain we can hold a few extra guests this weekend."

They talked and ate the rest of the food. Doug finally stood. "Thank you for trusting me in this new position." The cannoli seemed to settle as he thought about Dusty's weekend plans. "I'd like to be included in the team for this operation."

Dusty smiled. "You already bored with your desk job?"

* * *

After the acceptance he received from his brothers and friends, Bryce decided to approach his employer. As the work day wound down, he found Greg Chou in his office finishing up a meeting with Hank Seymour, the industrial waste company's owner.

"Do you guys have a minute?" he asked as they were clearing up the papers on Greg's desk.

"You want a raise?" Hank teased. "You keep up the good work and I'll consider letting you take a truck home on weekends." They all chuckled.

Bryce walked into the office and closed the door. "I got something personal." The two men returned to their chairs. "I thought I should tell you and you can decide if I still have a job." They waited. Bryce took a deep breath. "I'm gay. I've been telling my family and I thought you should know in case I'm not someone you want around the place." He stood, waiting.

"For crying out loud," scoffed Hank, "who cares?" He used his leg to pull out a chair for Bryce to be seated. "Someone around here giving you trouble?"

"No."

"A couple of them will," said Greg, with a frown. "I want to know if that happens. It's probably the same two who have not liked a Chinese guy at this desk."

"Someone gave you trouble?" Hank was shocked. "I thought my guys were all right with different things. Or at least kept their meanness to themselves."

Greg didn't want to tell Hank what some of the drivers had to say about Hank's daughters and about his dead wife. "Let's just say, they don't appreciate diversity."

"Should I fire them? Or talk to them?" Hank seemed surprised at the information.

"I've handled them," said Greg. "And I'll handle any problem they have with Bryce. I run this operation for you. I can't look like I run to you when things get tough."

"Some of these boys have been with me a long time." Hank shrugged. "I guess we work too hard to talk politics and stuff. I've always felt they think just like me." He thought over that statement. "I guess they just give me what they think I want to see." He sighed, sadly.

Bryce was beginning to understand that the world harbored many different kinds of prejudice - sexual orientation, skin color, ethnic bias. This was just the beginning. "I'll keep it to myself. I like this job."

The men talked for a while longer then Hank took them out for a beer.

* * *

Before Rachel had taken her nap, Owen had offered to bring in carryout when he returned from his office. As he had said, "Let me handle dinner this evening. I learned all the best carryout menu offerings while you were gone."

"This is lovely," she said as he opened a Bistro meal for two - prime rib dinner-in-a-box. "Our local restaurants have certainly learned to be creative."

Owen chuckled. "You have no idea what you can find for dinner these days."

"Maybe I should take another trip?"

"I missed you." He gave her a shy smile. They worked together setting out their meal in silence. Once settled he asked, "How was your work?"

"I enjoyed it. The people were great. But I don't think I want to do it every week." She told him some stories from her experience and they laughed at her recollections. "What happened here while I was gone? Did you hold wild parties?"

Owen replied, "I went to sub for you at the cancer fundraiser last weekend. There was a lot of talk about Kip and his wife. And his announcement about running for mayor."

"Really?"

He looked at her, embarrassed. "Your friends gave me an earful. About your work in town and about their low opinion of Kip."

She laughed. "I guess you believe me about no affair with him." Rachel thought about his remark as she offered him another serving. "Do you have any information on Anita? Is she healing? How is she handling this news?"

"I believed you when you said you weren't having an affair." He unwrapped the dessert and placed it on a separate plate.

"And you had it all substantiated at the cancer booth?" Rachel poured more wine.

"As you might expect," Owen admitted, "I heard a lot of gossip. The volunteers at our booth said Anita has a private detective looking into things. She has exonerated you and told everyone so, and she's closing in on Kip's secret life." Owen passed her the last piece of the cake. "I wonder if it will affect his campaign. Those women aren't happy that he's running for mayor."

Rachel laughed. "How did you get talked into working at the booth?"

"Someone called and needed help and you weren't here and I didn't have anything to do, so I went." He topped her glass of wine.

"Did you have fun?" She finished dessert and carried her plate to the sink.

"It was okay. I was the only guy. I'm glad you're home." He cleaned and stacked the plates without more discussion, then went into the den where he turned on the TV and flopped into his recliner.

Rachel finished cleaning up after dinner, sighed and went out for a walk.

CHAPTER TWENTY-TWO

Audrey and Bart Decker settled the children down for the night. There was a tension she hoped the children hadn't sensed. But evenings were becoming difficult. Her guilt, his attitude. They should talk. But that would rock the boat and she thought that by ending her affair, she could resume her old life and her relationship with Bart. But something was different. Had she changed with the affair? Had he changed for some reason or as a response to her affair? How much did he know about James? Was he having an affair of his own? Was he into something else that caused him to be a different man?

She walked into the den and sat in her usual place and picked up her crocheting. She laughed to herself. Her mother was an avid crocheter and always said that it was a great way to calm down of an evening, better and less worrisome than drinking. Audrey nodded to herself. She understood that wisdom this evening. Bart was sitting in the husband designated recliner. In happier days they had referred to the chair as the mandatory piece of furniture that proved he was a great husband and father. Those days seemed to be only a memory. He still interacted with the children. And sometimes even seemed to enjoy them and enjoy attending their activities. She reviewed the last year or two. His moods seemed to be in a repetitive cycle. Several weeks or even a month or two of energy, she hadn't really marked a calendar, then a week of withdrawal from the family. He would be quiet, as though he had a difficult challenge in his job and then he would be back teasing the kids, home for meals. But he was mentally gone from their bed. Maybe he was having an affair and that had pushed her into James' arms. No. She didn't think Bart was having an affair. He just seemed uninterested in her, in sex, in their marriage.

Her hands worked automatically with the small needle and the thick thread as she thought. He might tease and be present with the children, but it had no depth. Now she didn't even know what she was thinking. No depth? She tried to get a handle on that impression. Something else was behind his eyes, she thought. He was only half in the family and he had begun a year or two ago to find fault with her. Nothing evil, just unkind comments, given in a manner that suggested he was the parent and she the child. She had accepted it as long as he stayed kind to the children. The more she thought the more she felt she had become a beacon to him - some place to channel frustrations and worries. She was, on the other hand, finding her value more and more in her work and statewide success.

Maybe she was to blame for his attitude, his distance. She decided to make an effort to salvage their marriage and family. She cleared her throat. "Thank you for helping solve Logan's math problem this evening. Online school must be a challenge to children who don't have smart parents."

"It was easy. I do those calculations often. It's just understanding what the story problem is asking." He shifted in his chair and said nothing more, returning to watch the TV program.

After more silence he said, "I was surprised you noticed."

"What?" The thread got tangled in her fingers.

"You're always wrapped up in your work. You have that big job and disappear from here. You park the kids with your parents and are gone all weekend. I followed you, you know."

She gasped and waited.

He stood and came toward her in a menacing manner. "I got things I do and you got things you do." He knelt down in front of her and clutched her knees. "Don't bother me and I won't bother you." He stared at the speechless woman. "I got things to do this weekend. Don't you try to sneak off and expect me to watch those kids." He stood and left the room. She heard him climb the stairs.

How could she go to bed this evening with a man so hostile? But she had been in bed with him for over ten years. She crocheted a little longer thinking over their marriage, her mistakes, his secrecy. She yawned as the crocheting blurred. It was a king size bed. What difference did it make if they slept together. The bed was big enough. They never touched.

Tomorrow she would give some thought to counseling. The children didn't deserve a divorce. She had to continue in this marriage for a few more years. She had her job, she had her memories, she had her children.

* * *

"You're awfully quiet tonight," said Lynn as she brushed a kiss across Dusty's temple. He was sitting on the sofa in his office staring at a blank TV. "Can I help?"

He raised his eyes to hers and again wondered how he had gotten so lucky. He gave her a soft smile. "Nah, work will be taking up my time this weekend. Why don't you go on to bed. I'll be up later."

She kissed him again, "Good night," and left the room.

Dusty threw himself against the back of the sofa. Claire and her crew were ready for the raid this weekend. He knew they would be pulling in Kip and his girlfriend. But Dusty worried about Kip's customers. He and his staff had finally identified several well-placed citizens who were regular clients at the cabin. Claire said her research team agreed with Lonzo, theorizing the clients were getting some sort of maintenance shot that kept them sort of high and aggressively functional. When he had asked questions she had replied, "Just go with it. We need to know the formula before we'll say more. Think of it as something like people who get time released meds."

Claire had also given him some very off the record information. He hadn't shared it with his staff. She said her contacts were suggesting two things. One, this cabin operation was the tail end of a bigger operation. And two, the bigger operation involved a lot more than drugs. She promised him that she was initiating an undercover operation and as she had said at the end of the conversation, "Stay tuned. This will get interesting."

With her warning ringing in his ears, he climbed the stairs to bed, washed up and crawled in beside Lynn who was fast asleep. He pulled her to him, glad they only had a queen size bed. He could always find her when he needed her warmth and comfort. He held her tight and fell asleep.

* * *

Caught

It was a cool, moonlit evening. Owen drove silently through the quiet night. He and Rachel had visited some friends for a monthly dinner and bridge gathering. The evening hosts lived in the country club estates, a wealthy, quasi-retirement enclave. "George is starting to show his age," said Owen. "He's been my client and my golf partner since he and Rose moved to River Bend. I think they should think about moving into that retirement center."

Rachel straightened in her seat. Her mind had been miles away. "I noticed how slow he was this evening making his bids. Rose has confided that she has concerns." In the dimness she could see that Owen nodded his agreement. She sighed to herself. They could talk about their friends, probably even national politics, but, never, ever, talk about their marriage. They continued on home in silence.

Walking into the kitchen Rachel flipped on her electric tea pot. The water would be ready in seconds. "Would you like a cup of tea this evening?"

Owen looked at her, looked at the box of tea bags in her hand. "No, thank you. I think I'll catch the news and go to bed." He started to walk into his den but turned back. "Thank you for returning." She looked puzzled. "I mean for coming home."

"You didn't think I would?"

"I haven't known what to think lately."

She could ask if he wanted to talk about it, but she knew both he and she would rather avoid any discussion. For Rachel's part, she didn't have any idea what she would like as an outcome from a 'talk.' Maybe Owen was as confused as she was.

That made this evening the same as all the others. He would watch TV, she would have a cup of tea, glance at the remnants of the morning paper, and both would go to bed. Even though it was only queen size, they would never touch, never roll into one another, never meet in the middle. Never talk.

And tomorrow evening the kids would arrive.

* * *

Anita heard Kip come into the house. When she heard the automatic garage door open, she knew she had three or four minutes to put out the light at her bedside. She could track his movements as he entered the house. He would enter through the kitchen, hang up his keys, pour himself a quick shot of something, put the glass down on one of her cherished pieces of furniture. Hopefully, the new oil she was using would obliterate the stain in the morning. He would climb the stairs, not concerned about waking her. It had been several years since they had shared a bed. She hoped he enjoyed the king size bed, alone. Because she was certain that by the time they had been able to afford the bed, they had found no enjoyment in one another.

Anita felt safe in the darkness of her room. The bedside light was out. No hint of her awareness leaked under the door nor any telltale sign of life. She listened to him prepare for bed and snuggled under her own covers counting the days until she would be free. A talk with her attorney a few days after her accident had helped her formalize her plan. It was time to free herself of Kip Mahaffey.

CHAPTER TWENTY-THREE

Today was that luncheon the school clinic team had planned with the Congressman. Because her regional reputation was golden, Rachel had been able to set up the meeting. Every local and regional pol wanted to be photographed smiling with Rachel. Lynn thought to herself, I hope we can translate that into budget increases in child healthcare.

Piper walked into the country club lobby. She was dressed in a great looking business suit that had a waist length jacket in soft charcoal with a collar that stood away from her neck, allowing space for jewelry. She had topped the outfit off with a stunning necklace and earring set. On her feet were a pair of shoes that looked businesslike and fun at the same time. Rachel is teaching us all how to dress with style, thought Lynn. Then she reached for the scarf she had added to her own ensemble early this morning. She felt smug, remembering how she had checked the color to make certain it blended with her outfit, or pulled it together, she was never certain which was supposed to happen. She quietly let her fingers drift around her neck, hoping the folds defined her collar as she had intended. Her hands found . . . . nothing! No scarf? She had tied it, or pinned it or . . . oh, no, she forgot the pin. She sidled toward the window overlooking the parking lot. And there it was! Her designer, color coordinated, or blended, or . . whatever scarf, was waving at her from the door of her car. It was caught it the seam between door and car body - the place she usually caught her skirt hem, her purse, her heel. The 'car dragon' had won again!

Lynn decided she would resign herself to being blandly dressed amid the stylish assault of Piper and Rachel. Maybe she should just wear jeans and sweatshirts - she was so out of the fashion stream. "Am I late?" Piper asked as she smoothed her skirt and straightened her jacket, interrupting Lynn's thoughts. The country club was a busy place today. Several other maskless groups seemed to be gathering together in the lobby collecting stragglers before going to their tables for lunch.

"No, Rachel and the Congressman aren't here yet. And Zachary had to be out of town," said Lynn answering Piper's question. She stared out into the parking lot, tempted to wave back at her scarf fluttering in the breeze. And there was Rachel, dressed in all the style Lynn expected. She wore a bright blue dress that complimented her silver blonde hair. The dress was accented with a silk scarf of equally bright complimentary colors. Her shoes were spiky and as colorful as her scarf. "Here they come." Lynn watched and wondered how Rachel managed to walk with such grace in heels that high. Lynn had a lot more to learn about style. If she couldn't manage a scarf, high heels would certainly be a disaster!

Both women watched as Rachel and a short, balding man walked briskly into the club. The two women moved toward the door to greet the guest of honor as Rachel escorted him through the entry way. Before Lynn could get to the man she was nudged aside by Kip Mahaffey. He had his hand out greeting the congressman and wrapping an arm around his shoulders.

"Lowell," Kip said, as he held on to the man and insinuated himself between Rachel and her guest, "glad to see you. I didn't know you were in town. Why don't you come have lunch with me and some friends?"

"I'm here to have lunch with Rachel and her friends," replied Lowell. He tried to get around the eager attorney.

"They won't mind. Rachel knows we have important things to talk about." Kip laughed. Ignoring Rachel's scowl, he tried to move the Congressman through the lobby. "She knows that we always have important issues to discuss." He turned to her and said, "You and your friends can have a few minutes of Lowell's time after lunch. Have a great meal! It's on me."

The club dining room manager had seen the Congressman arrive and had sent a tray of drinks to welcome him. The drink of choice was a soft red wine to go along with a mushroom appetizer that was hurrying along behind the wine tray. Before Rachel could respond to Kip the tray of drinks was in front of the three of them. Lowell took a glass, handed it to Rachel, then took one for himself. Kip took a glass and said, "So let's get seated, Lowell. The girls won't mind. They'll gossip over lunch and have a fine time without you."

Caught

Rachel smiled sweetly at Kip and, turning slowly, she dug her spiked heel into the top of his shoe. He gasped, hopped backward and bumped the server bringing mushrooms into the lobby. The server moved quickly with the agility of a seasoned waiter and managed to get himself and the food safely into a far corner of the room. Kip, on the other hand, lost his balance and toppled backward, finding himself staring up at the ceiling.

Rachel bent down, tilting her glass so that his light grey trousers soon looked as though he had relieved himself. "Kip, are you all right? You acted as though someone shot you." She smiled sweetly, "but it only looks as though you've had an accident." She turned to her guest, "I think our table is ready, Lowell." The Congressman and the ladies walked into the dining room.

Piper and Lynn, controlling their laughter and staring at the floor, followed Rachel and their guest into the club dining room. Behind them they could hear the club staff helping Kip to his feet and apologizing for any inconvenience. They also heard subdued chuckles around the room.

* * *

When Rachel arrived home that evening she found a beautiful floral arrangement on her kitchen table. "Are these for me?" she called to her husband.

He padded into the kitchen in his stocking feet, holding his necktie in his hands. "Yeah, I just got in and was changing my clothes when it arrived."

That told her one thing. He didn't bring them as a peace offering or romantic gesture, or something else foreign to his nature. "I wonder who sent them?"

"There's a card."

She found the card stuffed between the fern stems and roses. It said, "Thanks. I laughed and laughed." There was no signature.

Her husband took the card. "What does this mean? Who's it from?"

"Hmm." She had her suspicions.

"What's this laughing stuff?" Owen asked her.

"Let me tell you about lunch." Rachel filled him in on the wine incident at the club.

"Who was in the lobby when it happened?" Owen wiped his eyes with his necktie squeezing his question out between great gusts of laughter.

She mentioned several names.

"I can think of about two or three of those folks who would have really enjoyed seeing Kip on his ass." He strangled through another laugh. "And wine in his crotch!"

"You're enjoying this too much," teased his wife.

"Who do you think sent them?" He nodded toward the flowers.

"His wife." Rachel sniffed at one of the yellow roses. "I told you we cleared the air when she was in the hospital." Here she stopped and looked at her husband. "She was being deceived, as well as you, by this man, at my expense, hurting all of us."

All of a sudden there was no mirth in the room. Watching his face Rachel knew that Owen understood. He hadn't known whether to believe the gossip or not about her and Mahaffey. He had shut down and surrendered to the handsome, charming Kip Mahaffey and not trusted his own wife. Now here they were, a shattered marriage with nothing much to say or share.

They heard a shuffling at the front door. "Mom, Dad," called their son. "Heather and I are here. You should read what's on social media." Jonathan Teague ambled into the kitchen. "Look at this." He held up his phone. "You know this guy, don't you? Mahaffey? Someone posted a shot of him wetting his pants or something."

Owen clasped the phone to study the screen. He made a gurgling sound, trying not to guffaw. Rachel said, "I think I heard he took a fall at the country club and spilled his drink."

"Wow, those are beautiful flowers," said Heather, their daughter-in-law. "What's the occasion?"

"Dad probably sent them," replied Jon. "He's a great guy." The young man grinned at his father. "Or you're in the doghouse trying to make amends."

Owen slapped him on the back. "That's for you to figure out. Why don't we run to Uncle Chicken and pick up dinner while the girls relax. Your mother had a busy day."

"We brought that coconut cake you guys like," Jon said. He tugged Owen out the door. "We'll be right back."

Caught

"Don't worry about us," said Rachel. "Heather can fill me in on the gossip from Greensboro." Heather had quite an extended family. Rachel was certain the gossip would last until the guys returned. With that she turned to her daughter-in-law and asked, "How's your mother?"

* * *

Will was laughing so hard he had tears in his eyes. "Stop," he pleaded, "you're making this up!"

Piper was still in her power suit but had removed her shoes as she sipped wine in Lynn's kitchen. "All true." She raised her right hand in an oath. "He fell backward and Rachel dribbled wine into his crotch." She turned to Lynn. "Tell him!"

Lynn was working at the kitchen sink with a stain remover to get grease marks out of her designer scarf. The one the car had tried to eat. She raised her head. "True." She scowled at the stain. "Lowell was a trooper. He ignored the whole thing, but all through lunch you could hear snippets from all the other tables in the dining room. Everyone was talking. Rory said he even saw photos on that local neighborhood website." Scrub. Rub.

Dusty walked into the kitchen. "Know what I heard?"

"It's true," said Piper as she finished her glass of wine.

Jason followed Dusty into the room. "Gramps heard this story and couldn't stop laughing. About some guy, Kip? What's for dinner?"

Will laughed some more. Catching his breath he said, "I sent the boys to pick up Chinese and Uncle Chicken. I'm celebrating the downfall of Kip Mahaffey!"

Everyone looked at him. "You don't like him?"

Will used a few words that he usually reserved for his shop floor. "When I first tried to raise money, he offered to help but wanted fifty per cent of my factory."

"What?"

"He said he would do all the legal work, be council for my business and I didn't have to pay."

"What nerve!"

"I told him my father was my legal counsel. And he said, 'You come from South End, you probably don't have a father.'"

Lynn gasped. "Did you hit him?"

"Almost." Will grinned, "I just said 'my father is Jim Hoefler.' He looked like he had a piece of gossip that was blackmail worthy, and so I said, 'he and his friends are investing in me.' That shut him up. It told him that others knew Jim was my father and that he better keep his distance from me and my inventions."

Lynn poured herself and Piper more wine. "How's Kip going to run for office with so many people coming out with negative stories?"

Dusty listened to the talk around him and wondered what everyone would be saying after the FBI raid tomorrow night.

CHAPTER TWENTY-FOUR

Rachel was putting a dish of scrambled eggs in front of Owen when her son, Jon, came into the kitchen followed by Doyle Hanby. "You boys hungry?" she asked. They nodded and sat at the table in their sweaty running clothes. The boys had been friends in high school. Though Jon was older, they had played on the same high school soccer team and maintained a friendship when they were in River Bend at the same time.

"Those detectives really work you out," puffed Jon. "Do you run all the time?" Mars and Danny along with Buck Rawlings ran a three-mile circuit through River Bend every morning they could manage when crime or sick children didn't intrude. The college crowd joined when they had the energy.

"Not me," answered Doyle, "but I try to join them when I'm in town. I can still do three miles." Rachel placed eggs and toast in front of each of them.

"Doyle, congratulations," said Owen, "graduation and soon marriage."

Yes, sir." He grinned. "Will offered me a job and Lori is going to work for Kevin's IT business."

"Wow," said Jon, "You'll be right back home. That'll be great."

"So how's marriage for you?" Doyle asked his friend.

"I've only been married eight months," replied Jon as he buttered his toast. "Can we have some milk, Mom?" Rachel served the drinks then sat at the table with her own breakfast - toast and black coffee. Doyle looked around the kitchen, then looked back at Jon.

"She's still asleep," he said after sipping his milk. "She works, too, and said she wanted some time to sleep in while we're visiting." He took a bite of toast, moved his eggs around his plate, then asked, "What's the secret, you guys?"

"What secret?" asked Rachel.

"The secret to staying married as long as you and Dad."

Rachel looked at Owen. He looked down at his plate and became busy finishing his eggs. She finished her toast and carried her cup to the sink. "Talk to one another," she offered, "Don't let misunderstandings grow to big problems."

Owen wiped his hands on his napkin. "And be proud of your partner's success. Several weeks ago I subbed for your mother at the cancer booth. I learned a lot about her community work. I was surprised to hear things about her work that I didn't know." He thought about the many comments regarding her sense of humor and her joy of life. "And about some things I had forgotten about her." He toyed with a salt shaker.

"Like what?"

"Her warmth and humor. Her ability to ignore my faults and stay with me." Rachel kissed his forehead. A spontaneous act they both realized hadn't occurred for months maybe even years.

"Just love one another each day," said Rachel. As the boys grinned, she realized they thought she was talking about sex. She blushed.

"Way to go, Dad," cheered Jon as he raised his hand to high five his father. Owen turned a deep red as he returned the hand slap. "It can't be that easy."

"It's not easy," replied Rachel, "there's breakfast to get, kids to sort out, chores, other responsibilities. The danger is that you forget one another as the rest of life intrudes." After she said that she could feel tears collecting behind her eyes. Taking a deep breath, she cleared some dishes from the table and, tousling her son's hair, left the kitchen.

"Any more advice, Dad?" asked Jon.

"I think your mother summed it up." He stood and carried his plate to the sink. "You boys enjoy breakfast. There's more milk and some cake from last night." He put the cake dish on the table. "I've got to run some errands." And he was gone.

"That's the first time I ever asked my parents such a personal question," Jon confided in Doyle. "Do you think I made them uncomfortable?"

"I wouldn't want anyone asking me about my sex life," said Doyle as he sliced a piece of cake.

Caught

"I wasn't asking about their sex life," argued Jon, "I was asking about the secret to a long marriage."

Doyle smiled, "I'm happy to hear it involves a lot of sex." Marriage in a month seemed even brighter.

* * *

Earlier in the week, Lynn had returned from the whirlwind graduation event. The dog had spent those days with Emily Jacobs and her grandchildren. It was Saturday and he looked a little peaked. She thought he needed to walk off all the food and treats he had been given. She had noticed that he just seemed to stay at home vegetating under a tree or on her bed. So today she had him on a leash and was walking him through the park. "Hey, Lynn!"

She turned and saw Tovah Fleischer, a new addition to the widows' group that met at Frank's Tavern. Lynn mused, it was becoming more than just widows, but it was a group she enjoyed. Her new friend was with a little girl. Lynn waved as the dog went on alert - anticipating an ear rub from the strangers. And maybe a treat. "This is Chips," she told the little girl who was hiding behind Tovah. "He likes to be petted." The child reached out tentatively. Chips licked her hand, wagged his tail and sent the youngster into delighted giggles.

"Rebecca, this is Miss Lynn. Can you say hello?" The little girl held out the hand Chips had just licked and Lynn took it.

"How are you, Rebecca? Chips likes you." She asked Tovah, "May we walk with you?"

In a wry wit Lynn had noted at their first meeting Tovah replied, "She'll enjoy him more than my company, I'm sure."

"I hope you liked our group last week."

"I did." Tovah smiled at Rebecca who wanted to help with the leash. "We're slowly making friends."

"Why did you move here from New York City. It's got to be cultural shock."

"Any number of reasons," replied the young woman. "My divorce, this guardianship," she nodded toward Rebecca, "and the ability to work remote."

"But working remote can be isolating," observed Lynn, "especially if you're new to an area."

"I have family here."

Lynn was shocked. "Family?" She became flustered. "That didn't come out right. I mean, everyone has family." She frowned. "Sometimes it seems like too much family." Then she smiled. "More than you want to hear?"

Tovah laughed. "You know my family because they talk about you." Lynn sputtered. "They like you. In fact, I think they're all your friends." Now Lynn was curious. Tovah gave her a teasing wink. "Meyer Levine?" Tovah referred to an elderly gentleman who had caused problems and confusion for Sean Hennessey in the past but who had become Sean's friend. Meyer, in his usual inept way, had been responsible for getting Sean to return to River Bend several years ago to claim the wealth he had inherited from his father's lottery win. As Sean liked to point out, he owed Meyer millions of thanks.

Lynn laughed. "And Camille, his daughter and Ernie, her husband." Proving that Lynn knew the family tree. "But I've never understood why Camille is Stein and Ernie is Bromstein."

Tovah nodded. "I think much the same reason you are still Powers. Camille had been married before and wanted the same name as her children. She has two. She and Ernie have no children together. He has a son in the state department."

Lynn did understand. She stayed Lynn Powers after her marriage to Dusty because her son was still Jason Powers. "All that family makes you networked in town. You didn't move into isolation when you moved here. And you didn't come alone." She cast an eye toward Rebecca.

"I am Rebecca's guardian. Her mother died and her father travels a lot." Tovah wasn't interested in giving up more information.

Lynn would respect her reticence. "Let me know if I can help you with anything."

Tovah laughed. "Maybe help me hide from Gramps who thinks I should be his personal secretary and Aunt Camille who thinks I should be as active in the community as she is."

Lynn nodded. "Feel free to hide out in my office."

Tovah guffawed. "I've been warned about you, too. I can almost feel your tentacles pulling me into something."

Caught

Lynn didn't even blush at that characterization. She saw the younger woman as a potential Philanthropies donor and volunteer. She hung her head, reminded again that a fundraiser had no conscience, and maybe not even a soul.

* * *

Dusty had worked hard to keep the raid secret. He had needed a staging area and finally asked Will to allow the team to use his factory. It had just what Dusty needed, a large warehouse to hide the FBI cars, and plenty of floor space to organize gear, and a few offices where the agents had brought in cots for afternoon naps and a great break area so there was plenty of space for food.

Will was standing beside Dusty as the last car pulled into the warehouse. Closing the door he asked, "You still won't tell me?" He scanned the visitors. "Claire!" he gasped. He rushed over to the special agent and gave her a hug.

"The other handsome man in River Bend," she said as she returned his hug.

Looking back at Dusty, Will asked, "FBI? This is serious shit, isn't it?"

Dusty nodded. "You'll hear all about it tomorrow. Just keep an eye on my house tonight. Jason is home but I still worry about Lynn when I'm involved with this stuff." Dusty slapped him on the back. "Thanks for your help, but you gotta leave."

* * *

"Where's Dusty?" Marianna dragged a stranger into Lynn's kitchen. Lynn was just reading his text: *Won't be home for dinner. Talk later.*

She looked at her guests. "He's tied up with something and won't be here for dinner." She sized up the stranger and if she had to guess she would say he reeked of law enforcement. He was almost as tall as Dusty, as muscular as Mars, and as silent and observant as a stereotypical investigator. "I'm Lynn." She held out her hand.

"Casey."

She was right, silent, probably brooding. She looked at Marianna for an explanation.

Marianna almost hugged him as she said, "This is Casey Handel. He's my consultant for my script."

Lynn's eyes bugged out. Wow, was she wrong! "I thought you looked like one of my husband's detectives. I didn't suspect you were an entertainer."

"I'm not!" The tone of Casey's voice said a lot.

Marianna laughed. "Casey is the police consultant for my script. He's here to look over River Bend and local policing to see if it's real or something." She sounded confused because she was. Casey's arrival had been a surprise. The producers who had an option on her scripts and concept had tried to explain his assignment but had only confused her more.

"Please have a seat," Lynn urged her guests. "Can I get you anything?"

"Your father's bringing dinner." Marianna looked around the kitchen. "I guess we won't get to meet Dusty." She turned to Casey. "Why did you want to meet him anyway?"

"Because Marianna's scripts refer to Dusty and his colleagues, the producers wanted my evaluation of the local team." He accepted a soft drink from Lynn and took a sip while he seemed to absorb the atmosphere of the house. "I have a law enforcement training and consulting business. I was a detective until I took a bullet and had to take medical leave." It had been three bullets but who was counting. "In my business I have recruited other law enforcement types and we offer trainings to other professionals and consulting on process for the entertainment industry."

"Like Mars and Dusty helping others in the state with trainings." Lynn smiled as she started to understand. "Mars was doing a training in Raleigh when that assassin chased us."

Casey looked at Marianna who said, "That's my third script."

He nodded. "So that really happened? Who crawled through the tunnel?"

"Me and Grover and his dog. But she died and Grover's daughter made him move to a retirement community in Virginia."

"The dog got shot?"

"No, she died of old age. Her name was Lavender. Mars shot the assassin."

Jim walked into the kitchen. "Dinner!"

Jason bounced in from the front of the house. "Dinner?"

As Jim and Marianna put out the food, Lynn introduced Jason to Casey. She squinted at her guest. "I'm still not clear about why you're here." The family stared at him.

"I work as a consultant on some scripts and advise producers and directors on police procedures. Sometimes my staff has to come in and train actors on technique for raids, interrogations, searches." He shrugged, "Routine police work." He sipped his drink and took a plate of food that Marianna passed, helping himself. "I've been sent here to compare scripts to reality and look over the detectives modeled for the series."

"You don't believe Marianna?" challenged her husband.

"Scripts are usually make-believe," Casey reminded him. "But the producers got a vibe from the initial scripts and want to know more about the community and the detectives featured in Marianna's scripts."

"Why?"

He shrugged. "I didn't ask. My job is just to report what I find and they will use that information to answer their questions." He sampled the salad, took another piece of chicken. "But I have to say, Marianna and her friends submitted some interesting scripts."

"It's all true," she cried. "Dusty and Lynn always solve their cases." Casey raised an eyebrow at Lynn.

She dithered in her explanation. "I don't solve cases."

"No," laughed Jason, "she usually gets caught in the middle of them. Like when someone shot the senator's son."

Casey studied her. "You the one who fell through the ceiling?" Lynn nodded. He smiled, "Damn, I wondered if that was true." The smile did it. Everyone had to relate stories of Dusty's cases and Lynn's interference.

They finished up the meal with some cookies and ice cream out in the backyard. "Where is your husband tonight?" Casey asked.

Lynn replied, "I don't know. But I've been expecting a raid or something because the FBI has been around."

"FBI?" Everyone asked that question.

Lynn sighed. "I think it's a secret, but Claire came to dinner one night."

"Conti?" gasped Casey. Lynn nodded. He grabbed his phone and punched some numbers. "You in River Bend? . . . . . I'm with his wife. . . . . . Okay." Ending the call he said, "Claire's an old friend. One of her guys is picking me up." They stared at him. "And I can't tell you anything because it's a secret."

CHAPTER TWENTY-FIVE

Dusty and his unit and the FBI were ready. They had kept this raid secret from the other members of the regional drug task force. Claire had promised that she would inform them all tomorrow that she had initiated the raid and asked Dusty for help. He thought there would be hard feelings, but Claire had her mandate from federal law regarding investigations involving those working with NIH, DOJ, Medicare and Medicaid. She could always hypnotize them with the alphabet. Because neither she nor Dusty wanted to share their concerns about a leak in the task force.

Dusty was just happy that Doug was in the loop and also hiding behind a tree in the forest with the rest of the unit waiting for the last customer to leave the cabin. They had a list of those to expect tonight. After some investigation, the unit knew all the customers, prosperous folks from a three-county area who wanted the 'elixir' that Mahaffey and the nurse distributed.

There was a click in Dusty's headset. The last customer was on the move. Mars and his team would do as they had been doing all evening - halt the car and take the individual to a quiet spot to be interviewed by the FBI. The euphoria of the inoculation, Dusty was certain, would be erased by the panic of an FBI interview.

Another click. Mars had the man. A double click. Tee, watching from Hank's cabin indicated Kip and Margaret were closing things up. "Now!" came Claire's voice through the headset. The team moved.

"FBI!" came the demand, order, and identifier, as the door crashed and bodies moved into the drug cabin in a practiced, staggered wave. "Freeze!"

Dusty didn't pay attention to the rest of the shouted orders, he just got on with his part, making certain no one tried to leave through the back door. He watched from his vantage point as the FBI arrest team moved in, secured the back door, and waved him to join the fun. He didn't see it as fun. He saw it as blowing up several families, threatening the viability of a needed health clinic and ending the career and reputation of a long-time community leader.

But Doug said it best. "Damn, one of those guys goes to my church."

* * *

Lynn had been waiting for Dusty to come to bed. She knew this was the evening of the joint effort with Claire's FBI team. And she suspected that by morning it would be a gossip fest. She stayed awake because she wanted to know everything before everyone else. What was the point of being married to Dusty if she had to wait for the morning paper to hear the news? Lynn snuggled against him when he climbed into bed after taking a quick shower. "So?"

"Hmmph!"

"Dusty." By the sound of her voice he knew he had to talk or else.

"We raided that cabin near Hank's place and arrested Kip Mahaffey." He sighed into the darkness. "We got some others, too."

"Wha-a-a-t?" She sat up giving him an electric look that even in the dark of the bedroom said start at the beginning and don't leave anything out.

Dusty thought, *interrogation*. He could either answer now or . . . or else. He sighed and struggled to a sitting position, the cold headboard against his back. "A while back," he said, "we were doing that stakeout for the state guys."

"When Mars and I were helping Grover?" Lynn was referring to the incident when she and Mars were in Raleigh and ended up in a shootout with a hired assassin. More correctly Mars was in the shootout, she and Grover and his dog were crawling through a tunnel.

"Yeah, then." Dusty pulled at the blanket. "After that little episode, the regional drug task force guys came to town and suggested we set up surveillance. That's when we set up in Hank's cabin watching another cabin that we suspected was being used for drug trafficking." He cleared his throat.

"It wasn't?"

"Well, we didn't think it was, but -

"But?" Lynn was beside herself with gossip anxiety. She knew she was going to learn something good.

He rubbed his face with the hand not gripping the blanket. "We saw that Kip and that lady Margaret Eliason met up at the cabin. It seemed we had discovered his love nest, not a drug drop."

"Kip and Margaret Eliason???" Lynn was almost floating above the bed. "She's the CEO of the South End Health Clinic. How do you know it was sex not drugs?"

Dusty grinned at her. "I think we threw out the drug idea after we saw the way he greeted her when she showed up at the cabin, three nights in a row."

"How?" Lynn liked all the details.

"They lip-locked as soon as he opened the door and sometimes didn't turn out the lights or close the blinds."

"Oh." She was quiet a moment. "Did you get pictures?"

"Not that I can show you."

"Why not?"

"It's part of an investigation."

"But you said, it was sex, not drugs."

"Tonight it was drugs." Dusty slipped back under the covers. "Claire's people conducted the raid and we helped. We caught Kip and his lady and a half dozen or so of their customers."

She slid down beside him. "Anyone I know?"

"I think so. But the full list will be published tomorrow."

"Can't you tell me now?" she wheedled.

He pulled her close. "I don't want to give you wrong information. Claire's people are making the arrests." He kissed the top of her head. "Some families are going to have some major hurt in the morning."

She could tell by the sound of his voice that this raid would have painful ramifications to people in town. She kissed him back. "Poor Anita Mahaffey."

"Yeah."

They clung to one another. Dusty always hated when crime touched their friends.

* * *

In another part of town a woman was awakened from a deep sleep. "Bart, what do you mean, you've been arrested?" Audrey Decker tried to make sense of this late-night call.

"This is all your fault, bitch," he screamed into the phone. "Get me out of here!"

CHAPTER TWENTY-SIX

"Holy shit!" The young man slammed his phone down on the breakfast table and stared at his parents.

"Jonathan Teague," gasped Rachel, "that is no way to talk at the table."

"Mom, you gotta see this." Jon waved his phone in her face. Owen put down the Sunday paper intrigued. They both waited. The young man explained, "I get headlines on my phone from the River Bend Chronicle. That guy you know, Mom, that Mahaffey guy was arrested in some drug sting!"

Rachel and Owen stared at their son. Owen cleared his throat, hoping when he spoke he sounded only mildly interested. "I think we need more information than a startling headline." Rachel gripped the skillet handle while she waited for the rest of the story as Jon read, "In a well-organized effort, early Sunday morning the FBI arrested the South End Health Clinic director, Margaret Eliason and the clinic board chair, prominent local attorney, Kip Mahaffey. The FBI arrested two other members of the clinic's administrative team at their homes. Charges include drug trafficking and misuse of federal funds." Jon looked at his parents. "Don't you know this guy? I thought he was some big-shot."

As her daughter-in-law brought toast to the table, Rachel took a deep breath and lifted eggs from the skillet onto breakfast plates. "Yes, we know Kip Mahaffey."

Heather Teague handed her husband some toast as she asked, "If he's such a big-shot, why was he selling drugs? Or was he using?" She had only been Jon's wife for less than a year and River Bend politics weren't as interesting as the local news from her own home town. "Did he try to sell drugs to you?" She looked at her in-laws.

Owen sipped his coffee as he formulated a response. "Kip did a lot of high-profile community work like Rachel. We've never heard anything about this other side of his life. I guess the raid was too late to make the Sunday morning paper."

"Poor Anita," gasped Rachel. The kids looked at her for an explanation. "Kip's wife. She's a lovely woman and probably had no idea he had these other interests."

"According to the new information popping up on this website," her son reported as his finger danced long the phone screen, "he was involved with the lady arrested with him." Jon squinted at the cell screen and repeated her name. "Margaret Eliason? Do you know her?"

Rachel plopped on a chair suddenly concerned about the school-based clinic committee since Margaret was a member. "From the health clinic?" Jon nodded. "Kip was her board chairman," Rachel mumbled, stunned.

"Yeah," her son reminded her, "I already told you that." He waggled his phone to indicate the source of all knowledge.

Heather, who worked for a nonprofit in Greensboro, said, "The clinic must receive federal funds, that's why the FBI is involved."

"You're right," chimed Jon. "It says the FBI led the raid because of fund irregularities." He looked at everyone at the table. "They keep adding more information on this website. There'll be a great story in the paper tomorrow." He could hardly wait.

Owen reached across the table and squeezed Rachel's hand. She gave him a tepid smile. "I guess that will answer a lot of questions," he said. She nodded.

"What questions?" Jon liked being on the fringes of local crime.

Rachel took a deep breath. "Kip's wife had confided in me and your father that she had suspicions about her husband and other women."

"Why don't you invite her over?" Jon suggested. "Then we could get the full story."

"I think I'll phone her," said Rachel. "I'm sure she'll want to be in seclusion."

"I bet the FBI will be going through their house with a fine-toothed comb." Jon was a high school soccer coach just beginning his teaching and coaching career. "You know Heather's brother is with the Greensboro police. We hear all the procedure stuff." He gave them a knowing look. "And all the gritty stuff, too."

Caught

Heather rolled her eyes at her husband. "My brother blabs everything and my husband laps up every word. My mother says she's going to ban them from Sunday dinner."

* * *

"The Sunday paper didn't have anything," said Piper as she walked into Lynn's kitchen clutching her laptop to her chest. "But my boys get their news from some app and they told us all about that raid." She looked around the kitchen. "Where's Dusty? Why didn't he tell us?"

Lynn yawned, because her phone had started ringing at six when the River Bend Chronicle posted its first update. "He's arresting Kip in the forest."

Piper snapped, "According to this app, he did that last night. I want details." Her eyes bugged out as a light dawned. "That's why Claire was here!"

"She used my factory for her staging area," bragged Will as he walked into the kitchen followed by the three boys.

"FBI Claire?" said Jason who was trying to have a quiet breakfast as he read the River Bend Chronicle app updates on his phone.

Piper's sons grabbed cereal boxes from the pantry, bowls from the cupboard and whatever else they thought they would need for breakfast and got comfortable at the table. Will poured cups of coffee for himself and Piper. Everyone looked to Lynn.

"All I know is that Dusty told me Kip was having an affair and it wasn't with Rachel and he couldn't talk about it and I couldn't tell Piper." She wondered if she had the ingredients for a mimosa, decided orange juice and vodka worked just as well and mixed a quick morning drink. She continued, "Rachel must have suspected something because she didn't want Kip on that clinic committee."

"Remember what she did to Kip at the country club," Piper reminded her. The boys wanted an explanation so Piper related the wine spilling episode.

By evening the country club story would be all over town, expanded by the delighted witnesses from the club, and the story would evolve into a true detective tale of Rachel helping the FBI bring Kip down. Which morphed into Rachel spending years working for the FBI to trap

Kip and to close a drug ring. Gossip was like wild fire - uncontrolled. And that was the Sunday social media entertainment throughout River Bend.

Of course, Rachel and Owen only caught the social media gossip when their out-of-town children called for explanations. FBI undercover work, indeed! Owen chuckled.

Everyone was anxious to read the full story Monday morning.

* * *

Anita Mahaffey scanned caller ID - again. Everyone she had ever nodded to was calling. She knew they wanted all the gossip. She was very selective answering the phone. "Good morning, Lynn," she said as she sipped her third cup of Sunday morning coffee.

"Do you need anything?" Lynn had finally understood all the hints Dusty had been throwing her way for the last several weeks. "I'm also calling to apologize for my husband's behavior."

Anita chuckled. "Dusty only did what the taxpayers pay him to do. Kip brought this all on himself."

"Can we do anything for you?" Lynn sounded so sincere, Anita was warmed by her concern.

"Thank you. The FBI agents are searching the house. Kip is in jail and I plan to stay someplace else tonight." She knew Lynn probably had the lowdown on the raid and arrests, so she ended the call saying, "Lynn, thank you for your concern. Tell Dusty I'm not mad. I'm fine." Click.

Almost immediately the phone rang again. Caller ID said it was Rachel Teague. "Good morning, Rachel," Anita gave a resigned sigh into the phone. "Big surprise this morning!"

"Anita, what can I do for you?"

"Nothing. Since our encounter at the hospital, I have been making plans to move out and end this farce of a marriage." She chuckled and was surprised that she could. "I have a place of my own and I've been moving my things there since I left the hospital."

"So soon?" Rachel was startled at Anita's swift action.

"Not soon enough," admitted the woman. "But a year ago I bought a condo at the country club and have been remodeling. After meeting you I hired a private investigator and an attorney and started making plans to move."

"Don't give me any more information," said Rachel. "I just want to help you if you need us. I recommend that you keep your plans to yourself. You know how gossip travels around town." Rachel would be shocked later when she learned of her metamorphosis into an FBI super undercover agent!

Anita was silent a moment. "Thank you. I think that's great advice. I'm not interested in Kip finding out my plans. Thank you again for your offer. I'll call if I need help." Click.

Anita finished her coffee and made another pot. She walked into Kip's home office and offered coffee to the FBI agents going through his files. Then she went back into her kitchen to finish her interview with that FBI woman, Claire Conti.

Returning to the kitchen Anita sat and waited. Claire sipped a fresh cup of coffee then continued, "I see you have a lot of friends here in town. Are they as surprised as you?"

"Oh, yes. I suspected other women, but not drugs and a whole other life."

"Let me explain what will be happening," said Claire in her non-judgmental investigator manner. "We will be looking into Mr. Mahaffey's files here and his office. We'll be combing through your joint finances, and other properties to determine what was purchased with misappropriated federal funds and drug funds."

Anita waved a hand to halt the discussion. "Let me be of some help. Several years ago, as I became unhappy in this marriage, I asked Kip to separate our funds. There is not much that is joint anymore. I think Kip agreed because he thought with funds separated, a divorce would be easier and if no divorce, at least separate accounting kept his activities hidden from me. I have personal wealth that I inherited before our marriage. My father set up a trust for me and my sister. I own this house and pieces of furniture for which I have receipts."

Claire gave her a considering look. "You were planning on leaving?"

"I have been for a few years, but never had the courage, even though I have had suspicions of other women. A few weeks ago, I had a car accident and the time in the hospital opened my eyes." Anita had no interest in explaining the meeting with Rachel.

Clare nodded. "We'll want to see your financial records. Did your husband have his own personal wealth coming into the marriage?"

"No." Anita crossed her arms not interested in saying more.

The agent smiled. "You're still his wife, until you're not. I won't pry. You're a loyal woman and he doesn't deserve you."

"I know."

CHAPTER TWENTY-SEVEN

Special from the River Bend Chronicle:
In a well-organized effort, early Sunday morning the FBI arrested the South End Health Clinic director, Margaret Eliason and the clinic board chair, prominent local attorney, Kip Mahaffey. The FBI arrested two other members of the clinic's administrative team at their homes. Charges include drug trafficking and misuse of federal funds.

The FBI spokesperson Special Agent Claire Conti reported that a months' long investigation had been prompted by federal regulators who suspected mismanagement, illegal use of the clinic's credit cards and questionable records maintenance in the pharmacy regarding controlled substances. Agent Conti declined to explain the character of the evidence stating, "This is an ongoing investigation."

Those arrested are being held without bail per the recommendation of the federal attorney's office in Asheville.

The FBI also arrested and held for questioning customers of Eliason and Mahaffey who received unspecified drug treatments. All persons arrested are being held in the James County jail for further questioning. Release will be determined by the federal attorney in Asheville.

Vice-chairman of the clinic board stated that members had met early Sunday morning and elected Franky Kaiser as the new board chairman. Ms. Kaiser stated, "The board has accepted the resignation of the director, CFO and pharmacy director. With the help of our board and our federal partners we will continue to operate the clinic at the quality of service River Bend citizens expect."

The report in the River Bend Chronicle then listed all those arrested and the pending charges. Jasmine Fuller, reporter for the FBI story, had begged for more details but had been advised that the new monthly magazine, yet unnamed, had first right because of their staff assistance in the investigation. Jasmine called Trina. Negotiations began.

* * *

Jim was delighted that he had been vaccinated. He had really missed the breakfast crime wrap-ups in Lynn's kitchen. He had even stopped at the bakery to pick up his offering for the anticipated crowd. "Muffins and crullers," he announced waving the box as he walked in.

And the gang, plus a few strangers, cheered. Piper was at the stove with cartons indicating three dozen eggs would be sacrificed this morning. Lynn was pouring coffee. Emily Jacobs was seated beside Nathan Taft, saying, "This is my first crime breakfast." Looking as delighted as any youngster with a new toy.

Dusty walked into the kitchen and froze. "What are you doing here?" He demanded of Claire and two of her agents.

She raised her cup of coffee in salute. "Word gets around. We wanted to hear your after-crime report." He growled and accepted a cup of coffee from Lynn.

The college crowd were seated at the island with bowls of cereal and eyes on the Chronicle phone app. But the most unsettling part of the breakfast crowd were Flora Reid and her sons, zooming in from the farm. Someone had placed a laptop near the mini bar area, getting a panoramic view of the breakfast table. A tinny voice shouted, "Speak up, Dusty!" He found the source of the voice and scowled.

"Are you this grumpy every morning?" asked Claire. "Not even a good morning kiss for your lovely wife?"

"Thank you, Claire," said Lynn.

"He does behave like a bear, and all we want is a briefing," offered Will.

"Well, I can do that," said the FBI agent. "It was a success. That Mahaffey fellow and his girlfriend are under arrest in your jail. Their trial will be in federal court, all to be determined and organized by the federal attorney in Asheville. We'll be moving them to another holding facility in a few days after the bail issue is resolved."

"How's his wife?"

Lynn spoke up. "Rachel and Owen are with her. She's doing fine. Herbie is helping her sort out assets." She looked at Claire. "It seems the FBI wants to claim some of them."

"This early? Who had time to look at assets? The arrests were only two nights ago," groused Jim.

Lynn shrugged. "Apparently Claire never sleeps." The breakfast crowd scowled at the agent.

Claire smiled. "It's what we do. We move quickly to take back what was taken from the taxpayers. You'd be surprised how fast people can transfer assets electronically." The breakfast crowd started to turn hostile. She added, "We suspect he kept his drug earnings away from his household accounts. We've found some funds held jointly with that nurse. His wife wouldn't have claim to that." The information seemed to calm the crowd.

"Who else got arrested?"

Dusty finally finished his eggs and two crullers. "We're responsible for the locals because this was a joint operation. We've got eight men in jail who purchased the drug supplement the other night." He saw several mouths open as he said in a snarky manner, "Yes, you'll know all of them. Three attorneys, two from Asheville. One doc from our hospital. And four businessmen from around the area. The list is in the morning paper."

"Audrey Decker's husband was one of them," Lynn advised the group. "She's coping."

"What a tragedy," sighed Nathan. "She does such good work in this town."

"I don't think that will stop," said Lynn. "She may have to lower her profile for a time and let others in her agency be more visible." Lynn knew that would be a challenge. Donors gave to Audrey because her work was very successful. That was the risk of fundraising getting too personality driven.

Dusty eyed Claire. "Is this the official debriefing?"

"Sorry, handsome. We'll meet you at your office." She glanced at the other two agents who quickly finished breakfast. They took their plates to the sink, rinsed and stacked them, then followed Claire out the door to farewells from the breakfast crimefighters.

When the FBI left the kitchen Dusty spotted a stranger hanging back. "Who are you?"

"Casey Handel."

Dusty glared at him. "Are you FBI?" Casey shook his head. "Then who the hell are you? I saw you at the cabin last night."

Lynn heard the tone of Dusty's voice and interrupted. "Casey is a script consultant."

"You make movies? And you were at the cabin?" Dusty was clearly disgusted. "We were doing real work. What were you doing trying to learn procedure?"

"I know procedure." Casey's voice was as clipped as Dusty's. The two men seemed to face off. Those remaining in the kitchen could feel the tension and waited for a fight or something.

Marianna intervened. "Casey is here to talk about my scripts."

"But why was he at the cabin?" Dusty asked Marianna, but Casey answered.

"Claire invited me." Casey seemed to have moved across the kitchen to stand toe to toe with Dusty.

"Claire?" Dusty wasn't backing down.

Neither was Casey. "She's an old friend."

Dusty pulled out his cell and punched some numbers. "Who's this Casey guy? . . . . Yeah . . . . . Yeah . . . .Okay." He ended the call and stared at the man whose phone rang.

"Yeah? . . . . Yeah . . . Yeah . . .Okay." He looked at Dusty. "She says you're okay and we should behave."

"Yeah." Dusty put his phone back in his pocket. "You want to come to the debriefing?"

"Yeah." Without another word both men walked out the door.

Jim sat back in his chair. "What a morning! Glad to see nothing stops crime. And our breakfasts." Everyone raised a cup.

* * *

After the breakfast crowd cleared, Lynn texted Audrey Decker. *Can I help?*

Audrey replied immediately. *Yes. Come to my office.*

Caught

Lynn arrived at the Exceptional Children's office as quickly as she could. Audrey saw her drive up and met her at the door, falling into Lynn's arms and sobbing. With a warning look to the rest of the staff, Lynn walked Audrey into her office and closed the door. "I knew something was wrong," Audrey cried as Lynn settled her on the office couch and sat opposite on a visitor's chair.

"Have you spoken to your husband?"

She wiped her eyes. "Yes. He is very angry. He's blaming me, saying because you're my friend, I told the police what he was doing!"

Lynn gasped. "That's ridiculous! This was an FBI raid. They just asked Dusty for some manpower." She was not happy that Dusty had kept so much information from her during the last weeks. She could have been prepared to help Audrey . . . and the other women in town whose husbands were arrested. "How can I help?"

"He'll need an attorney. My board has called a meeting for this afternoon. I think they want an explanation. But I'm going to need this job."

Lynn immediately saw ways to help this sobbing woman. "I'd get H. Lawrence Grayson for his attorney."

"Is he already working for Kip?" Audrey knew that Mr. Grayson was a topnotch, high priced, in-demand attorney.

"No, Kip is going to need someone experienced in federal court. I think Bart will be charged and prosecuted here. That was part of Dusty's arrangement with the FBI." Lynn shrugged. "They seem to do this often, setting lines of jurisdiction. Anyway, contact Herbie. I also suggest that you invite Dusty to meet with your board to answer questions."

"Would he do that?" Audrey looked hopeful.

Lynn dug out her cell and called him. "Can you meet with Audrey Decker's board this afternoon? She doesn't want to lose her job over this." She looked at Audrey. "What time?" And repeated the answer to Dusty. She listened to his response and ended the call. "He'll be there or one of the detectives"

"Any one of them would do." Audrey smiled softly. "Mars is a generous donor. So is Danny's family. Tee has helped us when some of our clients have gotten themselves in trouble because they didn't understand laws."

Lynn stood. "As you can see, I'm ready to help. We all are. Your program is too important to suffer because of Bart's arrest. How are your children handling this?"

"They're going to stay with my parents in Brevard and finish the school year online."

Audrey gave her a perplexed look. "I was against this online learning with the virus but look how it's helping me now!" She was thoughtful for a moment. Then said, "My son commented that dad's behavior finally made sense. I was shocked that he had noticed. But it made it easier for me to send them off. They seemed to understand we would be losing our privacy."

* * *

"That was my story!" Trina screeched at her husband. Mars had never seen her so angry. "And my investigative reporter! She gave the FBI and *you*," Mars cringed at the look in her eyes and the sound of her voice, "all that evidence!"

He held the baby who was crying in terror. Brian and Holly were hugging his knees. "Please," he pleaded.

"But my investors!" she screeched.

"They only gave you money two weeks ago. They don't expect you to own this story." Mars tried to sound reasonable over the baby's squalls. "Besides they thought they invested in a monthly family magazine."

"But it was my story!" Trina was beyond upset. She was certain the baby was crying in sympathy with her plight. She had been scooped! She had given Jasmine Fuller a lot of the information for her stories. She paused and looked at her little family - Mars holding the baby and two children hiding behind him in fear and confusion. She took the baby and tried to calm him. Mars lifted the other two and carried them into the kitchen.

"I think we need a drink," he announced. Seating the kids at the table he got out milk and cookies. Pouring milk into plastic cups and placing Fig Newtons on a plate, he said, "Drink up, gang. Mommy has run out of steam." He popped a cookie in his mouth and took a gulp of milk. Trina sat at the table with the baby in her lap. "Jasmine did say that Delsey worked for the new regional magazine." The River Bend

Chronicle reporter had been delighted to reference a noted photojournalist as a resource for her story.

"Folks will be on the lookout for your first edition now." Mars was looking for any silver lining to this storm.

"But," she sobbed, "I won't have a story as big as this one. I was scooped!"

"You could do profiles on some of the characters," he suggested. "Maybe do something on drug stats for the region. The Chronicle can't cover all that in depth and keep up with daily news."

She gave his suggestions some thought. "You're right. We can at least do some follow up, maybe an interview with Delsey highlighting her travels and news awards." Mars was nodding his head and the baby was nodding off.

Things weren't as bad as they had seemed.

* * *

Anita Mahaffey marveled at all the calls she had received today. She looked around the house. Kip was in jail. It was time to move. Several callers had offered to help. She hoped they were serious because she just might need help today. Thinking through all the callers, she made a short list of those she thought sincere. Lynn, Rachel and her sweet husband, and Piper, so tiny but she had all those sons and Will's truck.

Before making the calls she walked through the house making decisions about possessions. She had her condo in the country club estates. She hadn't planned to make the move until she had more information from that private detective. She smirked, once her husband was in jail, what more evidence did she need? Completing her house tour, she called for help.

* * *

"Where's Casey?" Lynn asked as Dusty walked into the kitchen. She was almost ready to put dinner on the table. She had added a little extra effort because she expected Casey to return with Dusty.

"He went back to Charlotte to see Claire and catch a plane."

"Did you resolve your issues?" She looked at the chicken primavera pasta that she had slaved over and knew Casey would have loved it. Dusty and Jason would just eat it.

"What issues?"

"Dusty," she chided, "You almost attacked him. You didn't like him. We all saw it."

"He's okay."

She glared at him. "But why is he okay now?"

He shrugged. "He thought my unit was very professional. And he liked Uncle Chicken's jalapeño wraps."

Lynn was prepared to respond when her phone rang. She looked at Dusty and Jason, both eager for food. "Sure, Anita, we'll help." The two men looked at her. "I just told Anita Mahaffey we would help her move a few things to her new place." She lowered her voice. "I think she's leaving Kip." The men's eyes watched as she placed the bowl of pasta in the microwave to stay warm-ish.

Dusty opened his mouth to object then reconsidered. Free invited access to a felon's home? How could he say 'no'? "Sure, we can help." He tried to look sympathetic. "She's going to have some rough times ahead with Kip's trial."

"But dinner?" moaned Jason.

He got no further because Piper and her sons came into the kitchen. "I told my boys you all can eat when we finish. Will has a meeting tonight, but we have his truck." With that the movers left for their assignment.

Arriving at Anita's, Rachel waved to Lynn. "Owen and I brought our son and his wife to help," she explained. "Anita says she's only taking a few pieces."

"Is she divorcing him?" Lynn was curious. So was Piper, who sidled closer to hear the answer.

"She's starting. She said she's been planning and he just moved up her timeline." They all smirked. Kip was no longer golden in River Bend.

Anita welcomed everyone in. "This won't take long. I just have a few pieces of furniture that I told that kind FBI lady I have receipts for from my own account. And I'll take my own things." With that she pointed out the items to be moved and assigned Piper and Lynn to pack

Caught

clothing, saying, "I've been moving things out slowly so there isn't much left." Rachel and her daughter-in-law were assigned to rearrange furniture and vacuum as the select pieces were carried to the truck.

"Damn, these are heavier than they look," grumbled Dusty. He tried to do a little sleuthing but the boys wanted to get done so they could eat.

"I know what you mean." Owen stopped to wipe his face with his t-shirt. On the other hand, all the young men acted as though they were lifting clouds.

It only took an hour to get Anita's remaining possessions packed. She locked the house and led everyone to her new place. Another hour and the job was done. She turned to Bryce. "Here's some money. You take this crew to dinner on me." The hungry young people cheered and left the house. Anita turned to her friends. "Thank you. I haven't anything to offer. My cupboards are bare."

Rachel put an arm around her. "We're glad we could help." It was a solemn moment among new friends. No one missed the importance of this new alliance.

Except Piper who groaned, "They took my truck. You have to take me home." She poked Dusty. That antic broke the mood.

Rachel and Owen stayed behind as Lynn, Piper and Dusty piled into his SUV. Lynn glanced at Piper. "You did that on purpose."

Piper grinned. "They need time alone to heal all the damage Kip did."

"Hmmph." Dusty knew she was correct. He just wished he had thought of it.

CHAPTER TWENTY-EIGHT

The clouds had rolled in to create an ominous background to the hastily called press conference that was being held in front of the courthouse. Kip Mahaffey stood at the microphones and declared, "This is a witch hunt. The federal government is looking for ways to distract your attention from this virus debacle. They've picked me as the distraction. I'm better than that. I'm one of the heroes of this town, keeping the health clinic functioning for the poor, doing work for other groups to help children, the homeless and the elderly. They've targeted the wrong man!"

Jasmine Fuller of the River Bend Chronicle asked, "Sir, what about the evidence they promise to reveal?"

"Made up! Probably photoshopped pictures. We know how the media lies about good, honest people." He narrowed his eyes at Jasmine. "I'm not forgetting how your paper jumped on the bandwagon to discredit me. Mark my words, my friends and supporters will bring your newspaper to its knees."

After several more questions that Kip interpreted as assaults on his character, claiming they had no substance, he said, "I have posted bail and will be staying active in this community finishing the many projects I have started for the young and the elderly - improving their quality of life." He gave a sweeping gesture out to the cameras. "All of you might as well go home. Kip Mahaffey has a lot of work to do taking care of his community. The real story is my commitment to my friends and neighbors. My next venture - running for mayor. My life is community service!"

With that statement he walked off the dais followed by his attorney and a hired bodyguard. Walking across the courthouse parking lot he swore, took a swing at a hapless photographer who got too close and left the bodyguard to deal with the rest as he returned to his law offices.

Caught

His attorney stepped into his private office on their return. "You did a good job out there, old buddy, but we're going to need proof of your innocence and proof that this is a frame."

"I'm working on it," snarled Kip.

"And you've got to keep a low profile here in town. If you're out and about, you become fair game for reporters and anyone else who is watching you." He checked his watch, this discussion was billable. "I understand your wife has her own investigation going."

Kip snorted. "It'll amount to nothing. She'll realize I give her status in this town and call it off."

The attorney said, "That's not what I hear."

"Trust me. She doesn't have the friends in town that I do. She's a fat, sad woman. I'm golden in River Bend."

Not what I hear, thought the attorney. "I've got to get back to Asheville," the man replied. "I've given you my advice." He gave Kip a short salute and closed the door.

Finally alone in his office Kip reviewed his calendar. He was certain he could beat this. He thought he could set Margaret Eliason up to take the brunt of the charges. He began to fashion his defense alleging that she, as the knowledgeable healthcare professional, had misled him, had suggested that the services at the cabin were a stream of revenue for folks reluctant to receive services in a clinic that catered to the poor. Chuckling to himself, he jotted notes, reviewed his datebook and added notes and innuendo to past calendar dates with what he hoped would be interpreted as definitive evidence of her misconduct.

Kip sat back and stared at the ceiling. He was confident that he could blame Margaret but he needed positive support, too. He needed someone like . . . No, not like, he needed Rachel Teague. He had sensed that she had been ready to melt in his arms a few weeks ago. And she hadn't been involved with the FBI raid. He'd give her his side of the story and dazzle her with his charm. He might even have to sway her with his sexual prowess. He chuckled to himself. Why not? Margaret was out of the picture. He would need someone new. He began to plot Rachel's seduction.

* * *

Audrey Decker called Lynn. "Thank you so much for your help." She had spent several days working for her husband's release from jail. Bart out on bail with a trial date scheduled in a few months.

"Was Herbie able to help?"

Audrey chuckled. "He's so stiff and serious I can't believe you call him 'Herbie.' But yes, he was very helpful. Bart is out on bail. He may have lost his job." There was a sniff. "But I'm still employed. Dusty was very helpful when he met with my board. Thank you for that, too."

They talked for a few more minutes and ended the call. Lynn stared out the window of her office. Audrey and her family would face a lot of challenges over the next year. It would be difficult keeping the children isolated from the fallout.

"Hey, boss," Rory called interrupting her reverie, "Did you talk with Audrey?"

"I did."

"Can we do anything?"

"I can't because it's one of Dusty's investigations," sighed Lynn, "but you can help her."

He blushed. "She stayed with me for a few nights after she settled her kids at her mother's." He looked angry. "Then that fool made bail and he wants her home."

"Is she safe?"

"Yeah, she's his meal ticket since he lost his job."

"Just keep an eye on her."

* * *

After sending his Asheville attorney on his way, then plotting Margaret's downfall and Rachel's seduction, Kip began to organize his money. Many years ago he had reconnected with an old law school friend - CJ Kirtley. CJ had gotten himself married to a Templeton of the very rich Templeton family of Raleigh. CJ had figured out how to redirect money from the Templeton Foundation into his own pockets and had helped Kip do the same thing with his estate clients' funds. Over the years the men had, along with a few others, created fake nonprofits to accept funds - opening and closing the nonprofits as needed, always having an innocent sounding agency with appropriate tax ID ready to channel funds to a partner's secret account using benign account identifiers such as consultant or cleaning service.

The money had added up. In addition, Kip and CJ had worked a few side deals of their own. It turned out to be fortunate that they had maintained a funding stream away from the designers of the original scheme. A few years ago the real brains behind the scam, Stanwood Garson, had been blown apart in midair as he flew his private plane someplace. Kip suspected murder. CJ had agreed but said it wasn't related to them. Then one of the partners, Cory Estridge and another, Rupert Rothman had died - well, Rothman had engineered Cory's death then died himself trying to escape capture here in River Bend. Three mysterious deaths that Kip tried to ignore. He hadn't known them anyway. But CJ had scrambled to secure their funds, promising Kip that all the money was safe and it was business as usual.

The River Bend connection did give Kip pause, though, but CJ reassured him that it was only a geographical coincidence. Rothman was going to kill Estridge someplace. And the local police would have caught him, no matter where the killing had occurred. CJ had chuckled and said, "A good thing you weren't at the Senator's fundraiser. One of our partners might have killed you." Kip agreed that was something on the plus side.

It all meant that Kip had access to his own secret stash of funds. CJ had even hinted that over time they might grab Rothman's accounts once the heat was off. But that was a discussion for another day and a nice cushion if he needed more funds. Today Kip just wanted to start the process of migrating some of his own off-shore funds back into the country through some fake nonprofit. It was a process which CJ managed while skimming a percentage for his trouble. He would then deposit money in legitimate accounts giving Kip access to funds to pay attorney fees and to live a quiet life out on bail until Mahaffey figured out his future.

"This bank is OK?" Kip had asked CJ years ago.

"Yeah," came the reply. "We created this online bank just for partners. Remember we each put some money in and the bank has been operating under all the banking rules that apply." At that point CJ had chuckled. "We even have unrelated clients who like our interest rates and our disinterest in who they are."

Today Kip opened the laptop that he kept in the ceiling tiles in a storeroom at the office. Its case was covered in dust and hadn't been found by the FBI as they searched the office and his files. He grinned at the screen as the banking icon popped up. With a few strokes, he moved funds to CJ's fake nonprofit, watched as CJ skimmed five percent for the service and then deposited the rest in the innocuous online bank. Done!

Kip had funds. He started to plan his next steps as he packed up his things and headed home.

* * *

When Kip pulled up to the house, it was dark. He clicked the garage door and it rose slowly. No lights and no sign of Anita's car. Good, he thought, I don't have to face her. Walking into the kitchen and flipping on a light, he noted the disarray. Drawers slightly open, cupboards not really closed. Walking further into the house he noted gaps. There seemed to be pieces missing. Not possible! Anita hadn't had time to move out. Maybe she has rearranged the furniture. He stopped. How could she move anything? Some of those pieces of furniture were really heavy because as much as he hated the pieces, he had used them. Stepping into the dining room he noted that the antique credenza was gone or moved. In the living room the bird's eye maple secretary was gone along with the Chinoiserie cabinet. He raced upstairs. The writing desk was gone and the small armoire in the guest room - gone. Two old humpback trunks and one small trunk, also gone.

He checked Anita's closets. Her clothes were gone, all her dresser drawers were empty. Where was she? Where were his files? He raced back downstairs and out the front door, hoping to find a hint, a footprint, something that pointed in her direction. He tripped over the real estate sign. She had put the house on the market! He poked her number on his phone. "What have you done, bitch?"

"Nice to hear from you, too, Kip. I moved my things into my new place. I guess you found the sign. You know how real estate moves these days. I'd get your stuff out soon."

"I want the furniture you took. I let you have title to the house, but the furniture is joint property."

Caught

"I only took the old pieces that you didn't like. The ones you called my fake antiques. They have charm. I want them."

"I want them back. I want mediation for the joint property."

If he had seen Anita, Kip would have known he aroused suspicion. But her phone voice gave nothing away. "That's fine. Can we meet tomorrow afternoon and agree on a split?"

He calmed down at her willingness to discuss the property split. "Fine. Where are you? I'll come over."

"I'm tired Kip. I'll meet you at your office tomorrow about one. Does that work?"

"Yeah, sure."

Kip fell on the living room sofa and blew out his breath. Tomorrow couldn't come soon enough.

CHAPTER TWENTY-NINE

Several women were sitting in the Philanthropies conference room when Lynn returned from lunch. She looked at Nelda who shrugged, "They just came in and got comfortable."

"I called this meeting," began Judge Dunn "to talk about a candidate for Mayor of River Bend. Kip doesn't stand a chance. We need to nominate someone who will do a better job than he would do."

"Who?" asked Piper as she pulled her cup of tea from the microwave.

"We can't talk like this in my office," complained Lynn who had come in to chase them all out, "we're a non-profit. We can't get political." She pulled the drapes closed then shut the door. Why did all the women in town think this was the place to do political plotting? Lynn remembered a few years ago when they all met in the conference room to plan Bev's political career as a county commissioner. She looked around the room. Some old faces, Emily and Sophie. Some new faces, the next generation of women community leaders - Penny, Michelle and Trina. Who was the mastermind behind this backroom group? She suspected Judge Dunn, but Bev, in a corner scanning her phone, was a close second.

"Who are we thinking about?" asked Amelia as she barged in on the closed meeting. "I'm here to write a check." They all stared at her. "Zachary told me a few days ago that he was sorry he ever encouraged Kip to run and then he said if someone else threw their hat in, we should help that campaign along." She looked around the table. "Who do I write the check to?"

"Not me," said Michelle, "starting this magazine is enough work."

"Count me out, too," said Judge Dunn, "I've got my re-election campaign for district court already organized."

Caught

With that statement they all turned to look at Rachel who was busy texting on her phone. When the room got quiet she looked up, "What? Did I miss something?"

"We just nominated you to run against Kip for mayor," announced Piper.

"No," she said in a disbelieving whisper. "I couldn't beat him."

"Yes, you could." They all turned to watch Anita Mahaffey walk through the door. She smiled, "I hope you're not sorry that you didn't lock it." She glanced back at the door she had just closed.

"What are you doing here?"

"I want to help. It seems that infusing your life with honesty does wonders for your health. My therapist says I was turning all my anger and hostility into physical problems." Anita filled a cup with water and heated it in the microwave. "That's when I fired the therapist and hired a private investigator. Life looks better. So, what's our plan? Are we taking down that bastard?"

"I have to talk with my husband," said Rachel, "I can't blindside him with this new venture."

"That's definitely not a *no*," grinned Michelle. "You are giving it serious thought?"

"I am," admitted Rachel. "I can do the job. I have a great statewide political network. I can make certain our issues get some attention. Besides I received a call from Lowell this morning suggesting the same thing. He said the party is disgusted with Kip and he was sent to talk with me."

"Do you have time to file?" asked Trina. "I'm not familiar with North Carolina elections."

"It's a municipal election and filing will occur next month. If there's to be a primary it'll be in September or October," said Penny, the lawyer.

"Kip's dropping out?" They marveled at the political machinations.

"I think that's the plan," nodded Judge Dunn, "whether he wants to or not."

"It has happened," announced Anita. "Lowell brought a delegation over to Kip's office. I was there because Kip had called me yesterday when he got out of jail. He isn't happy and he's blaming me and that Margaret woman for everything." Anita plunked a tea bag into her hot water. "My divorce attorneys will set him straight. It seems Jim - -"

"Dad?" gasped Lynn.

". .and H. Lawrence - -"

"Herbie?" asked Michelle.

". . . told Kip that they were withdrawing their support of his candidacy in favor of someone else."

"Who?" cried the group of women.

"Rachel." Anita smiled as she danced her tea bag in the cup.

The gang cheered.

Lynn scanned the room. Was there someone in the room who looked, well, looked not surprised, or looked smug, or, . . . ? And there she was, Sophie Grayson, quiet and smug! She hadn't offered any comment this afternoon, but Lynn was certain she had called everyone together or at least made suggestions to get everyone in the room. Hmm, thought Lynn, this is how old boy politics works - and Sophie can 'old boy' with the best of them. She smiled, made certain the conference room door was closed, then joined the celebration for Rachel's upcoming candidacy.

* * *

Rachel was sitting in the Philanthropies conference room stunned by the outpouring of support when her phone pinged with a text message: *Out of jail. Need your love and support.*

After glancing at the message and the sender, she cleared her throat. Everyone looked at her and waited. "Are you all sure about your information?" She waggled the phone in her hand. "Kip has just texted that he's out of jail and needs my," she squinted at the small screen, "my love and support."

Anita guffawed. "He can't turn to anyone else. He's going to try to make your imaginary affair a reality." She had finally caught on to his games.

"How did he get out of jail?" demanded Piper. Everyone scowled at Judge Dunn.

"It wasn't me. It was the judge in Asheville."

Anita scoffed at Piper. "Where have you been? He got out yesterday."

Penny, an attorney, cleared her throat. "The federal court can only hold him for so long, just like all courts. He isn't a danger. He may be a flight risk, but I doubt anyone is worried about that. He made bail." It was obvious to her, but the other women in the room were dismayed.

"Are Anita and Rachel safe?"

Anita chuckled. "I'm the last person he wants to see. He has his own resources for bail. In the last few years I have managed to separate my assets from his. In fact I don't think there's much we have joint any more. Kip isn't aware of the financial changes I've initiated." She looked at the women around the room. "That's probably more than you need to know. But I'm financially ok." She blushed. "I have family money. Kip has overspent for years and I've covered him with my funds. A year ago I bought a small condo. The house is also in my name and I put it on the market yesterday."

Rachel walked over and took her hand. "You are one tough lady. I'm sorry for all the grief I've caused you."

"You were as much a victim as me." Anita hugged her.

Rachel got a gleam in her eye. "What if I answered his text and set up a meeting place?"

"I don't want you to meet him alone," said Judge Dunn. "It could be part of his plan to muddy the waters of his charges by implicating you." Everyone gasped. She continued, "Meet him at the park. Emily can call some of her friends for an impromptu park gathering."

"Done," said Emily as she pulled out her phone.

At this point, Piper, the general, took over. "Rachel, tell him one hour in the park."

"What do we do at the park?" Emily asked. "My mahjong group is ready."

The general thought a moment. "Get there before Rachel. When Kip arrives don't let him take her out of your sight. If he does, you know, act like someone fell and needs help, or a heart attack. Nothing real serious, just time consuming."

Judge Dunn laughed. "Piper, I'm impressed." Chairs scraped and women scattered.

* * *

Kip was delighted to get a reply from Rachel. He checked his watch. He knew the FBI had searched his office. He shook his head and smirked.

They wouldn't find his important files. They were in a safe place. He thought about the day years ago when he started hiding files inside Anita's shitty antiques. Heirlooms he scoffed. Pieces of junk. But those pieces had deep drawers and locks. She had always said she couldn't open them but she loved the old wood and intricate carvings and finishes on many of the pieces. He learned to open the drawers and doors, always carrying the keys with him.

Searching through the office files he noted that not much had been taken by the FBI. He called together his young staffers and distributed his current billable work. "Keep these going." He winked. "I may need funds to pay my attorney. We need billable hours." Checking the time he concluded his instructions, "Keep the office running. I'll be available to consult but our clients might want me to keep my distance." They nodded and he was out the door.

Because his office was close to the park and knowing that the media was waiting in front, Kip walked out the back door and along the greenway to meet Rachel. Of course, he was dressed in jeans and an old polo-shirt, not his usual debonaire style, sort of his 'I'm out on bail' disguise. He spotted Rachel on a bench near one of the picnic shelters where a group of elderly women were engrossed in some activity. "Hey, sweetheart," he greeted Rachel. She turned and smiled. "That smile is just what I needed. I can't believe the mess that woman got me into." He flopped on the bench beside her stretching his arm across her shoulders and giving her a kiss on the cheek.

"Margaret Eliason?"

"The very one." He moved closer pulling her snug. "She had me believing that those people coming for drugs were patients who wanted to support the clinic but didn't want to be seen getting services in South End." He sat forward looking back at her. "I can't believe how stupid I was. I thought I was helping the clinic, helping folks get the medical care they need." He flopped back and had his arm across her shoulders again.

Rachel said nothing. She smiled again as the ladies in the shelter cackled over something.

He asked, "Can we go someplace more private? I need your help and support and maybe some special attention." He squeezed her shoulder. "I know we've behaved all these years but I've always felt something for you. And now I'm so lost and alone I feel I have to give in to that Rachel magic." He kissed her cheek and nibbled her ear. "What do you say?" He stood and tried to pull her to her feet.

There was a scream from the shelter. Emily Jacobs waved toward their bench. "Rachel, is that you? We need help. Glenda just fell. We don't know what it is. Camille is calling 9-1-1." Since Kip was holding her hand, Rachel dragged him to the shelter. Pulled along, Kip couldn't resist and fade into the shrubbery.

Emily grabbed him saying, "Help us, young fellow. Why, Kip, is that you? I thought you were in jail." She called to her friends. "Girls, look who's here. Kip, why aren't you in jail?"

The sirens signaled the arrival of the ambulance. Soon two EMTs were scrambling into the shelter. Rachel was giving all of her attention to the fallen woman. Emily hung on to Kip. "I'm so glad you're here," she mumbled. "I think I need a strong arm." And she slumped into him her eyes fluttering.

A lady who seemed to be watching Emily, screamed drawing the attention of the EMTs away from the woman on the ground and to the woman sagging in Kip's arms. They rushed to Emily as Glenda appeared to have recovered and was checking her phone. An odd activity, thought Kip as he held Emily while the EMT checked her vitals.

Rachel helped Glenda to her feet and led her from the shelter to the parking lot. Kip could only watch as his last hope helped an older woman into her car and drove away. The EMTs helped Emily to a bench but she continued to hang on Kip's arm. "Ms. Jacobs," he said, "I have to get back to my office. I don't have my car here or I would take you home."

She patted his arm and hoped she looked tired and at least one hundred years old. "Thank you, Kip. I guess you're not as evil as everyone says." She patted him again. "Camille brought me. She'll see me home."

With that release Kip dashed from the picnic shelter and quickly blended into the secluded greenway finding his way back to his office. He'd stay there until dark then go home trying to wait out the media at the house. He was disgusted. Nothing got done today. The political delegation, his fair-weather friends, interrupted his furniture discussion with Anita, demanding that he abort his political career. Then some old bags stopped his meeting with Rachel. He needed this evening at home to get ready for a rescheduled confrontation with Anita and to plan his approach to Rachel tomorrow. She looked ready to help him with anything he asked. He smirked to himself, tomorrow would be her seduction day. Golden Kip was coming back.

* * *

When Owen walked into the kitchen he was already pulling his tie from around his neck. He stopped when he saw Rachel sitting at the kitchen table with a glass of wine in front of her and an empty glass at his chair. "Are we having another talk?" he asked.

"Yes."

He sighed from the bottom of his toes and sat down accepting the glass after she poured some wine. "What is it now? Are you going to Siberia, or Tahiti, leaving in two days?"

"No. I've been asked to replace Kip on the ballot and run for Mayor of River Bend." She swirled the wine in her glass.

"Do you want to?" he asked.

"Yes."

"Then what's to talk about?" He stared at his glass.

"I don't want to take this on if you object," she replied.

He raised his eyes to her in surprise. "You wouldn't run if I objected?"

She nodded.

"You never asked my counsel before." He was puzzled.

"This will take over our life," she said, "and it pays a salary. You've always attached more importance to paying jobs."

"How will it take over our lives?" He was confused.

"It'll mostly take over mine, but you would be able to accompany me to dinners and out of town conferences." She teased, "You can be my arm candy."

His face lit up with a warm smile of his own at the interpretation of her comment. "I guess that's better than sleeping alone."

Rachel didn't know what to reply to his misunderstanding, but she thought they had reached a settlement, she could become a political figure, if she returned to his bed. There was no mention of any return to love making. She'd probably be too busy to notice anyway.

Caught

* * *

Another night of iPad cooking, thought Dusty as he walked into the kitchen. Lynn was bouncing around chopping zucchini. He winced as he watched her knife fly, waiting for a fingertip to bounce across the room. He didn't want to distract her because he feared such a disaster. So he pulled a beer out of the drink refrigerator and sat to enjoy the iPad inspired cooking show. The next scene showed some eager hands chopping onions; followed by the same hands skinning salmon. He closed his eyes, anticipating a sliced hand. Squinting he checked out the countertop. No blood.

Lynn stopped the tiny movie on her iPad and rushed around digging out a skillet and a small pot. She looked at him. "Almost forgot the rice." She got the water boiling as she gathered more items for the skillet. "This is salmon in a creamy tomato sauce." She ran to the refrigerator for something, grabbed some spice out of the cupboard, looked around for measuring spoons. "They were just here!" At last she was back at the stove adding rice to the boiling water to allow it to do what rice did in all that water. The skillet heated up graced with some olive oil. Dusty knew it was olive oil because of the fancy label on the bottle. One beer finished.

Lynn stared at the iPad and listened intently. She began tossing salmon around in the skillet. Soon it was browned or seared or something and she removed it from the skillet. Somehow she dropped a piece of salmon on the floor trying to transfer it from the skillet to the plate. "Just pick it up," drawled Dusty, "and put it back on the plate." She did a quick wrist flip and the salmon left the spatula and nested with the other pieces. The dog came over and licked the floor.

She returned to the empty skillet and tossed in the chopped vegetables along with everything else in the recipe, including some wine. Of course, adding wine to a recipe meant pouring a glass for the chef. She relaxed against the counter, sipping wine and stirring the vegetables. With half her drink gone, she took the next step - returning the salmon to the skillet. She nested the pieces among the vegetables and sipped her wine in triumph. She checked the pot on the back burner. The rice was ready.

Soon Lynn said, "Put out the plates." Dusty set the table for the meal placing a trivet for the skillet because he knew she wouldn't transfer the food from the skillet to a serving dish. As she always said, "It's only one more thing to clean." He did note that she put the rice into a serving dish.

She seemed to be getting to the finish line when the video chef said, "And sprinkle some fresh basil on top." She gasped and ran out to her garden with a scissors. She ran back in and snipped the basil leaves into strips and scattered the pieces on top of the salmon dinner.

"You didn't wash the basil," remarked Dusty.

"What does it matter?" she asked as she set food on the table. "The salmon came from the floor."

"Tough day?"

"You're lucky this salmon isn't raw." She went on to tell about the meeting in her office. "It was political! Don't they know the Philanthropies is a nonprofit and doesn't do politics?" She forked in some salmon and licked her lips. Another tasty recipe. "Rachel is running for mayor. And we're all worried about Anita because you let Kip out of jail."

"I didn't let Kip out of jail. He made bail." He dragged a piece of zucchini through the tomato-cream cheese sauce. "Besides we helped her move to her new place." He winced at his sore muscles from lifting that heavy furniture.

"She was at our secret meeting, too." She gave Dusty a squinty-eyed look. "She didn't expect you to let Kip out of jail, either."

"I didn't let him out of jail, the federal judge did."

"Yes, dear."

CHAPTER THIRTY

Because of the impromptu political meeting at Kip's office in the afternoon, Kip and Anita had not talked about his claim on her furniture. "I told you yesterday," shouted Kip as Anita pulled the phone away from her ear. "I want my share of the things you took from the house."

"Kip, I told you yesterday that the FBI only allowed me to take things that I could prove I paid for from my own funds." She took a deep breath. "I came to your office today to explain that to you and show you the receipts they approved. And I thought we agreed to reschedule."

Kip was beside himself. He needed the files that were hidden in that furniture. On the other hand, if the FBI had passed on searching the furniture, maybe having everything stay at Anita's was a smart idea. The files had to be destroyed. But he might not be under the pressure he had first imagined. He took a deep breath and softened his voice. "I'm sorry for shouting," he said in a modulated tone. "I've been under a lot of pressure. Do you think you could let us talk this over next week?"

"That sounds fine," she replied. "Call me next week." She didn't want to say anything else. She just wanted the conversation to end. However, when they met next week, she would have witnesses join them.

Anita ended the call with Kip and ambled into her new kitchen in her new home to brew a cup of tea. It had taken two years to finally find just the right spot. She loved the place. It was one of the condos in the country club estates, a gated community. After finding the place, she had had extensive work done. That took another year of manipulating funds to hide her expenses while making her usual donation to the joint checking account to cover Kip's spending, as he said, 'to keep up our image.' Kip always reviewed her trust fund reports. But the remodel was done, and just in time. The sale of the old house would be added to her cash account which, based on advice from her attorneys, she had set up out of Kip's access and control. She smiled to herself. Once she realized what a cad she had married, Anita had started her exit strategy. It had taken a few years to get her life and finances separated from his. Tonight she was rid of him and finally ready to live a stress-free, Kip free, comfortable life.

She sipped her tea and wandered about her new place. The antiques fit just as she had envisioned. She stopped in front of the small armoire and studied the doors. Why was Kip so interested in the furniture he had loathed all these years? She stared and she thought. She finally jiggled the doors. They seemed to be locked securely. Trotting back to the kitchen, she collected a few tools that she thought would work on the lock. Pick, jiggle, pull, scratch, pick and pick again. Finally the lock sprung and released the doors. Files tumbled to her feet.

Anita picked up one file and paged through. It was an estate. She recognized the name as a person who had died about five years ago. The file seemed to suggest that Kip had been the beneficiary of the estate. Really? Her mind reeled. Had he been robbing his clients? Is that how he made his money? Is that the money he placed in the joint account? She had spent money and paid bills from those funds. Had she been spending stolen money? Was she liable for his crimes?

In full panic mode, hyperventilating with guilt and confusion, she called a friend. "Lynn? This is Anita and I need your husband."

* * *

"What does she want?" Dusty asked as he drove up to the security gates at the country club estates. He turned to the security guard, "How you doing, Jake? We're coming in to visit Ms. Mahaffey."

"Let me check," said Jake. "I have a note that she wants no visitors." He called, spoke, nodded and hung up the phone. "She's waiting for you. You know where to go?" Dusty nodded as the gate opened.

"Maybe Kip got in and she's a hostage or something," offered Lynn.

"After the way you and your friends ransacked his house helping her move, you might be right."

"You were there," said Lynn with a smirk. "You thought you would find some clues or something."

He grinned at her. "You can't blame a guy for hoping." They pulled in front of the row of townhouses and Anita waved from her porch.

Once she had her guests inside, she burst into tears. "I'm a felon. I'll be arrested."

Lynn hugged her. "Tell us what's wrong, Anita. It can't be that bad."

"Yes, it can." She pulled Lynn into the small study and pointed to the files strewn across the floor. "I opened the doors and that all came out. He stole from estates. I spent the money. I'm going to jail." She sobbed. "I thought I was finished with that bum."

Dusty was down on his knees scanning the files and mumbling to himself. He pulled out his phone. "Mars, I need you at Anita Mahaffey's new place. . . . just you . . . .bring your laptop. I'll call Doug, too." He stood and explained, "Mars is coming over. He can make sense of this." He made a second call. It was to the interim sheriff. After a brief explanation to Doug, he asked, "Do you mind if I call the FBI?"

Anita shook her head but asked, "Do I need to call my lawyer?"

"Who is your lawyer?"

"Mr. Grayson handled the closing on this property. He's helped me with some other things over the years. He and Mr. Hoefler are working on my divorce."

Dusty scrolled through his contacts again. "I need you at Anita Mahaffey's new place. . . . . yeah, the place she bought. . . . .NOW!" He pocketed his phone and smiled at Anita. "Why don't you make some coffee or something for everyone dropping by? I'll tell the gate guard."

Lynn and Anita went to the kitchen and started a pot of coffee. Anita found some cookies and put them on a plate. Dusty stayed by the files, whispering into his phone. The two women sat at the table waiting for the second act. Lynn asked, "Why did you open the armoire? Did we break something when we moved it?"

Anita shook her head. "Kip called this evening really angry saying I took things that were his when I moved. I told him I had only taken furniture that I knew he didn't like. He said he considered it joint property and wanted to have a discussion about who got what. When he hung up I started thinking about how strange he was acting and stared at the lock and then decided to open it. And all those files fell out."

"Are there other pieces he didn't like that you moved?" She nodded.

Lynn dashed to the study to say something to Dusty just as the doorbell rang. He let Mars and Doug in as Lynn said, "Dusty, Anita says there are more pieces of furniture with locks."

"Let's wait for Herbie to get here."

Herbie walked in behind Doug, growling. "Where's my client? Are you harassing her?"

Doug turned to greet the attorney. "I don't know why you put on that act." He shook the man's hand. Last year Doug's son had shot Connie's ex-husband, just before Connie and Doug married. H. Lawrence Grayson, in all his pompousness, had worked with Doug, Toby and Child Protective Services, winning an outcome favorable to Doug and his son.

"Oh, the new sheriff," snarled Herbie with a twinkle in his eye, "Here to use a rubber hose or something?"

"Whenever we can get away with it," said Doug. "But I have to talk with the detectives first." They separated, Herbie to the kitchen to see Anita and Doug to the files Dusty had sorted.

"You didn't have to come," Dusty said to his friend. "I just called to keep you informed."

"I appreciate it," replied Doug, "but I'm curious about your findings." Dusty handed him a file. As Doug scanned it his eyebrow almost met his hairline. "Damn, that guy was a real scumbag."

"Claire said she'd have some agents here in the morning. The SBI and the state AG are also interested."

"How many more people will be involved?"

Dusty shrugged. "We're just starting.

* * *

After Bart Decker's release for misdemeanor drug charges, Audrey Decker did a lot of thinking about their marriage and their future. On the one hand, he had lost his job and he would need financial support through her salary and their savings until he found another job. On the other hand, she found it more and more difficult to stay in the same house with him. Neither of them had any other place to go. He couldn't leave town for several months as a condition of his release. She had a job that must now support the family. Their budget had no room for divorce attorney expenses or alternate living costs, in addition to the usual mortgage payments, car payments, and credit card payments.

She had come to Rory's place to think. Staring out the window she found no solution, only more problems. Children, money, a broken marriage. She heard Rory's car come into the yard. Soon he was in the house. "Hey, sweetie," he called. "I saw your car. Life too much?"

She ran into his arms. "You have no idea." She clung to him as he walked them to the sofa.

"Tell me all," he encouraged. And she did.

Concluding with, "I don't know what to do now. He's so strange. He knows about James. I've told him it's over. He implied several weeks ago that he would let my affair slide if I ignored his activities. I thought he meant another woman, but now I know he meant drugs. The attorney's fee took a bite out of our savings. I don't know what to tell the kids. My parents want me to leave him. But we can't afford to divorce with more attorney fees, and he doesn't have a job."

Throughout the confession Rory had made soothing sounds. When he thought she was finished he said, "Maybe once summer starts and you bring the kids back home, getting back to a normal life may be what you and Bart need. He might need family around him. And seeing you working hard for all of you, should assure him of your commitment to your marriage." Silently, Rory thought Bart was a creep and hoped he would do something to provoke Audrey to end the marriage.

"My parents are going on a trip in a few weeks. I was thinking thoughts similar to you. Try to get our family situation back to normal. Bart can help with the kids while I work. The folks will get back by early July. If things haven't worked out by then, I may have to find other solutions." She gave him a sad smile. "He might even have a job by then and we can go from there." It sounded like a fantasy.

Rory hugged her tight. "You're always welcome here. I don't have extra space for the kids but we could manage for a bit."

Audrey tweaked his nose and kissed his cheek. "What would I do without you, my friend?"

* * *

It was time to leave town. Delsey Ledges had received a potential assignment offer from CNN. She had to be in Atlanta in the morning to be briefed. And as the producer had pointed out, "Decline if it sounds too risky." Delsey wouldn't decline anything. She used her camera to point out the wrongs in the world. Sometimes viewers cared and responded with demands for action or donations for those featured.

But tonight she wanted to give a special good-by to Mutt. He had turned out to be a surprise, a young man with courage and kindness. She had watched him treat his patients, interact with his friends and with his mother. He was a man of quality.

"Where's Franky?" Mutt stepped back as Delsey entered his house and shut the door.

"She's at her church tonight. We already said good-by."

As he reached for the door planning to leave with the reporter for a promised farewell celebration, he finally noticed a different Delsey. She smiled. He looked again. The piercings were gone. "You look different." He put his hand on the door to open it. She stopped him. "I thought we were going to celebrate." He was confused.

"We are." She placed her arms around his neck and pulled him in for a kiss. "I thought we should take time for a private good-by." Breaking the kiss she said, "I know your mother is working tonight."

"She . . .ah . . . we . . .ah, can't." Mutt was a small-town fellow with very limited sexual experience. Mostly he stayed away from women because his mother had threatened him with all sorts of punishment should he get a young woman pregnant. He swallowed. Delsey pushed closer, pinning him to the wall.

"I . . .ah . . . I don't . . .I . . ." he babbled.

She moved as close as she could. "I can feel that you do." His erection was rigid. "In fact, I think we should take advantage of your interest." She kissed him. "I think we should enjoy saying good-by." She could see that he was both confused and aroused. "Let's find us a bed." She stepped away and pulled him through the small house into his bedroom. Each time he demurred she kissed and caressed. She removed her clothing and his. "That's a mighty eager fellow you got there." She scanned his naked body with appreciation.

After some coaxing and some quiet direction Delsey finally got Mutt with the program. "Ah . . . .ah?" he gasped. "Condom."

"I take care of my own protection," she whispered as she nibbled his neck. She pressed closer. "This is just my way of saying thank you. You

Caught

risked a lot. You're a hero, helping get the clinic in order, bringing down those crooks." She had him dazed and ready. With a little more encouragement, he finally did all she expected of a healthy, eager twenty-one-year-old male.

As they rested quietly in the aftermath of passion, she asked, "Your first time?"

"Could you tell?" He was embarrassed.

She rolled onto her side and looked at him, brushing her fingers along his cheek. "I thought it was everything it should be." She rolled on top of him. "But let me show you some other options." And she did. It was a night Mutt wouldn't forget.

But it wasn't to be all night. After catching their breath for, was it the second or third time? She said, "Gotta go."

"Wha. . .?"

"You're cute when you're confused." She kissed his cheek and slipped out of bed. He pulled up the sheets as she pulled on her clothes. "I gotta get to Atlanta. I should be there in about four hours. Catch some sleep and be at CNN by nine."

"You have a new assignment?"

"I hope. They want to talk about it first." She pulled on her shirt, slipped on her shoes and glanced around the room. "I got everything. I'll text you when to watch for the story." She tweaked his nose and was gone. He heard the front door close and a car pull away.

So that was sex, he thought. He had promised his mother years ago to be responsible. Between being worried about responsible sex and studying and working, he'd never had time to experiment with sex. Tonight he had learned and he suspected that Delsey had a lot of experience. He'd never see her again, but he would always remember her.

* * *

It was an easy drive to Atlanta on a dark night. The roads were empty. Delsey thought about the young man she had selected as the father of her child. She hoped her plan worked and that she would soon be pregnant. Her partner, Constance, Con for short, was an Atlanta based producer for CNN. They had a plan. Con would be the stay-in-town parent. The baby would be looked after and Delsey could still travel for assignments. Win-win. She hoped she was pregnant. Mutt was a good man.

CHAPTER THIRTY-ONE

Dusty and Claire sat in Anita's kitchen sipping coffee and making notes. The team of FBI agents had appeared with coffee and egg and bacon muffins at Dusty's about seven this morning. With a nod to Lynn, still in her bathrobe, they dragged Dusty to Anita Mahaffey's place. Last evening Dusty had secured the files and assigned Tee to spend the night to protect the integrity of the files but allow Anita to sleep in her own bed.

Now it was time to get to work. Arriving at Anita's, everyone was delighted that there was coffee ready to refill their to-go cups. "Morning, Anita," Claire greeted her hostess. "I see you did a little investigating on your own."

Anita rolled her eyes. "I never expected to be on a first name basis with an FBI agent, Claire. But, yes, Kip's behavior made me suspicious." She threw her arm toward the den where the armoire looked as though it had vomited files. Anita continued her explanation. "He called and seemed so interested in the furniture when all through our marriage he had always disliked it." She shrugged as Tee came into the kitchen.

"I'll see you, Anita," said the detective as she clutched her overnight bag. "Lonzo needs help getting everyone off to school."

"Bring the family by," invited Anita, "I'd love to meet everyone." After Tee left the house Anita turned to Dusty. "She told me an amazing story about adopting those children."

Dusty nodded. "It was special. They're a great family."

"Stop!" Claire waved her hand, "I'll cry. That story always does me in." The agent knew the story behind the children's adoption. But she was also FBI and her tear threat only lasted a nanosecond. "Okay, let's finish this up."

"Will Kip stay out on bail?" Anita asked.

Claire shrugged. "That's up to the federal attorney and your state attorney general. I'm not certain who has jurisdiction over these files. Your county Clerk of Court may have some role." She made a gesture to dismiss the thought. "I just catch the bastards. Someone else worries about prosecution." She refilled her to-go cup. "What kind of files did you find last night?" Claire asked Dusty.

He shrugged. "Mars said some estate files and some civil cases where Kip seemed to take most of the settlement. You know, the company or person paid a hundred thousand and Kip gave his client ten thousand."

"But do those clients need the money Kip took?" Anita had worried all night about the victims of Kip's scams.

Dusty took a stab at the answer. "Last night Mars scanned some of the files. He said that Kip never took the whole estate but just chunks of money probably overcharging for services. He hid the final files so that the families could never gain access to read the real costs." Dusty nodded to his listeners. "He did the same with the civil cases. Mars said this took a lot of work for Kip to manage. It seemed he worked only a few clients a year. But twenty years in practice adds up."

"What does this all mean for me?" asked Mrs. Mahaffey. "Are you going to take my house?"

Claire reached across the kitchen breakfast bar and patted Anita's hands. "Don't worry. We've already vetted you and your finances. We'll just catalogue and take files."

Anita brushed a tear from her eye. "Thank you. But what will this mean to Kip?" Dusty cast his eyes down to study his coffee. Claire did the same. Anita finally begged, "Please tell me."

Claire answered, "The state guys are picking him up today. He'll have another bail hearing on these charges. They'll probably allow bail to continue while his attorney negotiates with everyone about jurisdiction and timely trials."

"He'll think I did this to him." Anita panicked.

"You did," Dusty reminded her.

"But we're taking the blame," interjected Claire. "We're telling his attorney that the FBI became suspicious that you moved some furniture out of the house. When we finish here today, we'll tell him that we're satisfied that we have all the information. If he argues, we'll threaten to do another search of the law offices."

Caught

Dusty stood, finished his coffee and said, "I've got to get to my office. Mrs. Mahaffey, call me if these FBI folks get carried away." Claire scowled at him.

"Thank you," said Anita, enjoying the kindness of the two law enforcement officials.

* * *

Another golf date. But the crisis within Varney's organization overshadowed the scenic course. "Yeah," he growled, "that Mahaffey is a shit head. He's been skimming from his estate clients and who knows what else." He shook his head. "Once the FBI finishes with him, we'll all know everything about him."

"Are you safe?" Ebetts worried that Mahaffey's downfall would lead right to Varney's operation.

"Yeah," Varney replied, "He only dealt with Big Fish with the cabin operation." Varney referred to a man who worked for the organization but lived in Gastonia. "I got a couple of guys contacting Mahaffey's cabin clients. Maybe they want to change up their drug of choice."

"Good idea," nodded Ebetts. "It's money just left on the table. Someone should pick it up."

* * *

Trina was still disappointed. It had been over a week since the raid occurred and the story broke. And the magazine hadn't been ready for publication. Her first big story and nowhere to publish it! She was alone in the loft. Well, not alone, her three children were playing or napping while she sat and felt sorry for herself. She heard the ping. Someone was coming up in the elevator. Sigh. She wasn't in the mood to explain to her partners how they had missed this golden opportunity.

The door opened and Jasmine Fuller walked into the loft. She looked around. "So it's true. You're going into publishing."

"I wasn't ready for the big story," groused Trina. "You got all the press."

"And thank you for all the material you shared." Jasmine did one more look around the magazine's newsroom. "The River Bend Chronicle has been sold."

Trina gasped. "To who, er . . ..to whom?"

"That's what I like about you. No matter what, you follow the rules of good grammar." She took a seat at the kitchen bar and looked around at the childcare/newsroom vibe of the roomy loft.

"What does that mean for you? And for local news?" Trina was a journalist above all else.

Jasmine shrugged. Her delicate brown skin was taunt and worried over her expressive face. "They say we'll go on as usual. But you and I have seen this a thousand times. The local newsroom will slowly disappear."

"You shouldn't have any problem finding work. You're really good." Trina gave the reporter a searching look and the light dawned. "That's why you're here!"

"You need some diversity in your newsroom. And you need another reporter with experience to work with your students." The journalist stated her case.

"Jasmine, we haven't even gotten our first issue out." Trina almost moaned. Her frustration with losing the big lead still burned.

"And I still have a job," replied the reporter. "I just want to be on your radar when The Chronicle reorganizes and I find myself unemployed."

Trina's mind was swirling. On one hand if the new owners let folks go, she could find some talented staff with experience in marketing, ad sales, distribution. A small voice whispered, *Get your first issue out, then think big!*

Trina's two older children came running into the room. Holly smiled at Jasmine. "Hello, sweetheart," the reporter greeted the youngster. "Remember me?" Holly nodded. "You were so brave when I met you the last time." Holly nodded again. Jasmine had done a great human-interest story on Holly being lost and found about a year ago.

"Mommy, the baby opened his eyes," said Brian.

"Did you wake him up?" Trina sagged at her desk. Three kids and a career. She looked at Jasmine. "Call me when the axe falls."

Caught

Jasmine smiled. "That's all I wanted to hear."

Trina gave her a speculative look. "And when the time comes, tell a few others that you think we might like to hire."

"You got it, Chief," promised Jasmine in her retro Jimmy Olsen imitation.

"Don't call me Chief," mimicked Trina channeling Perry White. They both laughed and the children laughed, too.

* * *

In a quiet western North Carolina cove, several of the residents gathered to talk over the events of the last weeks. Many of them had received gifts from the estate of John and Anna Gillespie, an elderly couple who had spent years among them. Today they had gathered to look over the new SUV Lucas had received as part of his inheritance. He was to use it to attend the university and become a nurse in the valley.

Bundy, the local mechanic looked over the vehicle. "I'll be mighty proud to help take care of this car, Lucas. I know you got no sense about maintenance."

Lucas good-naturedly cuffed the mechanic in the ear. "You keep those greasy hands off my car." Everyone laughed. They all knew that the cove residents only trusted car maintenance to Bundy.

"When you starting on your new house?" Mickey, the local vendor of fresh vegetables, asked Bundy.

"That Sean fellow sent a contractor over. Some fellow named Carl Reid. He said he had some ideas he'd draw up and bring back." Bundy looked at his friends. "He just said we had to tell him how many bedrooms we would need." The young mechanic blushed as his friends chuckled and teased.

An elderly woman slowly left the back seat of the SUV after a thorough inspection. She had been listening to all the talk. "Remember what Preacher says. He tells us every Sunday that the Lord will take care of us." She gave the men a scolding look because not all of them were in the pews on Sunday morning.

Mickey grinned. "I wonder that the Lord sent an old papist priest to take care of us."

Lucas grinned. "I think it just shows that the Lord has a sense of humor." The old woman smacked his arm and they all laughed at their good fortune and marveled that the Lord really did take the time to care for them.

CHAPTER THIRTY-TWO

Rachel came into the Philanthropies office looking dazed. Lynn who had been standing at Nelda's desk catching up on the latest Kip gossip with her assistant and with Rory, turned. She took one look at Rachel and swept her into a hug.

Rachel pulled back and gave everyone a dry laugh. "I feel like a walking disaster!"

"Not you, sweetie." Rory took his turn with a hug. "You're on top of the world."

"Thank you," she said, "But let me outline my life for the next several months." She placed her small briefcase on Nelda's desk and began to enumerate. "I have just joined the race for mayor and must begin to organize a political campaign."

"Done!" They all turned and noted that Jim Hoefler had just walked into the office. "Your campaign chair is Penny Rawlings. We thought you should have a woman as chair so no one in the opposition suggests something unsavory."

"We?"

He tilted his head toward the door. "Your campaign committee met this morning at the coffee shop. Nathan, Will, Penny and Judge Dunn. We'll recruit a few others." He winked at his daughter. "But we can't talk here because this office can't do politics."

Lynn guffawed, loudly and indelicately, but had no opportunity to speak because the rest of the school-based clinic committee streamed into the office. She turned to Nelda, "Hold down the fort." And she ushered everyone into the conference room.

Once settled in the room, Rachel took charge of the committee meeting. "Thank you for all being here on such short notice. As you know our clinic project may be at risk because of recent investigations." Everyone scoffed at the understatement. Rachel ignored them and continued, "I asked Franky to join us this morning because we needed a representative from South End Health Clinic. Do you all know one another?" She scanned the room. Jim, Piper, Sherry Vonder, Amelia and Dr. Noah all smiled at Franky. Lynn and Rory as staffers to the committee were busy pouring coffee and passing a plate of pastries.

Amelia who was seated next to Franky gave her a hug. "That's from all of us. We're glad you joined us." Virus germs be damned.

Franky gave her an answering hug. "I'm glad to be here." She turned to Rachel. "I know all these folks."

Rachel nodded. "Good. Because we have a lot of work to do. We want this school-based health clinic model to succeed."

"But first," interrupted Franky. "You all have to help me keep the clinic going. Those arrests have taken a toll on administration. And the board has lost its chair. I was elected chair at a hurried meeting because everyone was numb. When they recover they may rethink leaders."

"I don't think so," said Jim. "You're the best choice. But I can see that you might need some outside consultants." He waved his arm to include the committee. "We can help you with some ideas."

"We need a clinic director. And we need a CFO and chief of pharmacy. We have a great medical director. She's a doctor who has been with the clinic for years. She has no interest in becoming director." The room was silent. Franky had given them a lot to think about.

"Well, of course, Noah has to take the job!" announced Piper sounding as though no other solution would be acceptable. They all looked at Dr. Noah.

"Hmmph." His greying black hair curled lazily over his head and his eyes twinkled. "If the position is interim, I'd like to apply." Franky started to cry. Amelia stretched an arm around her. Dr. Noah smiled at Franky. "Is that an objection?"

Franky dabbed at her eyes with a tissue Lynn had passed to her. "You're an answer to a prayer. We need someone to hold us together and rebuild respect for the clinic. You would be perfect."

"Perfect or not," said Noah, "that clinic does so much good. We have to keep it going."

Everyone clapped. The meeting went into overdrive. And true to Rachel's organizational skills, within ninety minutes everyone had assignments and Franky had a plan of action to present to the clinic board as the meeting adjourned.

After the other committee members left the office Lynn turned to Rachel. "I thought you said you were a walking disaster."

Rachel leaned against Nelda's desk. "I was when I walked in. But I'm leaving with a campaign committee and a clinic director and our school clinic project is still on track for success. This office must be magic!"

"Oh, sweetie," sighed Rory. "That's how I felt the day I walked in here and found this job!"

* * *

Kip had been out on bail for a week. Life was interesting. The nonprofits were keeping him at arms' length, but many businessmen were impressed by stories that hinted at his sexual escapades - a love cabin, sex in Margaret's office, secret trips with secret lovers. They were almost as bad as those women who ate up romance novels. Their lives were so boring he was becoming a cult-like hero.

Although he had been advised to keep a low profile, the demand for his presence at lunch, or card games, or golf matches where he could talk about his exploits filled his days. He was grabbing lunch at Pedro's when he spotted Rachel. He wondered if he had lost the opportunity to seduce her. After all, the party was quick to choose her as their mayoral candidate in his place. Maybe he could join her campaign and charm her using their relationship to shore up his community standing. Yeah, Rachel would roll over for him and then as a reward he might just give her a tumble. That husband of hers was probably worthless. She'd be grateful. He ambled toward her table.

"Rachel, sweetheart," he crooned as he bussed her cheek. "Mind if I have a seat?"

"I'm sitting here."

Kip turned and found himself facing Owen Teague as they both reached for the chair. At least he thought it was Owen. They rarely met. And Kip didn't recall that the man was so big. He squinted. And so angry. "Sorry, fella," Kip moved away from the chair. "I thought she was alone."

"She's not alone. She's my wife." Owen scowled and Kip moved back to his place at the bar. "Do you want to leave?" Owen asked his wife.

She smiled at him. "No. And thank you."

He blushed. "Maybe I was a few years too late."

"No," she said, "You were right on time."

* * *

Lynn sipped wine at her kitchen table. It had been another post-lockdown day on steroids. "Tough day?" Dusty asked as he walked into the kitchen. She rolled her eyes as he walked into the small pantry where he stored his gun and charged his phone. Back in the kitchen after his evening ritual he asked again, "Tough day?"

"Breathtaking day." She took another sip while he dug out a beer and came to sit with her and waited for an explanation. "Rachel came in for a clinic committee meeting and lamented about the work required for that as well as for organizing a campaign while keeping her other projects moving. Dad walked in and said the campaign was organized."

"Right," said Will as he and Piper walked into the kitchen. "I'm the treasurer. I have you down for a donation."

Dusty looked at Lynn. "I can't make a donation because the joint unit is both city and county funded. And Lynn is a nonprofit."

"That's all right. Jim will donate for both of you." He made a note on the list he pulled from his pocket. Lynn rolled her eyes at both men.

"Who's Rachel's competition in November?" asked Piper as she plopped in a chair with a full wine glass. Piper always looked out for herself.

"Lambert Weston," said Will. He had gotten a beer and was settling in a chair at the table next to Piper.

"I thought the whole point was to get him out of office," Piper said. Lambert was the current, uninspired mayor of River Bend.

"Yes. But someone has to run against him," explained Will. "His party likes him where he is. They discourage any challengers from within the party organization."

"That's not fair," pouted Lynn as she placed some snacks on the table.

"What's not fair?" asked Jason as he walked through the door.

"Lambert running again," said Will.

Caught

"That's all Gramps has been talking about. I've only been working for him for a week and its's been all politics." He grabbed a beer enjoying one of his college graduate adulthood perks.

"Rachel will trounce him," predicted Dusty.

"I thought you stayed out of politics," said Lynn.

He grabbed a cracker and dragged it through some hummus. "It's all over town. Lambert was closeted with Bergy all morning and Bergy is rumored to have told him to take this challenge like a man."

"What did Lambert say?" asked Jason, ignoring the hummus and grabbing the cheese straws.

"You mean after he stopped crying?" replied Dusty.

"Rachel still needs to campaign," observed Will. "Lambert and his party have a great network."

"We'll get the women's vote," boasted Piper.

Lynn stared at Piper. "Are you joining the campaign?"

"Of course, I work for the county. I can dabble in city politics."

"I think Gramps is counting on me campaigning, too," confirmed Jason. "He says you and Dusty have to stay at arm's length, but I can write a check and you pay me back. What's for dinner?"

* * *

Over the next several weeks Bryce found time to have very private conversations with Will, Dusty, Lynn and his grandparents. No one seemed surprised. But they had all cautioned him as Way Reid had about the meanness in the world. He was moved by their acceptance and concern.

He said as much to Beth during one of their almost nightly facetime calls. She replied, "Family. They love us, no matter what."

"I'm still not comfortable here in River Bend." He looked into his phone screen. His best friend smiled back. "But I think I'll keep my day job." He still marveled that the serendipitous friendship with Beth led to a great job in her family's business.

"Because Greg and I would panic if you left the company now!"

"Does this get me a raise?"

"Not yet, but probably a Christmas bonus."

"I do have to move on, you know." As much as he liked his quiet life in River Bend, it was really no life for a gay guy.

She nodded. "But stay with us as long as you can?"

"I will. But I want you to know, when live entertainment opportunities start opening up again, I'll be looking." He blew her a kiss. "Talk to you tomorrow."

He tossed his phone onto his pillow and rolled off the bed. Time for his nightly ritual - stare out at the stars and wish.

* * *

"Were you surprised by Bryce's announcement?" Lynn asked Dusty as they readied for bed.

"A little. I suspected he was gay but I thought he would take longer to tell us." He stepped into the shower and she heard the water spattering and soon the bathroom was as steamy as a sauna.

Lynn finished drying her hair and walked out into the bedroom and over to the sunroom windows to stare at the night. So many things had happened in the last few weeks. In January she was lamenting isolation and lockdown. Here it was the end of May and the family was getting ready for the graduation/engagement party tomorrow. She couldn't believe all the action that had been packed into the Spring months. What a Spring! So much had come out in the open. The pandemic and lockdown may have kept things hidden, but nature always finds a way to blossom, or explode or expose all its secrets.

First, Anita and Rachel hit head on - physically, then figuratively, then they joined forces and caught Kip. Well, the FBI caught Kip but those two ladies helped shine a light on him in his double or triple life. Kip was out on bail, out of luck, and out of everyone's hair. At that thought she fluffed her own hair and wondered if she needed a haircut.

Then she thought about Audrey. Bart Decker had been caught up as part of the fall out of Kip's arrest as one of the drug clients. H. Lawrence had managed to get him probation without going to trial but he lost his job and was relying on Audrey to support the family. Lynn vowed to stay in touch with Audrey.

And Bryce. What an announcement! She was proud of the way the family had accepted his news. After all, as Rory had pointed out to her, it's better to be open about things than to have to worry about getting caught.

Maybe Kip should have worried about getting caught!

She heard Dusty turn off the shower. She watched him walk into the bedroom with a towel slung low on his hips. She smiled.

THE END

Reset to Normal?
The River Bend Chronicles - Book 22

    After the big drug raid of the Spring and the family celebrations including the wedding of Piper's son, Doyle, the gang settles in anticipating a quiet summer returning to pre-pandemic normal. That is until they get involved in a criminal case involving offshore banking, fake non-profits and computer hacking. Those drawn into the investigation include one of the wealthiest families in the state, local IT consultants, and the FBI.

    All of River Bend is drawn into the drama as a new romance blooms, children are held hostage and River Dog Brewery is rob. As the story winds down everyone understands that the drug raid initiated in the Spring exposed only the tip of a regional crime operation.

About The Author

RENEE KUMOR was a stay-at-home mom for several years developing a personal ethic of community service. She began writing a political opinion column for the local newspaper, but retired from writing when she announced her candidacy for local political office. After eight years as a county commissioner, she returned to non-profit service and began writing a monthly column for the newspaper on non-profit management and service issues. The setting for the *River Bend Chronicles* series reflects her early life in Ohio and her later years in western North Carolina.

For sales, editorial information, subsidiary rights information
or a catalog, please write or phone or e-mail

AbsolutelyAmazingEbooks
Manhanset House
Shelter Island Hts., New York 11965, US
Tel: 212-427-7139
www.AbsolutelyAmazingEbooks.com
bricktower@aol.com
www.IngramContent.com

For sales in the UK and Europe please contact our distributor,
Gazelle Book Services
White Cross Mills
Lancaster, LA1 4XS, UK
Tel: (01524) 68765 Fax: (01524) 63232
email: jacky@gazellebooks.co.uk

Printed in the USA
CPSIA information can be obtained
at www.ICGtesting.com
LVHW010731170424
777536LV00013B/619